Justine Elyot's kinky take on erotica has been widely anthologised in *Black Lace*'s themed collections and in the most popular online sites.

She lives by the sea.

D0366099

Also by Justine Elyot:

On Demand
Seven Scarlet Tales
Fallen
Diamond

HEARTS AND DIAMONDS

JUSTINE ELYOT

BLACK
LACE

1 3 5 7 9 10 8 6 4 2

Black Lace, an imprint of Ebury Publishing
Random House, 20 Vauxhall Bridge Road,
London SW1V 2SA

A Penguin Random House Company

Penguin
Random House
UK

Addresses for companies within Penguin Random House can be found at
global.penguinrandomhouse.com

First published in 2014 by Black Lace, an imprint of Ebury Publishing
A Penguin Random House Group Company

www.eburypublishing.co.uk

A CIP catalogue record for this book is available from the British Library

ISBN 9780352347763

Penguin Random House is committed to a sustainable future for our business,
our readers and our planet. This book is made from Forest Stewardship
Council® certified paper.

Typeset in Janson Text LT Std by Palimpsest Book Production Limited,
Falkirk, Stirlingshire

Printed and bound in Great Britain by Clays Ltd, St Ives plc

Chapter One

From the front, it was easy to see that the house had once been handsome, almost stately, before the rot had set in. It might stand inside a barrier of weeds and its blank, shuttered windows might need a little care, but years of neglect could be reversed. There was hope for the place, and the hope was symbolised by the man standing on the front porch, painting the panels of the door.

Despite the paint-spattered overalls it was clear to see that the man was young and handsome, his rolled-up sleeves revealing strong, tanned forearms streaked with pillar-box red. The photographers ranged about the front gate certainly thought he made for a good snap.

So a casual observer might think that there was cause for hope. Ruin was being averted by new and enthusiastic owners who would restore the house to glory.

Approach the rear of the house, however, and hope would not be the dominant emotion. The wild and unkempt state of the gardens was one thing, the splintered window frames and sporadic roof tiles another, but the eye was inevitably drawn to something more sinister. A fence of yellow tape, rustling in the summer breeze, surrounding a square-shaped hole in the patio. Beside the tape stood a temporary tent, in and out of which people in plastic overalls came and went.

A helicopter, hovering overhead, had a good position from which to observe proceedings. Its occupants must have seen an attractive woman in her mid-thirties come out of the sparkling new patio doors with a tea tray, which she set down on a low wall before conferring privately with one of the plastic-overalled crew.

She looked up, so quickly it was almost over before it could be perceived, then ran back inside.

'Did you get her?' The helicopter co-pilot's tone was anxious. 'That's the first time we've seen her all day.'

'I think so. Just.'

'Great. Something for the evening edition.'

That same photograph, of the woman looking up at the helicopter while a forensics expert stood beside her, was in all the next day's papers.

'CURSE OF HARVILLE HALL'

Jenna Myatt read the *Gazette*'s headline aloud as she sat at the kitchen table waiting for the coffee to brew.

'More tabloid bollocks,' said her lover and front-door-painter, Jason, with dismissive contempt. He cracked several eggs aggressively into a basin and beat them to within an inch of their life with a fork.

'You don't think this place is cursed then?' Jenna put aside the paper with a sigh.

'How can I?' He turned to her, his head on one side. 'It's where we met.'

'You're right.' She smiled at him, glowing. 'My biggest bit of luck in years.'

'Mine, more like. You were already living a charmed life.'

'Yeah, well, it was losing its charm rapidly, or I wouldn't have come here.'

'From LA talent scout to Bledburn hermit,' said Jason. 'Riches to rags. Hero to zero. Sublime to ridic—'

'All right, I get your point.' Jenna's tone was slightly frosty. 'And it's none of those things, because it was my choice to leave LA and *Talent Team*, and I'm certainly not in rags yet. In fact, I'm still what you might call bloody loaded.'

'The new Lady Harville.' Jason whipped up the egg so vigorously the yellow mixture slopped over the side of the basin.

'I'm hardly that. I bought Lawrence Harville's house, that's all. It doesn't make me a member of the family. Just as well, given what a dodgy crowd they've turned out to be.'

'Even dodgier than their lodger,' said Jason with a grin.

'Their *unknown* lodger,' said Jenna, mirroring his smile, remembering the moment she'd discovered him in the attic of her new house, lying on his sleeping bag, unshaven, unkempt and surrounded by painting paraphernalia. Some people left lampshades or curtains in their houses after they'd sold them. Not many left a living, breathing, secret sitting tenant.

Jason tipped the beaten egg into a pan, tipping it this way and that so the yellowish mixture filled the foaming surface.

'Your sabbatical hasn't exactly been relaxing so far,' he said.

'No. I may need another one to recover.'

He smirked over the omelette pan. 'You need to take up yoga or tai chi. Aren't they meant to be good for stamina?'

'I wasn't talking about *that*,' she said, her cheeks heating in memory of the vigorous wake-up call he'd given her earlier on in bed. 'I meant generally, in terms of stress and constant bloody argy-bargy. First all that stuff about Lawrence Harville trying to frame you for his own stinking drug crimes, now a mysterious skeleton in the hidden cellar. I can see why the papers are going gaga over it all. I'm like a walking copy of *Now!* magazine.'

'Are those forensic guys coming back today?'

'No. They got everything they needed yesterday. It's all lab work from now on.'

'D'you think it's that chick Harville told you about? The one who was meant to have committed suicide? Fairy Fay or whatever he called her?'

'Could be. I've no idea. Harville might have been making it up to freak me out. That would be typical of him.'

'He must have known that cellar existed. He lied about that. Got any ham?'

'Some prosciutto, I think, in the fridge.'

Jason gave her a look.

'Is that ham or not?'

'Yeah. Wafer thin Italian ham. It's nice. Try it.'

Jason went to the fridge mumbling something about British pigs being good enough for him.

'I wonder if he's been charged,' said Jenna, her mind

still running on the Hall's former owner and Jason's near-nemesis.

'You know he was.'

'No, not with the threatening behaviour towards me. There's bags of proof for that. I mean the drug stuff.'

Jason shrugged, peeling open the packet of prosciutto.

'Up to the CPS now innit,' he said. 'And Kayley holding her nerve. And Mia finding hers.'

'I feel for those girls. He manipulated them.'

'Don't let your heart bleed too much. They knew what they were doing – Mia especially.'

Jason's tone was bitter and Jenna succumbed to an urge to go over and wrap her arms around his waist from behind, resting her head against his shoulder.

'What? I'm OK.'

'You're still hurt. She really let you down.'

'Yeah, well. These things happen. Especially on the Bledburn estate. Anyway.' He pulled her round to his side, resting his forehead against hers. 'Landed on my feet, didn't I? Now I'm here with one of the most gorgeous women in the world and she's banged up waiting for a bail hearing.'

'I'm not one of the most gorgeous women in the world,' said Jenna, laughing. 'That's all make-up and camera angles.'

'You're the most gorgeous woman in *my* world.' He gave the pan a shake, making sure the egg was set. 'Are you sure you don't want one of these?'

'I'll do myself an egg-white special once I've had coffee.'

'How can you have an omelette without the yolk? That's just weird.'

'It's the LA way. Can't go getting fat, can I?'

'Are you fucking joking? You could do with putting a bit of meat on, girl.'

'Not if I want my career back at the end of this year.'

'What? Don't be stupid. You're saying that you're only famous because you're thin? Get lost. You're famous because you've worked flat out for it. Don't put yourself down.'

'I've worked flat out, yes, and part of that was working to make sure I had a flat stomach for TV. You can't be less than perfect in my business, Jay. A few extra pounds could finish me on *Talent Team*.'

'But don't you think that sucks? What about that dude on the team, the one who was famous in the seventies? He's about the size of this house.'

'That's different.'

'Why?'

'It *just is*.' She could feel her patience wearing as thin as the rest of her. 'Besides, I thought you liked my body. My scrawny arse doesn't seem to put you off exactly.'

'It's not scrawny.' He cupped it in both hands, as if to make sure of this. 'But I sometimes think I'd like a bigger target. When you're bent over my knee.'

She swallowed, all her indignation melting at the low, drawled words.

'That's because you're a dirty pervert,' she said.

'Guilty as charged.' He rubbed her silk kimono gown over her curves.

God, I can't be turned on again, not so soon after . . .

The thought was scattered by a kiss, which became long and slow and involved tongues and fondling.

The smoke alarm screeched and they leapt apart.

'Shit!' Jason rescued the pan and its lightly charred contents from the hob. The scent of burnt coffee joined that of barbecued egg. 'Looks like breakfast's off. Better find another use for that table, eh?'

Keeping his hands beneath her buttocks, he jolted her up so that her legs were wrapped around his hips. She clung on about his neck, falling eagerly back into the kiss while he hefted her across the floor to the big shiny Corian-topped table in the centre of the huge room.

Before he sat her down on it, he lifted the hem of her gown clear of her bottom, so that it landed on the cold, sleek surface with no protection, causing her to squeal.

'Oh, it's cold,' she said, when he moved his lips from her mouth to her ear.

'Good,' he whispered. 'You'll want warming up then.'

She was naked beneath her robe, so it took Jason mere seconds to open his own dressing gown and introduce what lay beneath to her parted legs. He leant over her, laying her down flat between the salt cellar and the pepper pot, and eased into her, a knife into butter.

She was not exactly sore, but she felt a tingle as he pushed himself in, a reawakening that reminded her of how they had already been hard at it only an hour earlier. Nothing seemed to tire him or put him off. Sometimes she thought he would keep going all day and all night if she let him.

A fork clattered across the table as he thrust, thrust, thrust, his eyes gleaming with their purpose. She held on to his shoulders, crossed her ankles behind his back and pulled herself into him in rhythm. The pace was bruising and intense and soon they were both gasping, feeling the heat of the warm summer morning mingle with their exertions to bead sweat on their brows.

No amount of perspiration would deter Jason, though. When it came to sex, he was single-minded. There would be no deviation from his course. She would get shagged ragged and that was that.

'Feeling it, babe?' he groaned. 'Want it, do you?'

'I want it, give it to me.'

She was burning up, her throat dry, her bottom sticking to the Corian, but nothing beat the feeling of him, large and thick in her narrow channel, owning it, taking possession of her.

They came in a burst of slapping hands and pinches and growls, Jason sunk as deep as he could get inside her and straining to go still deeper, not that it was possible.

'Fuck, that took it out of me,' he panted, kissing her hard. 'But you could get it all over again.'

After all the LA sophistication and veneer, his simple animal passion was the best tonic there could be. It had revived her, made her see life in colour and depth again, something she hadn't done since the early days of her relationship with Deano Diamond. She hadn't had a bruised back or a sore bottom or a raw smart between her legs in fifteen years, but she was certainly making up for it now.

'This kitchen table is going to break my spine,' she moaned, only now realising how ill-suited it was to frantic sex. 'Next time bring a cushion down, eh?'

He withdrew slowly, grabbing a handful of kitchen roll to mop up the mess he'd made of her.

'That was a bit more spontaneous than I'd planned,' he said, sheepish now for reasons that were slowly dawning on her.

'Well, by definition,' she said, a little sharply, trying to struggle up to her elbows. 'But you mean . . .?'

'Didn't think to bring the rubbers down, babe. Is it . . . OK?'

'OK?' She sat up, wincing.

He stood against her, wrapping her in his arms, rubbing her poor back and shoulder blades with an expert touch.

'You know . . .'

'I won't get pregnant, if that's what you mean. I have the implant.' She stopped, a stray little pang piercing her from nowhere. She had been going to have it removed, a year ago. She and Deano had discussed having children. She had felt ready. And then she realised that he was too far gone in his addictions and had given up on the idea. It still hurt, even now that they were over and she was with this phenomenon of sex and creative talent.

'Right. But, even though I haven't slept with anyone but Mia in seven years, well . . . There were things she wasn't telling me, and . . . I suppose I ought to . . .'

'Get tested?' Jenna screwed her face up in his robe. She didn't want to think about this. It was too horrible, too real. She'd earned a bit of holiday fantasy time. How dare the mundanities of life intrude on it like this?

'Just to be safe,' he said, cradling her head and stroking her hair.

'Oh, that's weird,' she said, looking up at him.

'What is?'

'You being the responsible, sensible adult one. I thought that was my role.'

'Why did you think that? What have you done that's been sensible since you got here?'

She felt stung, but then she saw the justice of his words. She'd behaved like a cross between a hormonal teenager and a bad amateur detective ever since setting foot in Bledburn.

'You're right,' she said. 'I'll make us an appointment. At a *private* clinic.' They rested, lulled for a few minutes, in each other's embrace before she spoke again. 'Jason.'

'Yeah?'

'Do you think it'll change us? Being "out"? Public?'

'It'll be different. But we don't have to do anything we don't want to, or see anyone we don't want to. We can stay tucked up here as long as we like, can't we?'

She could hear the trace of anxiety in his words, though. He didn't want the secret idyll to end either.

She put a hand to his cheek. It was stubbly, and the stubble was growing out into a fuzzy beard. It felt soft, the hairs bending into her palm.

'Are you going to finish your paintings? In the attic?'

'I suppose. I thought you wanted me to sort out the garden.'

'I want you to do what you want to do.'

'Stay in bed forever then?' he said, his lips seeking hers and finding them.

The embrace was broken by the buzz of Jenna's phone. This was the phone she used for people she actually wanted to talk to – only half a dozen people were allowed access – so she sighed and fished it out of her robe pocket.

'Oh,' she said, looking at the caller display. She went out of the back kitchen doors and stood on the warmed stone of the patio, putting the phone to her ear.

'Tabitha? Hi. You've caught me at breakfast.'

'Have I? It's half past ten, you know. I've been at work for nearly three hours.'

'Well, things have been a bit intense round here lately. I've got a lot of rest to catch up on.'

'Quite.' There was a pointed pause, then Tabitha continued, 'Did you see the feature in *The Times*?'

'Oh God! Yes. Yes, I did.'

It was like rewinding the last few days, past the discovery of the bones, past Jason's release from his wrongful arrest, past all the work it had taken to get him out of prison, past Jason's desperate last stand on the parapet of the house and the police arriving at her door. She could almost see the officers walking backwards down her path, getting into their cars and reversing up the road, blue lights flashing.

And before all that . . . the article in *The Times*, which had been about to cause an almighty row between her and Jason, but was pre-empted by all the other stuff.

'I thought I'd hear from you,' said Tabitha.

'You would have done. But things got very hectic around about then. Tabitha, why did you talk to the press about him? You knew we wanted to keep things quiet.'

'I know you *said* you did, but, darling, you have the potential new star of the art world on your hands. Why would you really want to keep quiet about that? I didn't think you could possibly mean it.'

'I did mean it! And he was furious.'

'Was he? I take it the mystery artist was this chap all the fuss was about? The one you were hiding in your home?'

'Jason Watson. Yes. It was him. And we still haven't discussed this . . .'

'Well, you're going to have to. I've had the most enormous amount of interest on the back of that article. An absolute deluge. Buyers, agents, experts, all clamouring to know who he is and get access to his work. I can't fend them off much longer.'

'Oh God, really?'

'Absolutely. You must bring him down to London, darling. Everybody's dying to meet him.'

Jenna took the phone from her ear, needing to take a few breaths. Just as soon as one furore died down, it seemed that several more barged in to take its place. If it was too much for her, how on earth would Jason take it? The dream of a quiet summer spent alternately renovating the house and making love began to fade.

'Look, I'll talk to him,' she said. 'But that's all I can promise. He wasn't wild about the idea when I first broached it . . . but then, some of the reasons for that no longer exist.'

'Legal reasons,' said Tabitha, with a kind of gloating glee. 'You couldn't ask for a better launch for an artist. Really, what a story. He's famous before he's even exhibited. Marvellous.'

'I'll talk to him,' Jenna repeated. 'It'll be his decision. And please – no more press until you hear from me, or I'll be approaching another gallery.'

'Darling!' Tabitha sounded stunned. 'You wouldn't.'

'I'm serious. This isn't my client – not yet. I can't make him do anything. But I'll work on it. Anything that destroys the delicate balance of our relationship isn't going to help, though – and that includes more publicity. So keep a lid on it.'

'I'll be silent as the grave. You can rely on me.'

'I hope I can. I'll be in touch.'

She pressed the end call button and wandered down over the patio, past the police-taped cellar opening and away from all the horrible thoughts it called to her mind. This morning, she wanted to be in the weeds, smelling their pungent, milky aroma, feeling the strengthening warmth of the sun on her bare legs and feet.

She was standing among the dandelions and cow parsley, suddenly feeling her lack of breakfast and morning coffee, when a pair of hands landed on her shoulders.

She jumped.

'I didn't hear you creeping up on me. Don't do that. This house isn't the place for surprises. It's got too many of its own.'

'Horrors, more like. Harville House of Horror. Who was that on the phone?'

She leant her head back into his chest.

'Jason, I need to talk to you.'

Chapter Two

'Why would I want to do that? Mingling with a load of poncey bastards who'll look down on me? Fuck it. No thanks.'

Jenna sighed. This was exactly the reaction she'd been expecting.

'Why would they look down on you? They'll see your work. They won't look down on *that*, believe me.'

'Then why do I have to be there at all? Just stick a few paintings up on the wall and put the wedge in my bank account when some twat with more money than sense buys 'em. Everyone's happy.'

'No, everyone isn't happy. Tabitha won't be happy and the gallery visitors won't be happy. They want to know the artist.'

'Do they 'eck. They don't want to know me. Nobody ever has done, so why would they start now?'

'Jason.' Jenna tried to keep the edge of impatience out of her voice. 'Get that chip off your shoulder and start living your life. You aren't the feral youth from the estate any more. You are a grown man with an exceptional talent, and the potential to build an international career and reputation. So stop being such a mardy arse.'

He smirked at the local epithet.

'Mardy arse yerself,' he said.

'All I'm asking,' she said, more calmly, 'is for you to come down to London and meet Tabitha. No press previews, no champagne receptions, no nothing unless you want it. Just a meeting.'

He tugged at a dandelion root, pulling it clear of the ground. Jenna watched as he gazed contemplatively at its fluffy head then blew on it, sending the seeds afloat on the warm air.

'I've never been to London,' he said.

'What, never?' Jenna knew, of course, that Bledburn had a high proportion of people who had never left the county. Some had never left the town. It still surprised her, though.

'Never. There was a school trip once, to some gallery. The Tate, I think. But Mum couldn't afford it.' He threw the dandelion stalk aside. 'Apparently Kieran Manning set off the sprinkler system. I wish I'd seen that.'

'Well, you can go to the Tate. And every gallery in town, if you like. Don't set off the sprinklers though.'

'Could do with 'em today.' He looked up at the sky where the sun was boiling away already, only halfway up to its zenith. 'OK. I'll come to London. No guarantees, though. But I'll listen to what your mate has to say, at least.'

'That's all I ask.'

She laid her head on his shoulder and they stood

together, held in each other's arms, swaying gently among the waist-high weeds, until the familiar intrusion of a helicopter sent them back indoors.

'You're wasting your time,' Jenna shouted at it from the patio door. 'The police have all gone. Go and pick on some other Z lister.'

'You aren't a Z lister,' said Jason, laughing and pulling her inside. 'You're a lot nearer the beginning of the alphabet, aren't you?'

'I don't know. All this controversy is keeping my name in the papers, but that isn't what I wanted. I wanted *peace*.'

'You should have bought a desert island instead of this place. Couldn't you do that? Go on. Buy somewhere nice and hot in the middle of the sea and I'll come and be your Robinson Crusoe. Sleep in a hammock and live on coconuts. Reckon I could handle that.'

'It's a nice thought, but . . .'

She sighed as her 'important contacts' phone rang again. This time it was the police.

Jason watched her, his head on one side, as she nodded and made non-committal noises into it. Halfway through, he got bored and started tinkering with the cafetière, making a fresh pot after the burnt offering.

'Not your mate again?'

'No, it was the police.'

He always tensed when she mentioned the police – she supposed it was hardly surprising, after what he had been through.

'It's all right, they aren't after you.'

'Good,' he said, giving her a wry smile. 'I always get that feeling, you know, that they're going to get me for something else, something I don't even know about. I can't shake it. I don't feel as if it's over yet.'

'They've got the right people this time. You're in the clear. Anyway, it wasn't about that. It was about the bones in the cellar. The forensic anthropologist had a look at them.'

'And?'

'Human, female, older than twenty but younger than forty, no obvious cause of death, probably died somewhere around the end of the nineteenth century.'

'Right.' Jason shrugged and shook his head. 'Poor cow,' he said. 'So, what are they going to do?'

'Nothing. I mean, what can they do? They can't go around looking into centuries-old cases, can they? They'll just shut up the cellar again and do . . . whatever it is they do . . . with the bones.'

'Shouldn't they have a decent burial? After being hidden down there all these years.'

'What's her name, though? How can you have a funeral for an anonymous skeleton?'

'We could try and find out,' he suggested. 'Bet Harville would know something about it. It's probably some great grandma of his.'

'No, the forensic people said she'd never given birth.'

'Probably one of their maids. Them Harvilles probably treated them like dirt and chucked their bodies into the cellar once they'd worked 'em to death.'

Jenna took some cups from the cupboard.

'I know we all love the Harvilles,' she said. 'But we shouldn't go making assumptions. I wish I did know though. Lawrence did mention something about a tragic first wife somewhere in the family tree who committed suicide. It could be her, couldn't it? I mean, the vicar would have refused to bury her in consecrated ground. Perhaps they just couldn't think of anything better to do with her.'

Jason snorted. 'They've got a bloody huge garden. Might have been better than leaving her down there with the rats.'

'True. It does smack of something that they wanted to hide. Whoever "they" might be. Oh God, I hate mysteries. I'm not sure I can cope with this one. I want to know who she is.'

'Perhaps darling Lawrence could help,' said Jason with a sniff.

'Er, I don't think he's going to have a lot to say to me, not now. Why don't we go down into the cellar again? See if there are any other clues in there.'

'Don't you think those forensic guys will have done that already?'

'No, and they aren't coming back. The body's been found to be too old for them to pursue it. I mean, we've all heard of cold cases, but this one is bloody freezing. They'll leave it to amateur detectives like us rather than waste their own resources.'

'Speak for yourself. When did I ever claim to be an amateur detective?' Jason folded his arms, apparently displeased with the entire affair.

'I'll go down by myself, then,' said Jenna, misgivings striking her as soon as she spoke the words. Did she really want to do that?

He raised his eyebrows at her but said nothing.

She swallowed. This had become a challenge.

'Seriously,' she said, but her voice faltered. 'Unless . . . you want to come with me?'

He laughed. 'No, no, sweetheart. This is your baby. I'll be upstairs finishing off my frescoes.'

'Right. I'll, ah, go and get changed then. Into something I can get cobwebs all over without caring.'

She turned and marched up the stairs.

'Hope there's nothing worse than cobwebs,' he called after her. 'Maybe some tough gloves in case of rat bites.'

She almost vomited on the step but managed to keep her gorge down. It was a good point, though, and she put on her toughest jeans, thickest socks and a pair of leather driving gloves, just in case. She covered her head with a scarf to avoid getting too much dirt in her hair, and put on a dust mask, thankful for the decorating supplies she had in the house.

Jason, happily, had gone by the time she emerged from the room, dressed for combat. He would have laughed at her, she was sure.

But when she came out to the kitchen patio, she felt his absence with a pang. It would have been good to have a companion for this task. Even though the bones were gone, she couldn't help feeling that there would be a disturbing vibe down there. It could be a murder scene, for all she knew.

Her skin crawled with dread as she crouched to tug at the iron ring in the floor. It was no longer locked, as it had been since she moved into the house. Now its darkest secret had been given up, there didn't seem much point in keeping it secure. Jenna hadn't given the remaining contents of the cellar much attention after the bones had made themselves so horribly evident, but she had a vague sense of lots of boxes and shelves, mainly containing paper and old books.

The slab took its time coming up, Jenna making sure she kept her spine straight and knees bent as she tugged. Jason had made it look easy, but then there was deceptive strength in that wiry frame. She thought about how impossible it was to escape from him when he had her pinned against the wall and the pleasurable memory did a little to dispel the scalp-tingling horror.

At last the paving slab eased up and Jenna was able to remove it. Seeing the black maw beneath it, she doubted herself all over again. Could she really go down into that gloom by herself? She activated the torch app on her phone, which reminded her of the time she'd done it last, going up into the attic and finding Jason.

What a moment that had been. She should have been scared then – after all, a living, breathing fugitive in your loft space was surely more frightening and definitely potentially more dangerous than a few dusty old notebooks and some mice. Yet she couldn't see it that way. Jason in the attic should have been alarming, yet it wasn't anywhere near as creepy as this subterranean vault.

It must be to do with the unknown, she decided. After all, once she had seen Jason, she knew the worst. It was the not knowing . . . but even that didn't make sense, because they'd been down there once before, when they found the bones. They'd seen the worst of the cellar too. Or had they?

She thought of the little message they had uncovered

beneath the bedroom wallpaper while they were stripping it. 'Help me'. Something or someone in this house had driven somebody to scrawl those words. And what about the noises Jason said he had heard during the night? Sobbing sounds, coming from somewhere lower down, under the floors.

If an unquiet spirit haunted the house, perhaps the removal of those bones might have satisfied it. Perhaps it would all be all right now.

What are you thinking, Jenna? Ghosts, unquiet spirits. You don't believe in any of that stuff.

Perhaps this place had turned her head. Life had certainly been overwhelming since she had come back to Bledburn. She was fatally disorientated. And people thought LA was the place that led to disconnection from reality. No way. To her, it was a place of substance, almost mundane compared to this drab little ex-mining community on the borders of Nottinghamshire and South Yorkshire.

It was Bledburn that was making her go gaga, not LaLa.

She took a deep breath, shone her torch into the inky depths and located the top rung of the iron ladder set into the narrow brick chute leading to the cellar.

She lowered one foot in its hi-top Converse sneaker and waggled it around until it landed on the narrow metal. OK. She had taken the first step. Now she just had to keep on going.

She clipped her phone to her belt so that the torch continued to shine downwards and made slow, painstaking progress down the ladder. It was a matter of no more than about half a dozen rungs and she soon stood on the cellar floor, its flagstones disturbingly uneven and crunchy underfoot. She supposed it might be mouse bones or beetle shells – she didn't particularly want to check, so she shone the beam upwards, where boxes and trunks stood stacked against the slimy walls.

She tried not to focus on the spot where the bones had been found, but it was still cordoned off with police tape, so it was difficult to ignore. She edged around it, grateful for her dust mask which kept the worst of the thick, musty air from clogging her throat. She lifted one of the boxes from the top of the pile and noticed an index card inside a little gilt frame on the side:

'Harville Hall: Bills etc. 2006–2008.'

Inside appeared to be a number of photocopies and originals of paperwork, mostly dealing with finances and legal issues. It was dull enough but in good condition despite mouldering down here for so long. There were many such boxes, and Jenna decided to look at each one. Most were, like the first one, full of official correspondence. Jenna shuddered at the thought that somebody had brought the boxes down here and walked past those bones – in absolute plain sight – in order to stack them. What did these archivists think of their resident skeleton? Had no member of the successive generations thought it might be a nice idea to remove the bones and give them a decent burial?

'Bloody Harvilles,' she said out loud. 'Bad to the bone. Bad to the *bones*.' Her little giggle at this silly piece of word play sounded deeply inappropriate and she apologised under her breath to who knew whom. And after all, she only did it to try and keep her dwindling stocks of bravado going. It was so *dark* down there, and so horrible. She could never be a subterranean dweller.

Box after box of printed matter was examined and discarded, the pile slowly diminishing until she came to very old documents. 1960s . . . 1950s . . . 1940s . . . on and on she went, occasionally taking off a lid to see inside, but never investigating much further than that. What she wanted was material dating to the time when the owner of those poor bones had died. Something must yield a clue – and if she found nothing, then she would laboriously and painstakingly sift through all these other boxes of more recent date, to find a reference, however oblique or obscure, to what must have happened here.

1930s . . . 1920s . . . 1910s . . . and now she felt her pulse quickening as she drew closer to the kind of time frame in which the death must have occurred. The final few boxes went very far back indeed, and contained the original documents relating to the building of the Hall. She picked up the oldest of the boxes, intent on taking it up with her to perform a detailed analysis of the contents. But perhaps she should get somebody from the Bledburn Museum to help – after all, she was no expert when it came to old documents. She might be ruining valuable artefacts. She would take the box upstairs, ring the museum and then . . .

She was still running through the options in her mind when her eye was caught by a loose brick, sticking out behind where the lowest row of boxes had been ranged. It had definitely been dislodged, and that was strange, because surely it had been hidden behind these boxes for decades. Who or what could have caused it?

She reached out with gloved fingers and pulled at it.
It came away, grinding against the neighbouring bricks,
slowly at first, then falling loose and revealing a cavity
behind it.

She thought she might vomit into her dust mask.
There was something in there, something bound in cloth
and tied at the neck. Perhaps an object related to the
bones, perhaps not – but whatever it was, somebody had
wanted to hide it.

Jenna took hold of the knotted top and removed
the item, as gently as possible, from its place of conceal-
ment. Inside the cloth was a rectangular object, hard
to the touch – probably a book or ledger of some sort,
she thought. The material surrounding it was oilcloth,
tough and virtually unblemished despite the long years
in hiding.

Forgetting the document box for the moment, Jenna
hurried back to the chute and climbed it one-handed,
holding the oilcloth wrapper and its contents to her
chest.

She placed it on the patio wall, replaced the paving
slab that granted access to the cellar and sat down,
breathing hard and shaking the dust and the feeling of
crawling insects from her scalp. It had been cold down
there but she noticed that she was soaked in sweat. She
needed a shower, and now.

But not before she had seen what had been hidden
down there. She picked it up, untied the loosely knotted
neck and unwrapped the oilcloth, which was wound
around the rectangle in layers. What she found inside
was a book. It was in perfect condition, bound in morocco
leather and decorated with a frame of gilt curlicues. There

was no title or other information on the cover or spine, so Jenna opened it to the first page and held her breath.

'*The Thoughts and Ideas of Frances Elizabeth Manning, Nottingham, 1886.*'

Frances? Wasn't that the real name of Fairy Fay?

Chapter Three

She shut the book at once, ran into the kitchen and began opening and shutting drawers. She wasn't even sure what she was looking for – perhaps some kind of thin protective glove, better than these goalkeeper numbers, to keep the dry paper from desiccating under her fingertips. Marigolds hardly seemed any more suitable. She pulled off the thick gloves and looked at the red, sweating skin at her wrist. It would be OK to read the book as it was, wouldn't it? After all, there were volumes just as old in many libraries, and this was hardly a priceless artefact, just some ordinary girl's diary. Except the ordinary girl was destined to be a Harville, and just might have ended up badly. If it was even her. Didn't everyone have the same names in Victorian times, after all? So many Annes and Victorias and Charlottes. Frances would have been just as common. Really, it could have been one of the higher servants, or . . .

Shut up, Jenna, and just read.

The first page revealed the book to be a diary, with a page for each day. Riffling through, Jenna noticed that some pages were full to overflowing, carrying on to the next day's page, while others were blank. Frances, it seemed, only wrote when something was worth writing. Not a bad plan, she thought. It didn't seem that there would be pages of dinner menus or terse accounts of who had visited and what was spoken of.

January 1st, though, as was traditional, held a page of reflections and resolutions.

I hereby express my certitude that 1886 will be the year my life begins in earnest. Every one of the preceding nineteen has been a kind of overture or curtain-raiser to this, the true performance.

For in 1886 I shall marry. I feel sure of it. It is what the gypsy lady at Goose Fair told me and I believe her, truly. What a great deal she knew of me, without my letting slip a single word in corroboration. She knew of Father's tribulations in business, and she knew of Mary's illness and she even knew of my fondness for books and music, though she could not name my favourite author. But then, perhaps she has not heard of Mrs Corelli. Her line of work, after all, is in the reading of palms, not novels.

But the words she spoke inhabit my imagination even now, echoing in my thoughts before I sleep and when I wake. 'Not a twelvemonth shall pass before you are wed, and he shall be a stranger to you.' So nobody I yet know. I still thrill with each contemplation of it. She could not have made it plainer.

But what shall his name be, and what then shall mine be? All will be known, soon enough.

I have made some resolutions, as follows:

*1) I must not eat so many sweets or my stay laces
may burst and then my new husband may turn his face
from me.*

2) I must try to be more patient with Mary.

*3) I must practise at the piano for an hour of each
day.*

*4) I must be helpful to Mama and try to bear the
small privations of our life with fortitude.*

5) If all else fails, I must find work.

*Oh, how the last one dispirits me, but it may well
come to pass. Father looked so sober and so whey-faced
when he tried to wish us a Happy New Year that I
feel sure the end is close for his business affairs. And
then what shall become of us? Useless and idle to
speculate. I will hold to my resolutions and, between
them and God and my new husband, I will find a
course through these times.*

Jenna put the book down and thought about what she
had read. In the space of one page, she had formed an
impression of the book's author. A young woman of a
romantic turn of mind, perhaps a little spoiled, certainly
middle-class at the very least and well educated, but not
serious-minded. Jenna already wished her well and hoped
her family's money troubles might not be too severe. As
for the prediction that she would meet a husband within
the next few months – well, it was intriguing enough to
make her want to read on immediately, to see if the
prophecy was borne out.

*January 2nd, What a hateful day. We have had to
dispense with Rose, for we can no longer afford to*

retain her services. Mary and I have cried all day long, for we have known her since babyhood and we love her as a comfortable aunt and confidante. I asked her if she had a situation to go to; she was very brave and did not weep or cuss but said she should be happy to spend the rest of the winter with her brother, until a position should be found. Imagine, we none of us knew that she even had a brother!

Mary is much consoled by this for the foolish girl had pictured poor Rose at the steps of the workhouse. She has much too lurid an imagination for a child of her age. We attempted to cheer ourselves with music and the reading of poems, but it was a dull sort of evening.

January 3rd had apparently had few attractions and the page was largely blank but for a large blot which Jenna thought might be the result of a tear falling on the opposite leaf.

Turning the page, January 4th held dire tidings.

The evil hour has come and I must apply for a position. I found some advertisements in the Nottingham Post *and sent away for a great many of them with a heavy heart. Father would not even come down for dinner, so ashamed is he of the 'disgrace' of having a daughter who must work for a living. He is much depressed in spirits. Mama does her best to maintain a cheerful disposition, but she is sorely tried. Mary does not help by crying the day away and declaring that she will die of loneliness without me, now that Rose is gone.*

Now there is nothing to be done but to wait. But

*where shall I go and what shall I do and to whom shall
I be tied? I cannot think of any single outcome that will
be favourable to my disposition. Mary suggests that I
will be like Jane Eyre and meet my Mr Rochester, but
of course she is speaking nonsense.*

A few entries of a desultory nature followed, describing
the weather and discussing a book she had read. Then,
on January 12th, there was something to make Jenna sit
up and feel her hackles rise.

*I have the offer of a post. It is in a place called Bledburn,
which I do not know and have never visited, but is only
half a day's drive hence. I believe they live by coal mining
in that region. The employer's name is Harville and the
situation is at Harville Hall. I am to be governess to
Lord David Harville's two daughters.*

Jenna put the book aside. If Lawrence was to be
believed, Fairy Fay was the short-lived first wife of a
Lord Harville. Clearly, the Lord Harville of 1886 was
already married, or at the very least, widowed, to have
children in need of education. She considered flicking
ahead, but resisted the desire. She wanted the story to
unfold naturally, at Frances's pace. Besides, these old
family myths were often a bit garbled or inaccurate. It
could well be that Lawrence had misunderstood or been
told half the story. She took the book back up.

*The girls are eight and eleven – imagine, Mary's age!
I should feel relief or gratitude, but at this time I can
feel nothing but terror. I cannot even think of the name*

Harville or Bledburn without the rising of my gorge.
Mama tries to instil courage by calling me the saviour
of our family and the one who will put bread in Mary's
mouth, but I cannot see this in a happy light. Mary
says perhaps I will meet my husband in Bledburn, but
I should not wish to marry a miner!

Jenna prickled with irritation at Frances's attitude,
but tried to quell it. For a middle-class Victorian girl,
marriage to a working man would have been unthink-
able and shameful. Frances was no more than a girl of
her time.

Oh, what will become of me? For the first time, I doubt
the gypsy's word. No man of quality will marry a
governess and I shall shrivel and grow old in this
Harville Hall. The years stretch ahead of me, arid and
unyielding. Alas. Where is he? When will he come and
take my burden from me?

Jenna snorted. 'Don't go relying on a man, love,' she
said out loud. As soon as she spoke the words, she cast
an eye up towards the attic where Jason was painting
away. Perhaps a little unfair to lump him in with the
great mass of mankind. She was still a little bitter over
what had happened with Deano, clearly. She should
perhaps try a little harder to put all that behind her.

And for Frances, marriage represented escape, para-
doxical as it might seem to regard being yoked together
to a man for life as escape. There was a qualitative difference in the forms of captivity, though: a married woman
could expect to be treated with respect and courtesy. The

same was sadly not true of a spinster, and financial security was as important then as it was now. A married woman simply stood a much better chance of living well and happily than an unmarried one. Of course, she would have to hope that she didn't marry a brute. But that was no different today.

However, something told Jenna that Frances's rosy dreams of love might not come true in the way she expected at Harville Hall. She wished she didn't have to read on with this feeling of misgiving and approaching nastiness in her mind. Maybe the bones were nothing to do with Frances. Perhaps nothing untoward would occur and all the updates would relate to work well done and perhaps a respectable courtship and subsequent happy marriage.

But Jenna's heart didn't seem to think so. She took the book back up, finding January 15th to be the next entry.

I cannot bear it. I have packed my trunk and it is fuller of tears than of clothes and belongings, I am sure, for I wept so much into it before it was shut and locked. Mary has given me her own beloved Loopy Doll. I refused, but she insisted and pressed it upon me so mournfully that I had no alternative but to take it. I wonder what will become of Mary without me? She is not a strong child and she has such strange fancies. I wish I could bring her with me and she might make a friend to the Misses Harville, but of course I cannot possibly make such a request. It would be quite mad.

Mama has given me likewise her cameo brooch of Grandmama's profile. I am to look at it when I feel homesick and remember that I am a Manning and I do what I do for the love and good of my family. Mama has never been demonstrative, but this evening at her needlework, she broke into such a rush of tears that we were all taken aback and some moments passed before Mary remembered to find the sal volatile bottle and we moved to comfort her.

Papa, alas, is as remote as he has been ever since the genesis of this crisis. He went out, nobody knows where, and did not return until we were all abed. Mama fears that he is falling into low company, but she tries not to speak such fears out loud, out of kindness to me, I think. She knows that I will worry.

But I am not to, for I will be sending money home every week, and it will make the difference between gentility and savagery.

This is what she tells me. But how can I know what will pass when I am not there to see it? I have such fears, and I cannot even look forward, for when I get to Harville Hall, I will be thinking always of what might be happening here.

It is too hard.

Yes, thought Jenna, it was too hard. But not as hard as life was for her own forebears back in the days of Bledburn's mining glory. She thought of her father and her grandfather and her great grandfather, all tramping off to the pit with their snapboxes day after day after day, taking their lives in their hands with each trip down in the rickety lift to the dark, shining bowels of the earth. None of them were killed in mining disasters, but one of her grandfathers and an uncle had died of lung complications from breathing in the thick coal-dusty air. Her father was still alive but she wondered how much of that was due to the closure of the pit before his thirtieth birthday.

And during the strike, she remembered the youth club being used as a giant soup kitchen, the miners' wives in their pinnies boiling up vast vats of stew with ingredients donated by well-wishers. Those communal meals had been exciting and vivid to her as a child, but looking back, it must have been so hard for those women, to know that they faced a choice between losing their husbands' livelihoods or carrying on like this, towards starvation. It had been no choice at all in the end. They couldn't have won. But at least they'd fought. At least they could tell their children they did what they could.

This Frances, on the other hand, thought sitting in a grand house teaching spoilt children where to find India on a globe constituted a hard life. Jenna sniffed. She knew nothing of the sheer graft and determination needed to make a mark in this world. But she shouldn't think ungenerously of the poor girl. After all, who knew what tribulations lay ahead of her?

She read on.

January 16th
And now I am here, at Harville Hall. I suppose I should draw a sketch and reflect upon my first impressions of the town, the house and its residents, so that is what I shall do.

Oh, this gloomy town! It is both as I expected, and worse. Coming nigh on the train, all one could see was the great pit head with its black wheel spinning at its apex. It was like a giant, bestriding the landscape Colossus-wise. Beneath it trembled a little town, all ramshackle and poor. A sacrifice to the malevolent Coal God, or so it seemed to me. The very air seemed dark and choked with the pit dust which, mixed with the smuts from the engine steam, made for a very unpleasant atmosphere. I was glad indeed that I was wearing a dark gown and shawl, and my white gloves were packed away for special occasions.

I did not have to wait long after alighting at the station. A fly awaited me, driven by a very taciturn old fellow, but he was obliging enough and I did not have to struggle with my trunk at all.

And then — the Hall. What shall I say of it? It is impressive without overwhelming one; a handsome building of fairly recent construction. Function is not sacrificed to aesthetics, but nor is the converse true. It stands in pleasant old grounds, stark enough at this time of the year, but in summer I should imagine it is quite beautiful. To me, however, it looked mournful. I suppose my own mood made it seem so, but there was a sadness in the windows and a kind of droop in the ivy that hung about them.

I was shown into the front hall by a maid and left there while she went to find the master. It was so quiet in there that I wondered if everyone had gone out, but it was the hour before supper and so it seemed rather unlikely. All the same, I felt that it was unnatural, thinking of our own home with its boisterous cheer. At least, there had been boisterous cheer before Papa's troubles.

In this house, only the ticking of the beautiful

grandfather clock by the stairs disturbed a peace that seemed made of years and decades and centuries. An unfathomable stillness. It was broken at last by the opening of a green baize door at the back and rushing housemaids, hurrying to put cutlery on the dining table. They looked at me curiously as they raced by, then lowered their eyes again as if the sight of me had burned them.

I heard the clatter of knives and forks and the whisper of conversation in the room beyond and I strained my ears to catch it, but in vain. I had tiptoed a little closer when a heavy tread on the stairs disturbed me.

'Miss Manning?'

I had no immediate impression of him beyond his impeccable dress and his aristocratic bearing.

'Do I have the honour of addressing Lord Harville?' I asked.

He came down and stood level with me, seeming pleased by my phrasing.

'I'm not sure it's much of an honour,' he said, 'but yes, you do.' He held out a hand and I thought he would shake mine, so I took it, but he did not shake my hand, merely held it for a moment or two, looking me up and down in a manner that made me feel cold and then hot.

He took me into the drawing room and explained to me that his wife was dead and his daughters had found it difficult to settle with any governess since then. I remarked that this was perhaps not so surprising and he agreed with me, but warned me that I was to be the last of these experiments. Should I fail to engage their attention, then they were to be sent away to school.

I felt for them then, thinking of how Mary might bear up if she were to be sent away to some strange place

*full of rules and routines. I do not think she would take
to it, especially in grief.*

*It had been three years since his wife's death, he said,
and that did astonish me, for I had imagined it to have
been more recent. Nonetheless, Susannah and Maria
continued to hold her memory close and dear, and I was
to expect them to treat me with suspicion, even downright
hostility. But I was to report all such incidences to him,
and he would do his best to deal with it.*

*I asked if I could meet the girls but he told me they
were abed. So soon? It was not yet seven o'clock and
Susannah, I believed, was eleven years old.*

*He told me that he never allowed them downstairs
after five or before ten in the morning. I wonder if he
ever sees them. It seems such a strange and unhappy
state of affairs that I am almost tempted to hand in my
notice here and now and return home. I will take in
mending, laundry, anything . . .*

*But he was civil enough to me and my rooms here
are perfectly satisfactory, if a little cold. I did take a
peek at the girls in their nursery beds, but they were
fast asleep, looking as angelic as you could wish. I can
scarcely imagine hostility tainting those sweet faces at
all. The older one made me think of Mary, although
she looks nothing alike. Poor Mary. I wonder how she
does this night?*

'Good book?'

Jenna looked up, almost startled out of herself. In her
mind she had been in this same room, but nearly a
hundred and fifty years ago, living Frances's life along
with her.

But she was sure Jason hadn't been in Harville Hall back then, leaning in from the door frame, casting her a sly smile, as if he knew she'd been up to something.

'Oh . . . yes. Quite fascinating actually. I found it in the cellar.'

'Give us a look.'

He came forward, reaching for the diary, but Jenna held her hand over it, protecting it from his view.

'It's fragile, Jay. The fewer dirty twenty-first century fingers all over it, the better.'

'My fingers aren't dirty,' protested Jason, but he looked at them all the same and could hardly have failed to notice the paint blackening his nailbeds.

'Yes, they are. I think this might be *her* diary, though.'

'Whose? Fairy Fay's?'

'Yes. Except she doesn't appear to be Harville's first wife. She's a governess, looking after his daughters by his dead first wife. Perhaps Lawrence got a mixed-up version of events given to him.'

'Perhaps darling Lawrence wouldn't know the truth if it hit him in the face with a wet paper bag full of fish.'

'No, very likely. He's either confused or deliberately misinforming me. Not that I can ask him now. God, I hope he gets remanded.'

Jason put a hand on her shoulder.

'Whatever happens, he won't be allowed near us. So what's going on with Fairy Fay? Is it dirty?'

She batted the tip of his nose.

'No, it is not dirty, for God's sake. She's a very proper, very well brought up young Victorian lady.'

'Ah, those are the worst, if you ask me.'

'Just as well I'm not asking you then, isn't it?'

The book lay forgotten as they entered into an energetic play fight, chasing each other around the house and bending each other into amorous contortions before giving up and going back to bed.

Chapter Four

'I'm still not sure about this.' Jason gazed bleakly through the window as field after flat field rolled past, each cow marking a step closer to London.

'It's just a meeting. Besides, we'll have fun. Are there any London attractions you want to see? London things you want to do? Go for it. You can do them all.'

'Soho?' he said hopefully. 'That's where it all goes on, isn't it?'

'You're probably thinking of its old reputation rather than today's reality,' said Jenna. 'Sorry to disappoint, but there's only a very small section of it devoted to sex shops and peep shows these days. Most of it's upscale bars, restaurants and shops. And the odd corporate giant creeping in to ruin the vibe.'

Jason kicked at the footwell, clearly uncomfortable.

'The Emirates Stadium?' he said hopefully.

'Oh God, must we? What about the Olympic Park? That's bigger and more interesting.'

'Yeah, I used to support Arsenal though. A bit. I mean,

mostly I was a Forest boy but I just liked the name. *Ars*enal. You get me?' He winked.

Jenna felt a little prickly at his determination to drag the conversation down to base levels. She knew their relationship thus far had been largely predicated on their outrageous sexual compatibility but surely it must be possible to have some intercourse of a different nature with him? Why must everything be sex, sex, sex? It was beginning to bore her.

'Maybe, if we have time,' she said vaguely. 'What about the London Eye?'

'Oh yeah, that looks boss. Do you get one of them little pods all to yourself?'

'I'm afraid not.'

He tutted. 'Bang goes another good idea.'

She concentrated on exiting the slip road and getting on the motorway then turned to him.

'Jason, is there anything *non-sexual* you'd like to do in London?'

'Why would I want to do anything non-sexual?' he asked, as if she'd asked him to consider joining the Nazi party. 'Especially when I'm with you. Can't we just stay in the hotel when we're not meeting your posh mates? Room service, en-suite bathroom, all that?'

Jenna wasn't sure whether to feel flattered or frustrated.

'I don't know,' she said, trying to keep her tone light. 'I bring you to one of the capitals of world culture and all you want to do is shag.'

'You *bring* me? What are you, my mother?'

'Of course not.' Jenna considered abandoning the conversation. 'I'm joking. Stop being so sensitive.'

'I am sensitive,' he countered. 'I'm a sensitive artiste, see. That's why you love me.'

'Well, that's a fair point.' A sign for some motorway services appeared like a mirage in the desert. 'Oh look, let's get a coffee or something. I hate long drives.'

It was an indicator of how annoyed Jenna was that she even considered this. A woman of her international fame was bound to draw a lot of unwelcome attention in one of these places, especially with her tabloid-bait boyfriend in tow. But perhaps they could scoot in, find a secluded corner and keep the rubberneckers at bay.

She parked the car, pulled her sunglasses right up the bridge of her nose, and stepped on to the forecourt with a defiant air that seemed to invite all-comers to 'bring it on'.

She strutted while Jason slouched. His posture was shocking, she realised. She needed to do something about it – that rolling gait made him look as if he were skulking around a street corner waiting for a drug deal.

'Straighten up a bit,' she said through a fixed smile, noticing stares and double-takes from people passing them on the way back to their cars. 'You look as if you have some kind of degenerative spinal cord condition.'

'Charming.'

Rather than take her advice, he wrapped an arm around her, his hand landing on her hips.

'I'll need you to prop me up, then, won't I?'

'Jason. All these people . . .'

'What? Ashamed of me?'

'Oh God.'

She took deep breaths, keeping her head down all the way to the glass-fronted building.

The coffee shop was the first concession on the left and she headed purposefully to the counter, catching nobody's eye and forcing Jason to up his pace if he wanted to keep her by his side.

'A regular skinny latte, please, and . . . Jason?'

'A coffee.'

The barista was studiedly polite.

'Is that a filter coffee or one of our espresso beverages, sir?'

Jason blinked.

'Like, y'know, a coffee. Brown stuff in a cup with a bit of milk.'

'I think maybe a regular Americano with some milk from the jug,' Jenna offered.

'Americano? What, like, American coffee? What's the diff?'

Jenna paid and steered Jason away from the counter before any more of this tedious encounter could play out.

'I'm only asking a question,' he said, giving Jenna a glare.

'Jason, it's just a black coffee and you add your own milk, OK?'

'Why don't they call it that, then?' he persisted. 'Why doesn't it say Black Coffee on the menu instead of all this unpronounceable shit?'

'I take it you don't frequent coffee shops, then?'

'No, I bloody don't. There's one in Bledburn High Street but it's a fucking rip off joint. Four quid for a cuppa, they want. I can get four boxes of fucking PG Tips in Poundland for that. They've seen the likes of you coming.'

'They're very popular,' Jenna said mildly. 'Or there

wouldn't be so many of them, would there? Obviously there was a huge gap in the market.'

'Can't believe there are so many people with more money than sense. Well, in LA, I guess . . .'

'Oh, so I have more money than sense, do I?' Jenna teased lightly.

'Much more,' he said, relenting a little. 'Or you wouldn't be here with me. Double whammy, doll.'

She leaned into him, and he gave her bottom a brief but unmistakable squeeze.

She heard giggles from behind them.

'Jason,' she whispered loudly. 'There are *eyes* everywhere. Behave.'

'You *are* ashamed of me, aren't you?'

He removed his hand stiffly and folded his arms, brooding at the counter end while they waited for their drinks to materialise.

'Of course not. It's just that anyone's cameraphone snap can be in the *Daily Mail* tomorrow, that's all.'

She put their drinks on a tray.

'I know you've never had to think this way – never had to take anything like that into consideration, and I don't blame you for not thinking of it. But I've had years and years of intense public attention and it's changed my behaviour. Changed my personality almost.'

They found the furthest flung alcove and took seats in it.

'It must be weird,' said Jason. 'Like being spied on twenty-four seven.'

'Yeah, it is, a bit. And I feel guilty for bringing you into it, to be honest. You're so frank and open about everything. I think it'll be difficult for you to get used to the circus I live in. When it was just us in the house . . .' She sighed, experiencing a melancholy sense of paradise lost. 'It'll never be like that again.'

'It can be. We can just stay at home,' he said. 'Wouldn't bother me.'

'Oh, Jason. The world wants your art. The world deserves your art. And you deserve the world's attention. We'll always have our bolthole when it gets too much – but I think the time for hiding away is over.'

'The world,' he echoed, ruminating. 'Hasn't done a lot to get me on side so far. I'm not sure why it deserves my . . . I can't say art. I feel so fucking phoney. I am a phoney. I'm not an *artist*, Jen. I'm not that kind of person.'

'But you are. That's just your low self-esteem talking.'

'Oh, give me a break! You sound like a fucking counsellor. I saw one of those when I were at school. Poor self-image this, low self-esteem that. What she didn't want to say was that I was a thick kid from a shitty estate and what did I expect?'

'OK, what I don't want you to feel is patronised. How can we stop that from happening?'

Jenna put on her most businesslike, don't-mess-with-me face.

'Well, I might have an idea,' said Jason, stroking the waxed rim of his coffee container.

'Really? Come on then. Out with it.'

'You're going to mess me up, aren't you? Do a make-over or whatever, except not just with my looks. You're going to do what you do to those people on the show – what did they call it? Starmaking. I did see a few episodes of it, and I remember you looking straight to camera, all cheesy like, with massive hair and saying,

"Time for some starmaking." It was, like, your catch-phrase, yeah?'

'Yeah.' She cringed a bit. It did sound cheesy, when he put it like that. 'There will be an element of that, I suppose. If you can look on it as part of the job, you know, dressing the part, working the room . . .'

'Whatever. I know. I know what you're going to do to me. And I know it'll piss me off, however necessary you think it is. I'm not a fucking dressing up doll.'

'I know you're not, I—'

But he waved a hand, indicating that there was more for her to hear.

'I haven't said what my idea is yet. Do you want to hear it or carry on with the Starmaker Manifesto?'

'No, sorry. Say what you want to say.'

She flicked her eyes over to the counter where a group of people were leaning in to the barista, talking and casting covert looks in their direction. She kept her sigh inward. Incognito was over for the day.

'Here's my proposal,' said Jason, leaning forward and holding her eyes with the pokeriest of poker faces, as if he'd watched too many films containing Bigshot Business Deals. 'If you mess with me, it's only fair that I should mess with you.'

'I don't . . . Not sure what you're saying.'

'You're going to ask me to change a lot of things – the clothes I wear, the way I speak, the way I act. I want to do the same to you. I want you to know how it feels.'

'I do know how it feels. Once Deano's band started getting press, we had to reinvent ourselves. We had to learn fast, and we didn't have anyone to help us. We had to use our intuition – to know when the journos were looking down their noses at us and making fun of our Bledburn accents, and to tweak accordingly. It's not easy, Jason, and what you don't seem to realise is that I'm trying to protect you from that. You might not want to believe it but the media in this country is still hugely London-centric and if you don't want to be classed with the bumpkins . . .'

'Don't get all arsey with me. I'm not refusing to do it, am I? Just listen. I do what you ask . . . and you do what I ask. Isn't that fair enough?'

'But I don't understand . . . What are you going to ask of me?'

'Nothing that'll make a difference to your precious public image, don't worry. This is a private game.'

He winked and light began to dawn on Jenna.

'You mean . . .'

'Fun and games for Jenna and Jason,' he said. 'Let's start one here. I've agreed to come to London and see your gallery friend, so you owe me one and I want to collect. I'm torn, though, between asking you to come over here and give me a proper snog with tongues in front of all those people . . .'

'I can't do that!'

'Why not?'

'It's just not professional. Not when we *know* we've got an audience. Outside or in the car, fine. But not in a coffee shop.'

Jason rolled his eyes.

'That makes me want to do it even more, but all right. Not that, then. Not yet. It'll have to be the other thing.'

'What's the other thing?' The trepidation in Jenna's voice seemed to please Jason. He dragged the anticipation out with deliberate enjoyment.

'I'm warning you,' he whispered. 'It's naughty. Very naughty.'

'Just tell me. As long as nobody over *there* knows about it.'

'Oh, they won't know. They might guess . . . but they won't know.'

'Jason! Cut it out with the suspense.'

'Go to the Ladies' and take off your knickers. Put them in your handbag and come back out again.'

'I can't do that!'

'Of course you can.'

'Jason!' Her face flamed red, but the idea was more exciting than she could ever bear to admit to him. Just the idea of sitting on that plastic moulded chair with nothing between the gauzy cotton of her skirt and her bare skin . . . That was a point – was the skirt definitely opaque enough? She would have to check in the bathroom mirror . . . but the restrooms would be thronged with people . . . there would be no chance . . .

'Non-negotiable,' he said. 'Do it or we drive straight back to Bledburn. It's up to you.'

'You bastard,' she whispered, looking over again at their growing audience. 'All right then. I will.'

She took a gulp of her coffee, then stood up and marched, eyes front, out of the coffee shop and towards the toilets.

As predicted, they were busy, even on this workaday weekday. Business-suited women refreshed their make-up at the mirrors while retirees in slacks and polo shirts chatted by the hand-driers. Small children were helped to the soap by crouching mothers and a gaggle of glossy-haired students – Spanish? – giggled and eyed her from a corner.

She ignored them all to find shelter in the nearest unoccupied stall. There was bank after bank of these. It was hardly the most private place for a private moment. She looked up swiftly on both sides to check nobody was peering down on her. It wouldn't have been the first time.

She put her bag down on the floor and stared bleakly at the poster on the back of the door, asking her if it was possible she might be diabetic.

'Hope not,' she muttered, then she raised her skirt until it sat rumpled around her waist and slowly lowered her knickers. It was difficult, in the space available, not to bang her elbows or head as she bent, but she persevered, catching them slightly on one kitten heel before they were all off and ready to be stuffed in her handbag.

She stood up again, keeping her skirt where it was, trying to assess how this made her feel. Vulnerable, she thought, and a bit furtive. She had the weirdest feeling that, even with her skirt back down, there would be some telltale sign on her face, some giveaway.

'No, there *won't*,' she whispered to herself. She smoothed the skirt back over her bottom and thighs. Oh, how different it felt now against bare skin. It wasn't skin tight, but it was fitted enough that the fabric would rustle and whisper against her naked curves with each step she took. And what about between her legs? What if she couldn't keep herself . . . dry? The skirt's pale colour would show anything up.

Better focus on not getting too excited, girl, she thought. Who knew what a telephoto lens might pick out?

She needed half a minute to clear her head and gather her nerve, to put on her Jenna Diamond face. She felt like Superman emerging from the phone booth when she finally mustered the courage to push open the stall door.

She marched purposefully to the basins, deliberately avoiding her own eye in the mirror. She was trying to ignore the way her thighs were pressed together when a young girl slid into position at the neighbouring basin and said, 'Please, I think you are Jenna Diamond.'

Jenna turned to the girl, one of the possibly Spanish contingent. She had eager brown eyes and a brace on her teeth.

'I used to be,' she said with a wry smile. 'Now I go by the name Jenna Myatt.'

'Oh, I didn't know. I watch all your shows. I am a big, big fan. Will you sign my book?'

She reached into her bag and brought out an exercise book with a picture of a patchwork owl on the front.

'Sure. Do you have a pen?'

The girl handed her one.

Jenna's fingers were wet and slippery and it occurred to her that she would never have agreed to this – to signing autographs at the washbasin in a motorway service restroom – if she hadn't been so preoccupied with the state of things under her skirt. Any distraction was welcome, even an annoying or impractical one.

'Perhaps should have waited until my hands were dry,' she said ruefully, watching a blob of soap drop on to the page beneath her message.

'Oh, it's OK, really. Thank you so much!'

'No problem – but please – don't send all your friends to me. I can't sign any more.'

Already a crowd of curious, cameraphone-wielding

adolescents lurked at the fringes of her vision. She needed to get out of there before it got too much.

Luckily, they parted to let her through. Outside the restrooms, surprise surprise, a few impromptu buskers had set up and were warbling popular songs in competition with each other.

Jenna wanted to laugh. As if she'd interrupt her toilet break to sign up a potential star act. Still, she had to admire their spirit of enterprise.

She found herself rushing to get away from it all, and the rushing made her more intensely conscious of the cling of her skirt and the rubbing of her thighs.

By the coffee shop entrance, Jason stood waiting for her, but he was no longer alone. He was chatting to a couple of lorry drivers, leaning back on a high stool, his expression one of satisfied vanity. Jenna knew that look. It was his swaggering I-am-the-dom look. What the hell was he telling those men?

She hurried up to him.

'So you were on remand for a while then?' one of the men said.

Ah. They were talking about the false drug charges that he'd been accused of.

'Yeah, thought I was going down, for sure.'

'But Jenna Diamond came to your rescue. Fuck, that's a story. What's she like?'

'Why don't you see for yourself?' she suggested, stepping up to the trio. She sensed that the lorry drivers were keen to find out a bit more than she wanted known, and Jason might be too puffed up with self-importance to hold back.

The lorry drivers did nothing but stare for a few

moments, while Jason held out his hand and pulled her into his side.

'Wow,' contributed one. 'Well done, mate. Pleased to meet you,' he said, more formally to Jenna. 'The missus loves that show of yours. Wait till I tell her.'

'Would you like a photograph?' she asked graciously.

She posed with each lorry driver while Jason took pictures.

'Lovely to meet you,' she said firmly, so that they could be in no doubt that the encounter was over. They mumbled thanks and shuffled off towards the burger bar, looking over their shoulders every few steps.

'Good lads,' said Jason.

'You can't possibly know that,' said Jenna, a touch tetchily. 'And you're going to need to learn the wisdom of reserve. Smile and chat, but don't ever discuss anything personal.'

'Don't get too close to the little people? Is that what you're saying?' He was teasing, but there was a smidgen of ice in it.

'Of course not.'

The makings of a tiff were soon forgotten when Jason, making sure their backs weren't visible to anyone, ran his hand over the curve of Jenna's bottom.

'So did you do as you were told?' he said softly into her ear. 'Mm, I think you did. Good girl.'

She tried hard to keep her breathing even but his hand felt so sinful and so delicious, running over her thinly-covered cheeks, that she had to focus hard.

'Let's get out of here,' she muttered. 'I feel like everyone that passes has X-ray vision.'

Jason chuckled.

'Perhaps they have.'

'Not helpful.' She wiggled his hand off her bottom and marched off towards the main entrance.

'I want proof, you know,' he called, hurrying to catch up with her. 'When we get to the car.'

She had a delirious vision of raising her skirt there and then while the crowds ambled around them, baring herself to the sun-bleached expanse of the car park and beyond. God, what put these things into her mind? Or his, for that matter?

She didn't feel quite safe until she was back in the car, and confident that there was nobody parked nearby who could see them.

Jason opened her door and peered in, looming over her.

'Never mind that,' he said. 'Get in the back seat.'

'What? Why?'

'Because I told you to.'

She reached down to her handbag and took out the knickers, waving them defiantly in his face.

'Put 'em down,' he said, taking hold of her wrist. 'And get in the back seat. Now.'

She wanted to argue with him, but his tone brought out that strange meek side of her she hadn't known existed before she met him and she climbed into the back, looking carefully out of the tinted back window to make sure nobody was peeping – not that they could see much through the opaque glass.

'All right,' he said, once she was seated in the back. He got in beside her and put a hand on her knee. 'Now, show me.'

'Jason! We could be seen.'

'No we won't. Lift up your skirt and show me what's underneath.'

He was calm and confident and she found herself reaching for her hem and shuffling it up her thighs. He slung an arm across the seat, leaning in to her to watch as closely as possible. When the cotton inched up to the top of her thighs, he stopped her with a hand on hers.

'Let me finish,' he whispered.

She obliged him by raising her bottom slightly off the seat to let him push the fabric all the rest of the way, then sat back, the leather cool and thrilling against her bare skin. Why did this feel so extravagantly dirty? It was surely no different than bare legs and yet it felt completely, decadently other. Her pussy was throbbing and she knew that she would feel the wetness of it if she clamped her legs together.

But that wasn't going to happen.

'Open your legs,' whispered Jason.

She spread her knees wide and sat, looking down on what went on lower down as if it were all happening to someone else. It wasn't her, Jenna Myatt Diamond, sitting in a car with no knickers on, letting a rough estate lad take a good, long look at the goods. She would never do such a thing . . . She would never let him run his hand up her thigh and push his fingertips into the slippery centre of her, rubbing and teasing and whispering dirty words into her ear all along. She would never sit there, clenching her hands and her sphincter, trying not to gasp or cry out while he circled her clit with such cocky self-assurance, knowing exactly what he was doing to her and how to make her beg for more.

And Jenna Myatt Diamond would never have an orgasm in a car.

'No, never,' she panted, as she came over his fingertips.

'Never what?' He gave her a puzzled grin.

She sat back, shut her eyes and let herself flop against the leather.

'Nothing. Don't worry. God. You're evil.'

'I know. But I'm good as well, eh?' He nibbled at her earlobe, then moved down to her neck. 'Like you. My good girl. Doing as she's told. Thought you deserved a little reward.'

She opened her eyes again.

'And what about you?' she asked, looking pointedly at his bulging crotch. 'That looks uncomfortable.'

'It is,' he said. 'Perhaps you might want to . . . give me a hand?'

She didn't need asking twice. She released the protrusion from its close confines inside his jeans and gave it all the loving attention her hands could provide, using some hand cream to enhance his pleasure. The car park, the motorway services, the entire world fell away as she devoted herself wholeheartedly to making him feel as he had made her feel. He half-climbed over her, burying his face in her neck, and when his climax came he spurted himself over her bared thighs and pussy, sighing low and long.

'What a mess,' hissed Jenna, fumbling in her bag for some tissues.

'Who cares?' drawled Jason, sounding half-asleep and fully blissful. 'Gorgeous. You're gorgeous. I love you.'

Her minor irritation faded and she kissed him, delicately removing him from where he clung so that she could get at the creamy residue on her skin.

'I love you too,' she said. 'But I really think we should

have waited until we were in the hotel. I hope nobody caught any of that.'

'You're paranoid,' said Jason with a yawn. 'Why would they? The windows are tinted out. It's completely private.'

'I hope you're right. Damn, there's some on my skirt.'

'Take it off then,' he said with a wink.

'Don't be ridiculous. I'm not driving to London naked from the waist down.'

'I'll drive. You stay there.'

'Can you even drive? Do you have a licence?'

'Yeah.'

'On you?'

'No.'

'Well then.'

'It's with a load of gear I have to pick up from Mum's. I have got one though.'

'Yes, but you can't actually drive without it to hand. So there goes that plan. Anyway, how long is it since you drove?'

'Dunno. Couple of years.'

'Did you ever have a car?'

'Not one of my own, no.' He took a tissue and helped Jenna finish off the cleaning operation.

'Well, if all this works out, I daresay you can have one.'

He shook his head, looking a bit disgruntled.

'What?' she said, tugging down her skirt preparatory to climbing back over into the driver's seat.

'You sound like a parent talking to a child. Behave yourself and I'll get you some sweets.'

'You know I don't mean it that way.'

'Don't you?'

'No.'

'OK, I know you don't. I just wish it could be me in the driving seat.'

She put her hands on the steering wheel and twisted her neck around to him.

'It will be,' she promised. 'We just need to do the groundwork first. Come on. Let's go to London.'

Chapter Five

'So, what do you want to do first? Shower, eat, see the sights?'

Jason was peering through the curtain at Hyde Park beyond from their penthouse suite in Park Lane.

'Aren't we going to see your friend?'

'Tomorrow,' said Jenna, coming up behind him and resting her cheek against his shoulder. 'I thought it'd be nice to have the evening to ourselves.'

He grabbed her swiftly into his arms so that they stood in the floor-to-ceiling window together, not that anybody could have seen them from below, unless they used binoculars. Jason seemed to realise this, because their kiss had not lasted long before he pushed a hand up her skirt, revealing the bare skin beneath.

'Jason,' she gasped, breaking off. 'We're right in the window.'

'Yeah, but it's not as if anyone can see. Unless a helicopter happens to come by, which isn't too likely. Or a window cleaner. Christ, that'd be a job, cleaning all these windows.'

He tried to look down, but the parapet of the building prevented any view of the many lower floors.

'All the same, I'd rather not show myself off to the world. This isn't an Amsterdam brothel.'

'I've heard about those. Some mates went over on a lads' weekend once. They just stand right in the window on the street, yeah? Weird.'

'And sad,' said Jenna. 'Come on, you haven't answered my question. Are we going out, and if so, where?'

Jason threw up his arms as if to encompass the whole of London.

'The place is too big,' he said. 'I haven't got the first idea what to do here.'

'Well, why don't we shower, change and go for a walk in the park. We can decide while we walk.'

'Fair enough.'

He opened the door to the bathroom suites.

'What the fuck's this? There's no shower.'

Jenna hurried up behind him.

'Oh, there is – it's a wet room.' She bit back the impulse to ask him if he'd ever used one before. Obviously he hadn't.

'A wet room?' He twisted his neck to frown down at her. 'What's the point of that?'

'It's just like a massive walk-in shower room, that's all. It's great. You'll like it. See, the shower fittings are over there on the far wall. Much better than being cramped up in a cubicle.'

'Doesn't the towel get wet?'

'No, the rail is out of range.'

Jason still seemed unconvinced. 'Don't see what's wrong with a regular shower myself,' he muttered, but then he brightened, pulling Jenna into his side. 'Plenty big enough for two, then.'

'Well, now you come to mention it.' She squirmed against him. A shower would be lovely; she'd been feeling icky ever since their interlude in the motorway services car park. Not that a shower with Jason was likely to be particularly cleansing . . . Enjoyable, though.

'Get in there,' he growled, nudging her through the door.

The pair of them stripped off in seconds, coming quickly back together for a warm, bare-skinned embrace. As they kissed and held each other, Jason moved them in a clumsy dance towards the shower controls.

He broke off to examine them.

'Don't want to get boiled alive,' he muttered, fidgeting with the settings, before turning a gaze of frank lewdness back on Jenna. 'How's this wet room thing working out for you?' he said. 'Wet yet?'

She elbowed him in the ribs.

'Don't be vulgar,' she said.

'Thought that was what you saw in me,' he said. 'Ah, right, I reckon . . . step back a bit in case the temperature's wrong.'

They were drenched straight away in warm water, gushing from the jets that surrounded them. Jenna laughed with the suddenness of it and the delight of being here, naked, in this lovely room with this gorgeous naked man. His hair was plastered over his eyes, dripping down his face and he looked full of life and joy as he turned to her and cried, 'I wasn't expecting that.'

She twirled around in the hot, hard rain, letting the bullet-like drops attack every inch of her body. The pressure was firm enough to make her nipples tingle – it was almost a massage.

'You're definitely wet now, anyway,' said Jason after watching her for a few seconds.

'So are you. Where's the shampoo?'

She found a neat row of luxury bathing products on a shelf set into the tiled wall but Jason caught her around her middle before she could uncap any of them. He pretended to bite into her neck, sucking off the water and growling. His big hands closed over her breasts.

'Mmm,' she said, shutting her eyes and pushing herself back against him.

'Ever done it in a shower before?' he murmured into her ear, nipping at the lobe.

'Actually, I have,' she said. 'Not one like this, though. A teeny tiny cubicle. Nearly broke the door off. It was super uncomfortable and I slipped on some soap at one point.'

'Better improve the experience for you, then,' said Jason. 'So you can forget all about that time.'

He spun her around so they pressed together, her breasts squashing into his taut chest, and kissed her. Rivulets of water flowed around their conjoined mouths and over Jenna's closed eyelids, adding another layer of sensation to the ravishment. Somehow it made it better. This was why people were romantic about kissing in the rain, she thought. It felt *so* good.

'What's this?' he said, breaking off and reaching up to the shelf of products. 'Willow Bark and Echinacea for luxurious volume and control? Who writes these descriptions? It's just shampoo. Probably the same as what you get in Poundland.'

'Probably,' agreed Jenna, but she tilted her head back all the same, inviting him to massage the unguent into her hair. 'Go on. Oh, it smells gorgeous.'

'Not bad, I suppose,' he said grudgingly, lathering it into Jenna's scalp. The suds rolled off his fingers and down her neck, between her shoulder blades and breasts. Once Jason had finished treating her head to a perfect massage – just firm enough without becoming painful – he followed the clots of soap bubbles down her body, rubbing them into her skin when he found them.

The slippery-soft smoothness of her body seemed to intrigue him and he explored it with intent focus, his hands travelling up and down.

'I'm jealous of this water,' he said gruffly. 'The way it gets to be all over you all at once. I want to be able to do that.'

'You're giving it a good try,' said Jenna, and he was like some pleasure-giving octopus, his hands and mouth everywhere. 'Is there any conditioner?'

He put back the shampoo and felt around for another bottle.

'If Luxury Crème Rinse Solution is conditioner, then . . .?'

'I think it must be.'

It was rich and thick, coating her hair heavily. Jason had to concentrate hard on working its traces out of her soaked tresses, but eventually the job was done.

'Now I get to soap you,' he said greedily, but she held up a finger.

'Let me do *your* hair first,' she said. 'We need to do things properly.'

She loved Jason's hair and how he had not succumbed

to the local fashion of a skull-hugging razor crop. He had a fine head of chestnut brown locks that teetered on the border of being too long but never quite crossed it. Lately he had cultivated a neat goatee beard that gave him a devilish, rather buccaneering air she liked a lot.

'I want to wash your beard,' she said, easing Willow Bark and Echinacea into the soft bristles.

'Don't get it in my mouth,' he flustered, trying to direct her hands.

'Keep it shut then,' she countered, laughing as he made a disgusted grimace. Apparently Willow Bark and Echinacea didn't taste too good. She let her fingers swirl up behind his ears and let the lather bloom there. She had to reach up to wash his hair, so he bent his head down to her, keeping his eyes screwed shut against stray suds.

It felt good to have his thick dark hair slip between her fingers, and to feel the firm surface of his scalp at the roots.

She relished her work, enjoying his little sighs of pleasure as her fingertips probed deeper.

He looked more desirable than ever once the shampoo rinsed out and left him standing, tall and shiny-wet, with heavy dark hair swept back from his high forehead. Little drops of water splashed from the ends of his long eyelashes, making his eyes seem to dazzle. His lips looked softer and more kissable than ever.

She couldn't resist, tiptoeing up for a smooch. He clamped her against him with a swift movement of his arms, his hands clapping down on her bottom.

Warm water dripped sideways into her mouth and blinded her eyes but she could not have cared less. All she was conscious of was his tongue pushing into her mouth and his long hard body glued to hers by the strangely sealing property of the gushing jets. And there was something very insistent prodding at her hip now too.

The problem with sex in a shower, she thought distantly, *is the height differential*.

But surely a wet room was different. There was space for them to sit, or lie, or crouch, or kneel, or take up any number of different positions. And the floor, far from being knee-torturing ceramic, was made of soft rubberised tiling. The possibilities, in fact, were extremely promising.

But first – conditioner.

She tried to reach behind her to the shelf, but Jason had her too caught up in him and she had to break the kiss and explain, very breathily, what she wanted to do.

'Don't you think I'm in good enough condition?' he teased.

'You're in tip-top condition,' she said, 'but I wouldn't want that beard of yours getting too scratchy, now, would I?'

He chuckled, running his fingers through it, stroking his chin.

'Good point,' he said, 'considering where it often ends up. Wouldn't want to go giving you any nasty rashes.'

He let her smear the thick cream into his damp hair and beard, helping her to rinse it out afterwards.

'Now the good bit,' he enthused. 'Or, the best bit, cos it's all good.'

'Not yet,' she said, grasping his wrist halfway back to the shelf.

'I want to rub that gel into you,' he protested.

'What's the point in getting clean if we want to get dirty?' she said pointedly. 'Surely we should save the washing part for . . . afterwards?'

He didn't seem to cotton on at first, but a slow, wicked smile soon spread across his features.

'Ah, I get you,' he said. 'You little minx. You want it, do you?'

He braced an arm beneath her bottom and jerked her into his pelvis. His erection indented her lower stomach, making her squeal with the shock of it.

'You were the one talking about doing it in the shower,' she reminded him.

'Yeah, I was, but I might have been joking.'

'You, joke about wanting sex? I don't believe it.'

'OK, I wasn't joking. Of course I want to have you right here under the waterfall. I just had a slightly different order in mind.'

'You might have had. But I don't think *this* did.'

She inserted a hand between their lower torsos and wrapped her fingers around his shaft.

'Mind reader,' crooned Jason, shutting his eyes in rapture.

'To be fair, it's not your mind I'm reading,' she teased, stroking the droplets off him.

Before she had a chance to be shocked, he had taken hold of her round her waist and tipped her on all fours on the soft rubberised floor.

'All right,' he said, his face pressed next to hers while he crouched at her shoulder. 'Let's do it your way.'

Within seconds, her way was being done.

Jenna blessed the wet room designers for not

installing a hard surfaced floor as Jason slipped inside her and began to thrust beneath the jets. How amazing it was to feel the massaging pressure of the water on her back, her scalp, her shoulder blades at the same time as Jason provided a similar but less escapable force within her. The water pooled in the small of her back and streamed down the crack of her bottom. She imagined it gushing over Jason's cock as it sawed in and out. Not that extra lubrication was needed. This hard, hot, wet and sudden coupling had done its erotic magic the minute her knees hit the rubber.

She ignored the drips off the end of her nose and eyelashes, shutting her eyes and glorying in what was happening at her hindquarters. She felt part of the shower, of a piece with its roaring gush and spray steam. She and Jason, too, were one. They were water gods, doing what came naturally in their element.

It took longer to come than usual, perhaps because they were distracted by the extra attention needed to cope with the water, or perhaps because it was perversely anti-lubricating, and Jenna needed to rub at her clit for a long time before she began to feel the familiar stirrings. The water, maybe unsurprisingly, was actually a bit of a dampener.

But they got there in the end, and lay afterwards in luxurious relaxation, letting the water pelt their spent bodies, lathering each other in expensive gel when they were able to think straight again.

'We should get one of these,' said Jason, once they had crawled beyond the water's range and enveloped themselves in thick fluffy towels. 'There's enough bathrooms. Turn one into a wet room, yeah?'

'You're a convert, then?'

'Aren't you?'

'I'd like that. It's officially on my list for the renovations.'

Jason smiled briefly, then bit his lip and turned away.

Jenna almost felt the breath of cold air from him. She wanted to ask him what was up, but she knew. *Her* house. *Her* renovations. *Her* list. She had graciously accepted his suggestion, and he hated that the final decision was not really his.

Jason, she was understanding on a deeper and deeper level all the time, was a proud man. For all his playing at being the council estate dropout and dosser, he was intelligent and craved independence.

He would get it, once the art career took off, of course he would.

But in the meantime, he had no alternative but to depend on her. She knew it was difficult for him.

She crept up behind him with the hotel-provided bathrobe and slung it over his shoulders, clasping her arms around his chest and burying her face in the soft fuzz.

'The rest of the day is yours, to do with whatever you like,' she said. 'You lead and I'll follow.'

'I haven't got the faintest idea where to go,' he said. 'Besides, I thought you said we were going for a walk in the park.'

'Would you like that?'

'I dunno. Would I?'

She tired of his prickliness and stepped away, looking for the hairdryer.

'I don't know. Let's find out, shall we?'

Hyde Park was just across the road and they walked up towards the Serpentine, mingling with late afternoon crowds taking advantage of the summer heat. Most had escaped offices and lay on the grass, ecstatically unbuttoned with shoes kicked off. Some ate ice-cream, some read books, some snogged with abandon.

'I could fancy an ice-cream,' said Jason.

'We'll go and find one then.'

Jenna felt light and happy to be back in London, suddenly loving all the people for not crowding round her or trying to follow her. People here were too wrapped up in their own lives to care about who was passing by. It was many years since she'd been able to take a simple walk in a park without at least one bodyguard. Perhaps Jason fulfilled that function, she thought. Actually, that could be an idea . . .

By the time they reached the Serpentine café, she was feeling jumpier and had noticed several people, mainly young teenagers, trailing in their wake. The little train of followers led in turn to more attention being paid from the deckchairs.

Her dream of a pleasant anonymous summer evening walk seemed to be over.

'Jenna,' called one of the teenagers, not aggressively, but loudly enough to be irritating.

Jason wheeled around, thunder-faced.

'Are you a mate of hers?' he said, and the threat in his voice was evident.

'Jason, don't. We don't want negative publicity,' she demurred, but his work was done. The teenager shook her head, lips trembling.

'Leave 'er alone then,' he growled.

The teenagers stopped following them, but Jenna felt that some damage limitation was in order. Seeing that they were all still lurking around by the edge of the lake, she bought them all ice lollies and handed them around, to their considerable excitement.

'Sorry he was gruff,' she said, 'but we are trying to have a quiet walk by the lake.'

They seemed to understand and a couple of them apologised in turn. A third wanted to know when she would be back on *Talent Team*, but she just laughed and shook her head before walking away.

'What did you do that for?' sniped Jason, watching them mooch off with their lollies.

'Good PR,' she said. 'Come on, let's find somewhere shady and completely secluded and watch the boats on the lake.'

They took their ice-creams to a hedge and sat in front of it, as inconspicuous as they could be.

'You must get that a lot,' said Jason.

'Yes.'

'Doesn't it do your head in?'

Jenna took a philosophical lick of her honey and stem ginger cone.

'I'm used to it.'

'How could you get used to it?'

She thought about it.

'Actually, I'd forgotten what it was like,' she confessed. 'Perhaps it was naïve of me to think that this – a simple walk in the park – was possible. Back in LA, I never went anywhere unaccompanied. Always travelling by chauffeur-driven limo, flanked by my bodyguards on the way to meetings or parties or anything. Didn't even go shopping unless the shops were closed to the public. It's not the public you have to even worry about there – LA people are so used to seeing stars all over the place, they barely turn a hair. It's the world press. The freelancers after something to sell to one of those woeful celeb mags.'

'Like living in a bubble,' said Jason.

'It just seems normal after a while. It's the ones with kids I really feel sorry for. Having to keep them hidden away in their walled mansions. I feel privileged – seriously, don't laugh – that I grew up on the estate and I could ride my bike wherever I wanted and get into fights behind the shops. Better that than what these kids have to call a childhood.'

'Is that why you and Deano never . . .?'

She licked around the base of the ice-cream scoop, considering how to put her answer.

'No, that's not the reason. At least, it's not *the* reason. It's one of them, I suppose.'

'Do you want kids?'

Jenna shrugged. 'The time's never been right.'

'Work?'

'Yeah, work. And Deano.' She paused. 'I mean, he's a kid himself. A thirty-seven-year-old kid.'

'I've heard rock stars don't make great dads. Not that I'd know what would. Great dads are in short supply where I'm from.'

'Where I'm from too,' Jenna reminded him gently. 'Though mine was good. I really ought to go out and visit him in Spain one of these days. Maybe when the weather gets cold, eh?'

'Why are you asking me?'

'You could come too.'

'Er, I don't think so. I don't do chit-chat with parents.'
He looked anxious and she rubbed his arm.

'They'd like you,' she said, though she wasn't really sure this was the truth.

'No parent has ever liked me,' he said. 'Not even my own.'

She scooped up a tongueful of luscious ice-cream and waited for it to slide down her throat before speaking again.

'You don't see yourself as a dad then?'

He laughed bitterly. 'I don't even know what a dad *is*. I mean, I like kids. I prefer them to adults most of the time. But I'm not sure I could eat a whole one, if you know what I mean.'

Jenna smiled. 'It just seems unimaginable, somehow, doesn't it? You see parents all around, yet their lives are mysteries to those of us who haven't crossed into that realm of experience.'

'I know a stack of dads,' said Jason. 'The estate's full of 'em. It's just that none of them ever see their kids. I don't know how they can do it. How can they carry on, day to day, knowing that their own flesh and blood is so close – and not seeing them? I suppose it's what I've always wondered about my own dad. Whoever he is.'

'Why won't your mother tell you?'

'Sometimes she says she's sworn to secrecy.' He rolled his eyes. 'Goes to show how much she cares about what I feel. I'm not worthy to know who my own dad is. Then other times she just says she doesn't know; it could be one of several guys. She has a different excuse for every day of the week. To be honest, she probably doesn't know. Probably too drunk to remember.'

He closed his fist around a clump of grass and pulled it up with vicious strength.

'But she does love you,' said Jenna. 'And she's proud of you.'

'For what that's worth,' he said. He crunched down on his cone. 'I've had enough of being angry all the time, Jen. I've been angry all these years, and look where it's got me? Wasting my life.'

'Not any more,' she said. 'Things are going to change for you. They're already changing.'

'I've got the one change I need, and that's you,' he said. 'I don't care about anything else.'

He leaned into her and they kissed. Jenna shut her eyes and let it be all and everything. The sounds around them, of oars plashing on the lake, idle laughter, the dull thud of a bat and ball game, merged inside her head into a delicious fuzzy melange. Until another sound shook her out of it.

'Jenna! Jenna! Is that your new man? Give us a smile. Give us a look.'

Later, over dinner in the hotel's Michelin-starred restaurant, she was able to laugh about it.

'Oh God, the looks on their faces when you got up and ran at them. It was as if they were being charged by a homicidal rhino. I've never seen a crowd scatter so fast.'

'Homicidal rhino, thanks. I've had better compliments.' He frowned at the soup, which was unexpectedly cold and had leaves floating on the surface. 'What the fuck's this anyway?'

'Watermelon gazpacho. I thought it'd be refreshing on a day like this.'

Mind you, the air conditioning seemed set to arctic, so maybe something hotter might have been a better choice.

'Gazpacho? Sounds like a Mexican bandit. "My name is Gazpacho. You knew my father. Prepare to die."'

Jenna laughed at his hammy Spanish accent.

'Don't you like it? I can ask for more bread, if you'd rather.'

'No, it's all right. Just . . . a bit weird.' He spooned some up, nodding his head as he swallowed.

'There's so much I want to show you,' said Jenna. 'So many lovely things in this world. Beautiful places to visit . . .'

'Where you get mobbed,' finished Jason wryly.

'Well, some of them are private,' she said. 'But . . .' She sighed.

'Yeah, well, I want to earn some money of my own before we start jet-setting anyway,' he said, swirling his spoon about in his soup.

'You will,' Jenna insisted gently. 'But it might take some time, and initially cost us more than we make. But you've got my services and contacts for free, and that will be worth thousands. We need to organise the exhibition first, and then—'

'No,' he cut in, rather harshly, so that Jenna was shocked into silence. 'No, Jen, you don't get what I'm saying. I need to earn some money *now*. I can't go on living off you. I'm not a ponce.'

She shook her head. 'I don't think of you like that! God!'

'You might not, but everyone else will. All they see is me, living the life of Riley, whoever he was, in your house, in your bed, on your cash. I'm not going to be your kept man. It was different when I had no choice. But I've got a choice now, and I'm going to work for a living.'

'Why change the habit of a lifetime?' said Jenna, stung by shock. She regretted the remark before it was out of her mouth.

He pushed away the gazpacho half-eaten and left the restaurant.

Jenna, swearing under her breath, more at herself than him, followed him to their room.

'I'm sorry,' she said, slipping through the door after him. 'All right? It just came out because you were being stroppy and I don't really see why it's a problem that your future brilliant career is funded by my money – just to start with. All the great artists had a patron, pretty much. It's been that way throughout history.'

'I'm not all the great artists,' said Jason, standing by the picture window, looking down on London at sunset. 'I'm Jason Watson. I've done nothing all my life and I think it's time I changed that.' He turned to face her. 'It hurt me, what you said, because it's true, Jen. I've spent twenty-eight years arsing around on benefits because I was scared to do anything with my life. I was scared. I'm not the kind of person who makes it. I'm not . . .'

He broke off and Jenna rushed over to him, throwing her arms around his neck and crushing him to her.

'It's OK. Everything's going to be OK. Come and sit down. Let's have a drink.'

The suite contained a huge cream corner sofa, on which they settled with a bottle of wine from the minibar and two glasses.

Jason nibbled at his fingernails while she poured, staring moodily towards the panoramic view outside.

'I could paint that,' he said. 'That's just about the best view I've ever seen. So much life, so much going on. I could just stand looking at it for hours.'

Jenna smiled and handed him his glass. 'That's London,' she said. 'My first days here I was overwhelmed. I almost couldn't face it. So much to take in all at once.'

'Do people get used to it?' he said. 'Did you?'

'I got used to it. And then, after that, every other place seemed incredibly, frustratingly slow. Until I went to LA. You become attuned to fast living, infinite choice, constant change. I never, ever thought I'd find myself back in Bledburn. I guess I had to crash for that to happen.'

'Crash? You mean, the thing with Deano?'

'The thing with Deano, yeah, and . . . just generally. I was so close to breakdown, Jason. I was this far away from it.' She showed him her finger and thumb, almost touching. 'I knew something bad was coming. I jumped before it jumped on me.'

'Like, mental illness or something?'

'Something like that, I think. Yes. And now I'm so much calmer. I feel I've regained myself, started to see more clearly. That LA life was warping my brain.'

'Yeah, all that money and luxury. Must be tough.' Jason laughed sardonically.

'Don't, Jason, I'm serious. I mean, I was starting to think like *them*. The people I'd vowed never to be like. I'd always told myself I'd keep my down-to-earth Bledburn attitude but after eight years in LA I was full-on LaLa. I had a nutritionist and a reflexologist.'

Jason laughed again, more kindly this time.

'Fuck me,' he said. 'I don't know what that even means.'

She put a hand on his knee. 'Neither do I, love. Not really. And the worst thing was, I was starting to do that thing *they* do. Of despising everyone who isn't in "the business". Turning my nose up at people who weren't perfectly buff and toned and tanned and rich and . . . ugh. So false. I hated what I was becoming. And I can never thank you enough for saving me from it.'

'Yeah,' said Jason thoughtfully. 'I saw a few episodes of that show of yours, back in the day. It wasn't my kind of thing really, but the bit everyone loved was where they take the piss out of people who are never going to make it. I always thought that was lame. I never liked that.'

Tears prickled in Jenna's eyes as she felt the justice of Jason's words.

'I wouldn't have done . . . the real me wouldn't have liked that either. But I lost her . . . somewhere along the way . . .'

Jason shuffled up closer to her, putting an arm around her, letting her rest her head on his shoulder.

'I'm all right,' she said. 'Pass us a tissue, eh?'

He dabbed her eyes and the tip of her nose, then put her glass of wine back in her hand.

'There you go,' he said. 'Anyway, whatever you thought was lost is back now, in full effect, yeah? The real Jenna Myatt.'

She took a slug of the wine. 'God,' she said. 'We were talking about *you*, not me. Sorry to derail. That's Hollywood again. Turns you into a self-obsessed idiot.'

'Stop being so hard on yourself.' He nudged her and winked. 'That's my job.'

'You were talking about how you felt about your life.

About how you'd been scared to do anything with it,' Jenna prompted, laying her head back on his shoulder.

'Yeah. At first, when I was at primary school, I had big ambitions, like all kids do. I was going to be a superhero, then I was going to be a ninja, then I was going to be a famous graffiti artist. So far so good. Then the usual Bledburn thing happened.'

'You lost your faith in yourself?'

'Exactly. That school teaches us we won't make it unless we toe the line and wear our ties straight and do what we're told. I'm not that good at doing what I'm told, so the message I got, day in, day out, was that I was heading straight for the scrap heap. You can only fight that for so long before you believe it.'

'You were a rebel.' Jenna laughed ruefully. 'I think we all were, at that school. Nobody saw the point, especially after the pit closed.'

'Exactly. It's all "do this, do that, if you want to get a job" but what jobs? There weren't any.' Jason gazed into the bowl of his wineglass. 'We all gave up, around year eight. Just pissed about in class or stopped going. I still thought I could make it as an artist, though. But I suppose, as the years went by, it dawned on me how I was from the wrong place at the wrong time and didn't know anyone who could help me. I suppose you could say I got depressed.'

'Did you see a doctor?'

'Well, no, because I didn't *know* I was depressed. I thought you had to be like my mum, sitting indoors day in day out drinking White Lightning and staring at the telly. That was depressed. I mean, I went out, I had friends, I had girlfriends, I had what I would have called good times. But behind it all there was this hopelessness. This feeling that there was nothing else to live for but partying till you threw up in someone's trashed living room. We pretended it was how we wanted to live, and by the time we worked out that we were pretending, it was too late.'

'Too late? You're a young man, Jason.'

'I don't feel young.'

'Well, you are. And you're luckier than most. You've got an amazing talent. Now you have a chance to get away from everything that was holding you back.'

'Yeah, and I'm going to take it, Jen, so don't go on at me. But in the meantime, I want to pay my way.' He stood up and gestured around him at the suite. 'I mean, look at this. This is way beyond anything I ever thought I'd have in my life. But I don't feel like I should be here, because I haven't paid a penny towards it. I should be out there sleeping in the park by rights.'

'Don't be daft.'

'It's not daft.' His eyes shone with righteous anger. 'It's time I grew up, Jen. It's time for me to be a man.'

'I know you are . . .'

'Don't joke. I'm serious. In ten years' time, my mates'll still be on the estate, sleeping all morning, sitting outside the off licence all afternoon, smoking weed all night in each other's houses, playing Call of Duty on ripped off Xboxes. That's not going to be me, even if the art thing fails.'

'Of course it isn't. And the art thing won't fail.'

'I owe you, Jen. Big time. And I'm going to pay you back.'

'I don't want your—'

'I'm going to pay you back,' he repeated, alight with the ferocity of his resolve.

'OK,' she said quietly. 'OK. I believe you. Now will you come and drink your wine?'

It was the right thing to say, she realised. It had been pointless to tell him that he didn't need to do it, that she was happy with the way things were, that she didn't begrudge a penny. The point was his resolution, his determination to overcome the wasted years and turn himself into somebody he could live with.

But there was nothing he could do tonight, so she tried to change the subject.

'I've been reading that book I found in the cellar at the Hall,' she said.

'Oh yeah?' His voice was blank, as if the impassioned speech before had drained him of expression.

'I really think the body is hers,' she said.

'Whose?'

'Frances Manning . . . Fairy Fay. She gets a job as governess at Harville Hall. I think she goes on to marry the lord and he kills her, or she kills herself.'

'Sounds like a good book.'

'No, it's really creepy to read, actually. I've only got as far as her getting to Harville Hall and meeting everyone, but I'm dreading what's going to happen next. I almost don't want to read on.'

'What, and you haven't even got to the good bit yet? Have you got it with you?'

Jenna nodded. 'I shouldn't have brought it, really. It's delicate. That's another reason I don't much like reading it. It smells so weird – sort of sour and dusty. It's a miserable smell for a miserable story. But I wrapped it up in a tablet cover and brought it all the same.'

'Give us a read. Do you think it's really the diary of the skeleton we found? Do you think she was murdered?'

Jenna rose to find her suitcase.

'I don't know, Jason, and I'm not sure I want to find out.'

'I do. Go and get it.'

Chapter Six

January 17th

I breakfasted alone in my room – comfortable enough, if a little small – and then the young ladies were brought in to meet me. Oh heavens, ridiculous that I should be nervous of a pair of little girls, but I was, very much.

Both of them wore expressions of milk-curdling sour-ness, such that I was grateful to have already disposed of the little jug of cream for my porridge. All my efforts at friendliness and conversation were met with severe rebuff. Not a word fell from their lips.

The lady who had brought them in was the family's nurse, Bertha – a lady who had performed faithful service at Harville Hall for many years, and indeed, it was evident, for she was very elderly. She reminded them of the master's decision that I was to be the last governess before the last resort of boarding school was reached, and this seemed to bring a weary resignation to the fore. Both girls then bade me good day and offered a species of reluctant curtsey.

It was not much, but better than the frozen silence.

Our first morning in the school room was a long and dreary affair. To elicit any response at all from them was the proverbial drawing of blood from a stone. And yet one sensed that, beneath their hostility, two unhappy and lonely girls existed, having only each other for comfort. I have determined to be a friend to them, even if I must crack away at their stubborn carapaces for a month of Sundays.

Saw very little of Lord H, who went out to the mine and then kept himself in his study all evening. It is lonely here and the staff, when I attempt to engage any of them in light discourse, oblige me with such a sullen air that I am quite put off.

Consoled myself in writing long letters to Mama and Mary. How I wish I could bring them here.

'I'd get out of there if I were her,' said Jason gloomily. Jenna shuddered.

'It's very odd to think of her, quite alone and adrift, in *my* house. I wonder which was her room? And where did the girls sleep?'

Jason shrugged. 'Perhaps in the room where we found the graffiti message that time? You know – "Help me". Maybe that was them.'

'Maybe it was.' Jenna's scalp prickled.

'Go on then. Turn the page.'

January 19th

Summoned to take tea this afternoon with Lord Harville, a most momentous occasion, for he has been all but invisible since our first meeting on my arrival here.

A miserable and rainy day but we sat in the drawing room that overlooks the garden, watching the raindrops course down each square pane in the French doors. Any glimpse of the garden was quite obliterated, but of course, my attention was focused upon my employer.

He was perfectly polite, if unsmiling, and seemed solicitous of my comfort.

Of course, his primary motive for our meeting was to ask after the girls and establish for himself whether my appointment was a success or failure.

I knew this, but was truthful with him, opining that, while progress was slow, it was at least progress and I intended to be steady and unwavering in my devotion to their education.

He seemed to appreciate this, but said I must inform him immediately should their behaviour decline or become unmanageable.

All this time, his eyes had remained upon his plate of scones, but now the quality of his attention changed and became something quite other. How, I cannot quite explain, but he held my eyes and proceeded to ask me a perfect barrage of questions about my own education, my likes and dislikes, my hopes and fears.

It was most peculiar to be the object of such a man's apparently sincere interest. What possible reason could he have had for wanting to know anything at all about a person of such little account as myself?

'I am a man accustomed to giving orders,' he said to me. 'But my own daughters are the only people I cannot make obey. Their conduct shames me.'

'No,' I said, and I blush at my presumption now in contradicting him. 'I think they only crave your

*attention. Your affection. If you were to invite them to
take tea with you, I am sure you would see a gentler
side to them.'*

*He stared at me, so long and so hard that I fully
expected to be dismissed on the spot.*

*But instead, he said, 'Perhaps I should. Perhaps I
will.'*

*We finished our tea in near-silence after that, save
some desultory remarks about the weather and the
newspapers.*

*Alone now in my room I cannot rest for thinking of
him and his strange manner. At first I thought him cold
and remote, but now I see how grief has laid its mark
upon him and changed what he once must have been.
A heart beats inside his stiff breast, of that I am sure.
But of what use is such knowledge to me? And why does
it affect me so?*

'Struck by the love bug,' said Jason laconically.

'Oh dear, do you think so?'

'Poor kid, didn't take much, did it? Just a bit of attention was enough. I bet he knew it too.'

'She seems very easy prey,' Jenna agreed. 'I hope he
doesn't take advantage of her.'

'I bet he does.'

'And those poor girls . . . bereaved of their mother
and ignored by their father. God. I'm so glad I didn't
live in those times. Imagine.'

'I'd have been in the workhouse,' said Jason. 'Or more
likely in prison. I think prison was meant to be better.
Better food.'

'Or you'd have gone down the mine,' said Jenna.

'Virtually every man in Bledburn did. I'd have probably married some miner and lived in a two-up two-down with a brood of screaming kids.' She laughed. 'I can't imagine anything worse.'

Jason put his hand over hers.

'What if I was the miner?'

She laid her head on his shoulder. 'Then it would have been bearable, at least.'

'You might not have wanted the brood of kids, but getting them in the first place might have been all right.'

She tried to picture it – living in a dark terrace in a cobbled street, washing down her front doorstep in a shawl while children screamed and laughed up and down the pavement. Jason arriving home from the pit, showered but still grimy, with dirt-blackened fingernails. A stew made of cheap scrag end with rough bread and a pot of beer from the corner house. A tin bath in front of the fire.

It sounded cosy in her imagination but she had no doubt it would have been hard, repetitive and possibly soul-destroying, especially if you weren't one of nature's matriarchs.

'Getting the first one, maybe,' she said. 'The other times, the bed would probably have been full of babies and toddlers. Not conducive to a romantic atmosphere.'

He chuckled and kissed her head.

'Good old twenty-first century, eh?'

'Yes,' she agreed. 'Just as many people living grim lives but at least they can have sex without being watched.'

'Unless they want to be,' said Jason after a beat.

She slapped his wrist and a playful struggle ensued,

during which the diary slipped off Jenna's lap and fell in
a dusty heap on the floor.

'Shit,' she said, sobering. 'I must be more careful with
this. It could crumble to dust if I don't look after it.'

She found the page they had been looking at.

'I wonder if Miss Frances Manning will be having any
sex any time soon,' she said.

'They didn't go in for it much, did they, the Victorians?'

'Well, we're here, so presumably . . .'

'I thought they were meant to be all weird about it.'

'I'm willing to bet the Harvilles were weird about
everything.'

'Good point,' said Jason with a laugh. 'Go on, then.
Let's read on a bit.'

January 22nd

*Such a trying day with the girls that I was obliged
to leave the school room and gather myself on the landing
before I lost my temper.*

*They can be charming, but today they have been
demons, deliberately obtuse and sly. I want very much
to like and befriend them, but they make it so terribly
difficult for me.*

*I called for Bertha to watch over them while I collected
myself. It occurred to me that perhaps an aggravating
factor had been the dreary weather. It has rained for
quite five days together, and not one of us has set foot
out of doors in all that time.*

*The wet weather having finally abated, I decided to
take the girls outside for a nature study lesson, in hopes
that all our spirits might be lifted by some fresh air.*

Alas, the lesson did not run as I intended it to. The

girls were quite ungovernable, escaping to the far corners of the garden, where they remained concealed in the woodland for more than an hour.

In despair, after much hunting and calling, I sat myself at the garden table and hid my face in my hands. I entertained serious thoughts of resigning my post and going home to Nottingham, even more so when Lord Harville appeared on the terrace.

I tried to dry my eyes and compose myself as quickly as I could, but it was too late. He had taken the measure of my distress and came swiftly towards me.

'Miss Manning, whatever is the matter? Where are the children?'

'A game of hide and seek,' I said, and may God forgive me for the lie. 'It has been so rainy lately, and they needed the air.'

'As do you, by all appearances,' he said, sitting beside me. 'You are pale and your eyes . . .'

Modesty dictated that I should look away, change the subject to one that did not concern my personal appearance, but I found myself meeting his gaze, which was of such genuine concern that my heart was pierced.

'Oh, I am quite well, I assure you,' I told him. 'A slight cold, perhaps.'

He did not believe me: that much was plain from the sober judgement of his fascinating eyes. I could not determine their colour. They seemed to hold a little of each, the predominant shade varying with the light.

'Miss Manning,' he began, but the girls chose that moment to reappear, and, oh! the sight of them was enough to make me cry out in dismay.

Their pinafores were torn and filthy, their faces

smeared with mud, their ringlets tangled with dead leaves and twigs.

'I thought you said hide and seek,' remarked his lordship. 'Not stick in the mud.' He paused. 'Well, I had come out here to invite these two young ladies to take tea with me, but it is clear that they are in no condition to do so.'

Even through the caked-on dirt, their faces could be seen to fall. In amongst my anger and distress, I felt a pang of sympathy for them.

'Oh, Papa,' remonstrated Maria, but he waved them away.

'Go and put yourselves into a bath. I will speak to you in my study after tea. And, since I now require company for that repast, I will invite instead Miss Manning here.'

Maria and Susannah stomped off with murder in their eyes, and all directed at me.

'Would you do me the honour?' asked Lord Harville, standing and extending his arm.

How strange it felt to enter the house on his lordship's arm – surely hardly appropriate, and yet also thrilling in the extreme. I am not a lady, but I certainly felt like one at that moment. I enjoyed it entirely too much.

At tea, he was terribly kind and managed to tease out from me the difficulties I had been having with the girls. I begged him not to be harsh with them but he made me no promises.

'But do you see your way to establishing a firmer footing with them?' he asked me. 'For Rome, of course, was not built in a day, and I fear even the architects of that eminent city might themselves have baulked at

*the challenge offered to them by my daughters. But I
think there is hope. I must allow myself that, at least.'*

*'Oh, I am sure it is but a matter of their becoming
accustomed to me,' I said.*

*I did so want to reassure him – and myself at the
same time – that I allowed a breath of optimism to
enter my hitherto despairing soul.*

*'I do not know how they can treat you ill,' he said,
his peculiar eyes upon me again. 'I am sure I never
could.'*

*By the time I was sure I had heard him aright, a
maid came in, breaking the unholy silence between us.
I excused myself immediately, claiming a headache.*

*What did I fear? Why did I leave so precipitately?
I scarcely know myself.*

'Woah, cliffhanger,' said Jason. 'He's a fast worker,
though, I'll give him that.'

'Lonely, I suppose,' said Jenna. 'Widower, rattling
around in that house with two wild daughters. I bet he
couldn't believe his luck when he got a governess who
was young and pretty.'

'Do you think he ends up marrying her, though?'
asked Jason dubiously. 'He could probably have talked
her into bed without all that.'

'Only one way to find out,' said Jenna briskly, turning
a page.

January 26th
*I have been in such torment, such precious torment,
and now it has been transformed into a sparkling ocean
of pure joy.*

'Wow,' said Jason with feeling. 'Carry on.'

These past four days I have kept as strictly as I can to the school room and my bedchamber, for fear of encountering Lord Harville. I could not bring myself to express aloud, or even in my thoughts, my reasons for doing so, but I can say it now. It is because I love him. Yes, I love him. I have been fascinated by him since the moment I entered this house. No man has ever looked at me so, with such a penetrating need to understand what he sees. To begin with, it frightened me, for I could not accept that such a man might have any interest in me. I suspected that he might have some nefarious intention and I made sure to be circumspect. Besides, Susannah and Maria took up quite all of my time, with their demands and their disappearances and their long periods of mute defiance.

I was exhausted and low in spirits this evening, having bade them goodnight and taken my place in my window seat with my work basket.

A mournful wind set about the house and I was glad of my little fire, though it was burning low and I did not want to disturb the housekeeper by asking for more fuel. They are unfriendly enough in the servants' hall; I have no desire to enter into any intercourse with them that is not strictly necessary.

Ah, but soon all of that will change . . .

But I gallop ahead of myself. There I sat, in my little nook, netting a new purse, when I heard a knock at my door.

Thinking it to be one of the girls complaining of an upset stomach or a quarrel with the other, I called for the knocker to enter.

*Imagine my confusion – and my blushes – when my
visitor proved to be his lordship. He was dressed formally,
for dinner, in a silk waistcoat and tails, his hair brushed
and curled.*

'Your lordship,' I said, rising from my seat. 'Is something amiss?'

'Yes,' he said, and his voice was so hollow it alarmed
me even more. 'A very great deal is amiss. Dine with
me, Miss Manning, and I will expand on the theme.'

'Oh . . . but . . . my dress.' I was so plainly attired, and
I possessed nothing suitable for the dining table of a lord.

'Your dress is nothing to the purpose,' he said, and
he was impatient, not his usual courteous self. 'Dine
with me, damn you.'

In my shock at his uncouth language, I could do
nothing but follow him downstairs.

The table was set for two and a bowl of soup awaited
me, together with a crystal flute of wine.

'I am honoured, my lord,' I said, taking my seat.
'But also somewhat surprised. Might I ask your reasons
for inviting me to dine with you tonight?'

'Yes, you might,' he said, eyeing me as he unrolled
his napkin. 'The fact is, Miss Manning, I have admired
you from the first moment I laid eyes upon you.'

The words were clear, and yet they did not strike my
ear in a manner that allowed them to sink in. I had to
ask him to repeat them.

'I see no reason to keep silent on the matter,' he
continued. 'You are unattached, and so am I. Therefore,
it seems nothing prevents me from making a declaration.
Miss Manning, I love you, and I want to make you my
wife.'

I stared down at the soup, which was a white soup, topped with a sprig of parsley so highly coloured I doubted its veracity. It swam before my eyes, green and white, with the suggestion of a skin forming at the edges of the bowl.

'I wonder if you can mean this,' I whispered. 'For it is so strange.'

'What the devil's strange about it?' He banged his soup spoon on the tablecloth. 'A single man proposes marriage to a single woman. It happens every day.'

'Not to me.'

'Well, I should hope not. Can't have any old Tom, Dick and Harry proposing to my sweetheart, can I?'

His sweetheart!

The words gave me courage to face him across the table.

'It is so unaccountable that you . . . should look at me,' I explained.

'You're a handsome woman,' he said, and I blushed anew. 'But I suppose you refer to our disparity in rank and station. Well, well, that's all the same to me. I am a man in need of a wife, and a mother to my children. You are a single woman in need of protection. Marry me, Miss Manning, and your family will never again know want or distress.'

The way he phrased it, like a bargain at market, wounded me. But I saw the sense of it all the same. And he had struck me with the hand of love already. I only needed the black rush of fear at the enormity of the decision to recede and then I would be able to . . .

I spoke.

'Yes, my lord, I will marry you.'

*He tapped his bowl with his spoon as if formally
sealing the contract.*

*'Good,' he said. 'That's settled. Now, will you take
some veal?'*

'What a romantic bastard,' observed Jason.

Jenna's laugh was a little rueful. 'What is she getting
herself into?' she wondered.

'Never mind her,' said Jason, removing the book from
Jenna's hand and laying it gently on the table before
cupping her cheek. 'What have you got yourself into,
eh?'

Jenna recognised the dark look in his eye and felt the
familiar thrill.

'What do you mean?' she whispered.

'You haven't forgotten that bargain we made, have
you? Back at the services?'

'Oh.' Her mind returned to that crowded, striplit café
and the way she had walked back into it, knickerless
beneath her skirt. 'No.'

'You get to drive my career. I get to drive *you*. And I
feel in the mood for a nice drive tonight.'

'What, after all that time we spent on the M1 today?'

But Jenna's voice wavered and she knew Jason wouldn't
be diverted with a quip.

'That was a boring drive. Too smooth. I'm thinking
of something a little bit . . .' He leant forward, his breath
advancing towards her ear, then his lips were there.
'Rougher.'

'A dirt track?' suggested Jenna, then she laughed with
shock and her hand flew to her mouth at the image that
came to mind.

Jason chuckled into her ear.

She could have kicked herself.

'If that's what you want . . .'

'I was joking,' she said hastily. 'I meant . . . more of a B road.'

'You want me to take the B route, eh?'

Oh God, this was even worse!

'No, the A road,' she said decisively. 'Jason, can we just say it straight out? I'm just being stupid, not issuing an invitation to you to . . . to . . . oh God.'

'Have your arse?' he murmured, kissing her eartip.

'Not tonight,' she said and she was firm.

'But you're not saying never?'

'I'm not . . . saying . . . oh, that feels good.'

He was kissing the space below her earlobe, pushing the tip of his tongue into the yielding skin of her neck. His teeth nipped, ever so faintly, at the dampened patches, sending tingles through her that made her want to swoon.

Moving swiftly and without hesitation, he laid her flat on her back on the sofa, covering her with his own weight. She enjoyed the stalwart heaviness of him, the breadth of his chest, the length of his legs as they slid into position between hers.

He was wearing jeans and his shirt had come untucked from the waistband so she could reach inside and put her palm to the warm, hairy expanse inside.

'You need a good suit,' she'd said earlier on when they dressed for dinner. 'For meetings.'

'Oh yeah?' he'd retorted. 'Well, if you get to dress me, I get to dress you. So watch it.'

She'd brushed the remark aside at the time as typical Jason chippiness, but now, as his lips descended on hers and she felt the domination of his body upon her, it returned to her. Jason needed some control over his life. He was going to make her pay for what she took from him in full.

The thought aroused her as she pictured herself made to attend meetings in tiny shiny miniskirts and fishnet bralets, Jason by her side in a sharp Prada suit, one hand on her tightly-packed bottom.

Of course it couldn't happen in real life. Imagine the press! But the thought of it made her breath come more quickly, and she wriggled urgently underneath Jason's bulk.

He released her lips and, to her considerable dismay, hauled himself off her.

'Get your clothes off,' he said gruffly. 'Come on. Or do I have to rip them off you?'

She struggled to her feet, conscious of how her skirt had ridden up and her shirt was half-undone already. She was hardly the image of elegance she'd portrayed in the hotel restaurant.

She shucked off her high-heeled pumps and got to work on the remaining buttons with fumbling fingers. She tried to retain a modicum of poise, keeping a level, challenging gaze upon Jason as she worked. He stood, smirking slightly, enjoying the show, trying not to draw attention to his bulging crotch.

'You ever seen a strip show?' he asked her as she began folding the shirt with fussy precision. 'They don't fold their gear up. Just put the bloody thing down and get on.'

'I've never seen a strip show,' she said, feeling a little prick of absurd pain at having to discard the shirt unfolded. 'It's not really my kind of thing.'

'I thought LA was full of sleaze. City of Vice and all that.'

'Not my LA. I didn't hang around Sunset Strip much.'

She unzipped her skirt, giving Jason an annoyed glare. Why would he expect her to have watched strippers? Did he think she'd spent her evenings snorting coke off hundred dollar bills in high end brothels? Nothing of the sort. She'd spent most of them on the phone, toying with freshly-delivered macrobiotic carb-free food in cartons. Wondering where Deano was.

The memory of all that loneliness washed over her as her skirt slithered down her stockinged legs.

Immediately Jason made a lunge for her, hooking the backs of her knees so that she tumbled on top of him, knocking scatter cushions everywhere.

'Can't resist a pair of stockings,' he growled. 'You put those on to get this, didn't you?'

'What if I did?' she said, straddling his hips, trying her best to pin him down although it proved impossible.

'All through that meal,' he said, 'you were thinking about getting me alone afterwards. I know you. I know what you're like. Sex mad.'

She giggled, bending her face to his ear to purr into it. 'Pot, meet kettle.'

He had her flipped over on to her stomach in an instant, and he crouched over her with his hands on her shoulders.

'Yeah, well, if you don't want me to be sex mad, you shouldn't be so damn sexy, should you?' he accused.

'I can't help it,' she spluttered, his weight on her back forcing the breath from her lungs.

'You do it on purpose.'

He braced an arm beneath her ribcage and pulled her up on to all fours. At least she could breathe again, but somehow her lungs didn't want to do it properly. And who cared what her lungs were up to when her stomach was fluttering like a butterfly farm? Not to mention the hot, soaked condition of her knickers.

'What do you want me to do about it?' she asked, hoping the answer would involve the rapid conjunction of intimate body parts.

'Absolutely nothing,' he purred, ripping down her knickers.

And with that, he was inside her. No ceremony, no sweet talk, no stroking and feathering, just the quick, hot connection they both craved.

She didn't know when or how he had shucked down his trousers and pants, but somewhere in those few panting, wanting moments between falling on the couch and getting nailed, he had managed.

What a talent, she thought, her head swimming with the delicious dirtiness of what he did to her. *Well spotted, Jenna.*

Now his hand was on her neck, holding her in position so he could thrust hard without fear of her collapsing forward.

She surrendered to everything: his control, her own desire for it, the primitive urgency of the coupling, letting herself fall into it and forget all else.

He let go of her neck and instead grabbed a ponytail of hair, wrapping it tight about his fist. She pushed her hips back, signalling how much she loved what he did to her, raising her bottom to him.

He smacked it, hard, but not too hard to break her intense focus on taking pleasure from her submission.

He grunted now with each thrust, plunging deeper. It was as if he was determined to find something hidden at her centre, a core of her, perhaps her soul. She knew he was demanding something of her.

She thought she knew what it was, too. She worked hard to sustain the rhythm they established and to make sure each forward drive of his cock rubbed against that crucial little spot inside her. He wanted her to come. He wanted her to feel that she owed him her pleasure. For that to happen, she must first let it overwhelm her.

'Yes,' she muttered, once she was sure she was on course to her orgasm. The first low stirrings rushed up from the pit of her stomach, then a tremendous climax radiated outwards from her g-spot, causing her to press her mouth to the arm of the sofa and howl into the buttoned leather.

'Yes, yes,' answered Jason, slamming into her. 'You love it.'

He still tugged at her scalp but she felt no pain, only a melting, maddening tingling all over.

'Yes,' she said. 'Give it to me.'

He grabbed her hips and emptied inside her, for so long that she thought there would be nothing left inside him, just a boneless shell of him lying limp on the sofa.

She was almost right.

When she managed to wriggle out from underneath him, he looked as if he might never move again.

'Are you OK?' she whispered, brushing his sweat-damp brow.

An exhalation parted his lips. It might have been some kind of laugh.

'Fuckin' hell,' he whispered. 'What do you think?'

'You look . . .'

'Shagged out? Yeah. There's a reason for that.'

He encircled her with a shaking arm and brought her down to lie, squashed between him and the sofa back, leather on one side, quivering flesh and hot blood on the other.

'I do love you, you know,' she said, rubbing her forehead against his.

She felt his eyelashes flutter on her cheek.

'Mutual,' he said. 'Don't ever stop.'

Chapter Seven

Jenna woke up the next morning feeling sore. Her bones ached and she needed a shower more than she needed air. Jason had kept her up half the night. If there was any justice, he should be feeling even worse.

She turned reluctantly to her side, ready to ask him, but he wasn't there.

Must be in the shower, she thought groggily, but no sounds of water splashing on to the wet room floor could be heard.

She yawned and tried to prop herself on her elbows for a squint round the dim room. Too much effort. She flopped back down and reached for her phone on the bedside table. That made her open her eyes. Half past nine already! And she had meetings scheduled for eleven and two o'clock today.

She edged herself into a sitting position, wincing at the sting between her legs.

'Jay,' she called. 'Jason.'

No reply. Damn. She was going to have to get out of bed.

Gone were the days when she could shag all night and spring back into shape like a bath sponge. A twinge of regret that Deano, rather than Jason, had enjoyed those years of insouciant flexibility added itself to all the other twinges as she hobbled around the room looking for her dressing gown.

'Jen, you're thirty-five not ninety,' she chided herself, stretching out her limbs before slipping on the silk robe. 'Get your act together.'

She was almost out of the bedroom and in the open-plan living area before it occurred to her that Jason's clothes were not where he had left them. He had obviously dressed. Perhaps, she thought with a burst of optimism, he had ordered a room service breakfast and it would be waiting for her, together with copious amounts of coffee, when she walked out of the room.

But no.

Nobody was in the living area, or the bathroom.

He'd popped out for some fresh air, perhaps, although there was a balcony for that. The sun shone brightly through the gauzy curtains that covered the balcony door. She would get some coffee brought up and drink it out there, she thought.

Before ordering, she grabbed her phone and tried to dial Jason on the contract smartphone she'd bought him the week before.

She swore under her breath as it chirrupped back to her from the other side of the bedroom. Wherever he was, he was incommunicado.

She took the coffee, once it was delivered, and went out to the balcony, deciding to try and enjoy her enforced wait. He'd be back soon, no doubt. Gone out for a paper or a quick stroll round the block. Freedom was still a wondrous novelty to him after all those weeks cooped up at Harville Hall. He was stretching his wings. It was fine.

From the balcony, the lush green expanse of Hyde Park stretched out before her, Kensington Palace visible at a distance above the flourishing tree tops. The London morning was busy as always. Down on Park Lane, cabs and buses filled the road. Speakers' Corner was already open for business, a small crowd building up around the soapboxes. On the pavement, artists attached their paintings to the railings, ready for another day's business. Here and there, a tourist or two stopped to admire the work of a pavement artist, drawing their portraits, or those of a famous person, in chalk.

Jenna's idle gaze stopped roving and she focused abruptly. She got up from the small table and peered from the balcony edge, squinting to make sure that she was seeing right.

'Oh *God*!' she said, abandoning her coffee and running to the shower for the quickest douse under the warm needling water before dressing and hurrying out.

'What are you doing?' she demanded, down on the pavement. She wore sunglasses and a headscarf tied in a fifties style under her chin, hiding her hair. Even so, she couldn't be sure a couple of faces in the small crowd that had gathered hadn't lifted in recognition.

Jason looked up from the chalk fantasy that now encompassed half a dozen slabs. His face was dusty, in several pastel colours.

'What's it look like?' he said carelessly. 'Earning a crust.'

He waved a hand over to a battered cap in which several coins and even a few notes lay.

'I tried to phone you,' she said.

'I told you,' he answered, in a tone of long-suffering patience. 'I'll use that phone once I've paid you back for it. You can call that your first instalment.'

He picked up the cap and proffered it to her.

She took it without further remark, for she had just noticed what the chalk art represented. Amidst a backdrop of orchards and birds and flowers and trees was her face, exquisitely rendered, like a da Vinci.

'That's . . .' she whispered.

'Yeah, Jenna Diamond,' he said loudly, so that she caught on that he was trying to preserve her anonymity amongst this crowd. 'Well recognised.'

'Looks just like her,' commented a woman at her side. 'Though I think she's overrated myself. I mean, she's no Cheryl Cole, is she?'

Jenna wasn't keen to hear much more of this.

'Have you forgotten?' she urged under her breath. 'We have an appointment at eleven. It's after ten already.'

'Right. The Italian bloke.'

'Alfonso, the best men's stylist in London, I think you'll find. Come on. You need a wash. I can't take you there all covered in chalk.'

Sighing, Jason packed up his chalks, waved to his admiring onlookers and took his leave.

'Shame the rain'll wash it all away,' he said, looking back at his handiwork.

'Yes, isn't it?' said Jenna, unsure whether to be annoyed with Jason or moved by the beautiful portrait he had made of her. 'That's why you should be concentrating

on making a proper, lasting career of your art, rather
than busking on street corners.'

'Every little helps,' he said. 'And you can stop telling
me off. I'm not some snotty kid in your class or
something.'

'Sorry. I just wish you'd let me know where you were
going.'

'I left a note.'

She stopped and looked at him.

'Did you?'

'Yeah. On the table in the living room.'

'Oh, God, I didn't realise. I didn't see it. Sorry.'

'Apology accepted,' he said, so loftily that she immediately wanted to snap at him again.

But she refrained and, once in the lift, offered him a
compliment on the portrait instead.

'You weren't working from a photograph?' she said.

'No,' he said. 'From here.' He put a hand on his heart
and all her residual irritation faded clean away.

It didn't return until, washed and brushed up, they
were in the cab heading for Alfonso's Shoreditch consul-
tancy office.

'So this is like a clothes shop?' said Jason. 'Where
we're going?'

'No,' said Jenna. 'Alfonso is a stylist. He doesn't sell
clothes. He suggests looks for you.'

'What's the point of that? Why not cut out the
middleman and just go shopping? If we must,' he added
in a sulky undertone.

'Jason,' said Jenna, slipping without realising it into a
professional lecturing tone, 'all successful people in the
public eye need styling. The days when you could get

away with wearing what *you* thought looked good on you are gone. With so many magazines and papers selling copies on the back of pictures of celebrities who made bad style choices, you can't afford to get caught out like that any more. Believe me, if you put a fashion foot wrong, it will be all the way around the world before you can blink. That's the frightening reality of modern celebrity.'

'Yeah, but it's shit, though. Just because something's shit doesn't mean you have to go along with it.'

Jenna couldn't even begin to formulate an answer to this, not least because, somewhere near the core of her consciousness, she had a nagging feeling that he could be right.

Instead, she chose to bluster. 'Trust me, Jason. This is what I do. I know what I'm talking about. Think about the pop music you grew up with. Which acts broke through the quickest? Was it the most talented? Was it the ones with the best songs? No. It was the ones with the strongest style. The Spice Girls, Take That, Britney and all those others. The public love their stars to be instantly recognisable, to be unique and yet also easy to copy. Madonna pulled that trick off brilliantly. So did Michael Jackson.'

'What about Susan Boyle? What about Johnny Rotten?'

'Johnny Rotten was styled to within an inch of his life,' she said, on surer ground now. 'Believe you me. But that's an interesting thought. We go left field, do something nobody's expecting. I'll discuss it with Alfonso.'

'You'd better not make me look like a tosser. I won't be made to look like a tosser.'

'Why would I want that?' Jenna snuggled her head into his shoulder. 'I still have to fancy you, don't I?'

'I should bloody well hope so. And don't forget. There'll be payback for this later.'

Somehow she didn't think threats of payback were meant to make her feel quite so hot and bothered, but this one did.

She was still tingling mildly when the taxi disgorged them and they mounted the narrow stairs to Alfonso's office in a converted warehouse.

The floor on which he held his premises was an open-plan space filled with small business units. In one, a group of women cut cloth and worked at sewing machines; in the next, a younger mixed group sat on a circular sofa huddled over iPads. Inspirational posters and strangely-clad tailors' dummies were rushed past until Jenna located the unit she needed to get to.

'Alfonso,' she called, and a short, dark man in an outsize pinstripe shirt and neon yellow skinny jeans burst out from behind a screen, arms spread wide.

'Oh my God, you *are* real,' he cried, tackling her into a hug. 'I thought someone had cloned your voice pattern or something when you made the appointment before. I didn't dare to hope.'

He stood back, laughing all over a good-natured, pointy-bearded face.

'Still a goddess,' he said.

'Still a bullshitter,' she grinned back. 'But fantastic to see you, all the same. I've watched your progress from behind my desk in LA. You've got some of the hottest clients in town. Congratulations on the Girl Crush gig.'

'Oh, those bitches are hell on wheels to work with,'

he exclaimed, then he lowered his voice, putting a finger to his lips, although his eyes still twinkled. 'But you didn't hear that from me. Come into my lair, darling. Oh God.' He stopped dead, staring at Jason. 'I'm *so* sorry. I was so bowled over by the goddess Jenna that I didn't even . . . Do excuse me. Alfonso Vannetti.'

He offered Jason a hand to shake. Jason took it and shook it awkwardly, muttering, 'Jason Watson.'

The three retired behind a pair of giant screens plastered all over with photographs of Alfonso's celebrity clients on various red carpets and podiums. In his large corner space, he had racks upon racks of clothes samples and little else beyond a desk on which a slim silver notebook computer lay shut, and a very large, very plush, very marabou-trimmed sofa.

'Take a seat on my sofa of the stars,' he offered, pulling out a mobile and speed-dialling. 'Freya, Alfonso. Champagne, please, and three glasses.'

Jenna could feel Jason's discomfort radiating out from him in waves. He was sitting stiffly, looking at the clothing rails with some dismay.

'She won't be a moment,' said Alfonso, perching himself on the corner of his desk. 'She's not my secretary as such – we all chip in here for a general receptionist, so Freya does this kind of thing for all of us. She's marvellous but we could do with three of her, to be honest. So.' He bent forward, scanning Jason with a professional eye. 'I take it this is my raw material?'

Jenna laughed nervously and held up a hand.

'Alfonso, you are awful. This is the most talented artist you're ever likely to meet, on the cusp of getting his first gallery show.'

There was a slight pause.

'Am I right,' said Alfonso slowly, 'in thinking that this is the same Jason that was all over the news recently, linked with you and your house?'

'I was fitted up,' snarled Jason. 'That's all done with now.'

'Oh, yes, I wasn't implying anything! I just recognised you, that's all.'

Freya appeared with a smoking bottle and three glasses. The diversion was welcomed by all.

'Well,' said Alfonso, raising his own flute. 'Here's to a fruitful business partnership. To you, Jenna, and to Jason.'

'To us,' said Jenna.

Jason said nothing but knocked back the champagne in one, then gagged as the bubbles fizzed in his throat.

'Horrible stuff,' he muttered, once he had spluttered himself back to equilibrium.

'Now,' said Alfonso, 'we can get down to work. Talk to me, Jenna.'

'Well, as I've said, Jason is an artist. He's a serious artist, so I want his style to reflect that, but I also want him to appeal to more popular tastes as well. The trick – the one you've mastered so thoroughly – is to give him a look that's distinctive and yet not open to ridicule. I so admired your work with Dial M on that music video you did with him. Toned him down, and yet made him even more watchable than ever.'

'OK. An artist. So, Jason, Jenna emailed me photos of some of your work. It's got a feel that's a bit modern, a bit street and yet also quite classical, even formal at times. I was really hard-pressed to categorise it. What would you call it?'

Jason shrugged. 'Art,' he said.

Jenna bit her tongue. Why did Jason have to be so awkward all the time? She realised, with a rush that touched her heart, that he was shy, even unconfident. She had seen this in some of her other protégés, raised to stardom from obscurity. They would start out so tongue-tied that they came across as rude. She usually sent them to an exclusive 'finishing' college for a course in etiquette and social poise. She'd have to get in touch with Georgina at the Margery Mountjoy Institute. In the meantime, it was up to her to give him a few pointers herself.

'Art,' repeated Alfonso, completely deadpan, giving him another chance.

Jason seemed a little shamed by Alfonso's good tempered tolerance, and he tried harder this time.

'Yeah, I mean, all those things you said. I've tried to learn whatever I can pick up from the old dead guys – Van Gogh and Rembrandt and all them – but I want to be me as well. I want to be what I am, and what I am is a deadbeat from a dead-end town. It's important that people know that. I want people to see and recognise where I'm from and how it's made me. And how it's making this country.'

'So . . . your work has a strong political slant? I was picking some of that up.'

'All art does,' said Jason. 'If it's going to mean anything.'

'That's a strong statement,' said Alfonso, raising his eyebrows.

Jason's passion brought Jenna up short, almost breathless. Whatever his shortcomings were, he was no pushover. He believed in what he did and he'd live or die by his beliefs.

'If you say so,' said Jason, keeping eye contact with the stylist.

Alfonso looked vaguely intimidated, which Jenna found both interesting and unusual.

He coughed. 'Yes, well, let's see what we've got to work with, first. Stand up, will you, Jason? I want to get the measure of you.'

Jason rose and stood with his chin out and shoulders back, as if modelling for a sculpture of a victorious general. His tight T-shirt and jeans showed off his tall, well-made figure to perfect advantage and Jenna thought she could almost see Alfonso's mouth watering.

'You could wear anything,' murmured Alfonso, darting around to take him in from all angles. 'In fact, you could model. If you're ever short of a pound or two and worried about starving in your garret, give me a call. I can fix you up with a photographer or two.'

'I'm not poncing around on no catwalk,' said Jason, thrusting his chin out still further.

'Well, the offer's there if you want it. What are you? Six foot? Six one?'

'Six and a bit.'

'Great shoulders, good legs, a dancer's build, almost. Do you dance?'

'Bit of head-banging at the disco on a Friday night.'

'That's a no, I take it?'

'I'm not Billy Elliot, no.'

'And what's your personal style? I mean, I love what you've got on now. Clean, simple. Very young Marlon Brando, James Dean. It could almost work just as is. If you had a big budget to spend on clothes, what would you buy yourself?'

Jason shrugged. 'Back home, I just wore trackies.

Hoodies. I never cared that much what I wore. I suppose I might get myself a decent leather jacket, but I dunno. More likely to spend the money on good paints, cost a fucking fortune, they do.'

'Right. I'm getting a Wild Ones vibe off you, Jason, if you don't mind my saying.'

Jason looked rather flattered.

'Sound,' he said. 'So what does that mean? What kind of dress-up doll do I get to be?'

Alfonso smiled widely, daring to put a hand on Jason's shoulder and manipulate him gently into a less aggressive pose.

'I think you have such a wealth of natural attractiveness and charisma that we can afford to keep it simple.' Ostensibly, he spoke to Jason, but Jenna knew that he was really addressing her. 'You've got a great body, a really strong face. You're sexy and you know it. There's no need to overegg that.'

'I agree,' said Jenna eagerly. 'And he looks like an artist already. Those eyes – such soul.'

Jason snorted. 'Yeah, baby. You know I've got soul.'

Alfonso stepped back, appraising his client as if fixing him in final memory.

Then he went over to the racks.

'I think I know what I'm aiming for,' he said, rummaging among the coat-hangers. 'But let me try a few things. Just for fun, and to perfect my focus.'

He came out with a checked shirt, a pair of very tight, bright green skinny jeans, a fringed scarf and a pair of Converse high-tops.

'Get bent,' said Jason, eyeing the jeans. 'They look like agony.'

'This is the current artistic look, Jason. Try it for size. You might like it.'

Alfonso directed him behind one of his screens and Jenna waited, grinning at the various exclamations of discomfort and disgust that filtered out from it.

When he came out, with legs like pea green poles, she laughed with delight.

'I look a right tool,' he grumbled, as Alfonso rushed forwards with a pair of spectacles and a beanie hat.

'There's nothing wrong with my eyesight.'

'No, but put them on. They've got plain glass in them. Honestly, people wear them to look cool these days. My God. You just need to cultivate that bit of beard you've got, and you're totally Hoxton Square.'

'I'm not sure he's meant to be,' cautioned Jenna, and Jason demonstrated wholehearted agreement by pulling off the beanie hat.

'I wouldn't be seen dead in this,' he said with finality.

'OK. I think you're right,' said Alfonso. 'It's so not you. But it was fun to try. Can I experiment with a different look?'

He returned to the clothes rails.

Jason stepped out next in a voluminous white shirt tucked into tight burgundy velvet trousers with riding boots and a black cravat. A big slouchy velvet hat perched on his head at an awkward angle, as if afraid of slipping off.

'This looks like the bloke on the paint-by-numbers kit I had as a kid,' said Jason. 'Art Master of Chelsea.'

'It is a bit stereotypical-artist,' Jenna agreed. 'Though I like the boots. And the shirt. And the trousers. Turn around for a minute, will you?'

'What, so you can check out my arse?'

Jenna smirked. That had been her exact reasoning. Alfonso didn't look exactly averse to the idea either.

But Jason had hidden himself behind the screen again.

'I'm not coming out until you give me something decent to wear,' he threatened.

'OK, seriously now,' said Alfonso, returning to his racks. 'I think we need a few different outfits that can be mixed and matched – blended into each other. This is just an idea – I can't give you these clothes, but I can tell you where to get them. First of all, a really good formal suit but with a twist. Something to express your essential subversion, but in a non-threatening way.'

He brought out a slim-fitting, single-breasted jacket with narrow lapels and a pair of matching trousers – not skinny jeans by any means, but certainly tight enough to define the legs.

'Get hold of those. You can put the trousers on for now – you can wear all kinds of things with that jacket. You can wear jeans with it for a TV interview, the suit trousers and a white shirt for a gallery opening, a patterned shirt for a date, a plain T-shirt for something more informal . . . so many different ways to style it.'

'OK,' said Jason, warily grateful. 'It's not too bad. Simple.'

'Yes, I thought simple would work. You don't need dressing up, really. People will be looking at your face, and taking in your body. The clothes are just icing on a rather scrummy cake.'

Jenna shook her head, smiling. Did Alfonso have a crush?

'Here,' he said, passing things to Jason behind the screen. 'This shirt – never mind if you don't love the pattern, it's just to give you an idea. Put a handkerchief in your top pocket and do up your jacket button if you want to look dandyish. And, of course, you can say so many things with your hair . . .'

'Like, "cut me"?' suggested Jason.

'People expect long hair on an artist, don't they?' said Alfonso indulgently. 'Oh. Shoes.'

He scuttled off again, returning with a handful of shiny leather and casual dark canvas.

When Jason stepped out a third time, Jenna rose to her feet and said, 'Oh, well, NOW . . .' before running out of breath.

He looked effortlessly elegant and yet also a little bit dangerous. His silhouette was lean and sharp with the jacket done up, but also raffish and sexy with the white shirt beneath undone to reveal a glimpse of chest.

'Oh God, you are *hot*.' Alfonso clapped his hands. 'Seriously. You look like you mean business.'

'But not in a corporate way,' Jenna hastened to reassure him. 'No tie, no tight collars. In an art-world way. You do look really . . .' She winked, and he brightened, losing the self-conscious glower that had hung about his face.

'Fuckable?' he said hopefully.

Alfonso clapped again.

'Believe it,' he purred.

'So that's settled then,' said Jenna. 'We go to town, buy a suit like this one and some accessories, a few shirts, some jeans, some shoes, some bits and pieces and there we have one beautifully-styled Jason Watson, ready to knock 'em dead.'

'Absolutely. I'll list the stockists I've used for you. I'll email them to your phone, shall I?'

'Please.'

They spent the next couple of hours in various gentlemen's outfitters, putting together the new Jason look, though Jenna could not resist buying a couple of traditional stiff-collared and cuffed shirts together with a silk tie and cufflinks too.

'I just want to know what you'd look like properly suited and booted,' she said over a snatched lunch in a suitably private little basement Moroccan restaurant in Knightsbridge. 'Just . . . out of curiosity.'

She blushed down at her tagine.

Jason's eyebrows shot up. He had understood her implication.

'Curiosity, eh?' He took a bite of his flatbread and chewed thoughtfully. 'You want to dress me up as a boss, yeah?' He swallowed. 'Perhaps we ought to get a big desk as well, then? You know. To bend you over.'

'A big desk might be an idea,' she said, lowering her eyelids in coquettish acquiescence.

He shook his head. 'I've cost you enough already today.'

'Don't start that again,' she pleaded quietly. 'You'll pay me back. You're already paying me back, by being here. By agreeing to do all this.'

'Well, don't forget, we've got a little bit of role-reversal to sort out later. We've shopped for my new look. Next up, we're going out to shop for yours.'

'Not next,' Jenna cautioned. 'Next, we're meeting Tabitha to thrash out the details for the show.'

'Thrash out? Don't put ideas in my head, girl.' He winked and her fork felt a bit wobbly in her hand.

'Honestly, we need to get on,' she said. 'Are you done with that lamb? I said we'd meet her at two, and it's nearly ten to now.'

'Fine, but it's a postponement, not a cancellation. Tabitha first, shopping trip after that.'

'I promise. I'm going to ask for the bill now, OK?'

They had to dash to Mayfair, but Tabitha was still at lunch herself when they turned up, ten minutes after two, with bright eyes and shining faces.

'Sorry, she won't be long,' said Shona, rising from her desk in the empty gallery. 'I'll get coffee, shall I?'

'A glass of water would be great, actually,' said Jenna, feeling the sour London air on her breath. 'It's gasping out there.'

Tabitha came rushing in as soon as Shona disappeared into the back room.

'So sorry, darlings, lunch with my accountant, always seems to drag on. Do come upstairs. You must be the famous Jason.'

She stopped mid-whirl to look him up and down as if he were a canvas she'd been asked to value.

'That's me,' he said. His new clothes seemed to have given him a burst of confidence because he didn't slouch or roll his eyes but returned Tabitha's gaze with a cool dark searchlight of his own.

'Well,' was all she said, leading the way upstairs.

Ensconced in her office with a jug of iced water and an electric fan whirring on the desk, Tabitha opened the meeting.

'You are a surprise,' she said to Jason.

'I thought you would have seen me in the papers. I made them all,' he said, with a hint of pride.

'This isn't the man I saw in the papers. I must admit, I was bracing myself for a tough sell. But . . .'

Jenna turned to Jason. 'You see what I mean? A little styling really does work wonders.' She spoke to Tabitha. 'We've been to see Alfonso.'

'Ah. Your miracle man. Of course.'

'Excuse me,' Jason cut in. 'I did all the paintings before I got the suit.'

'Of course you did,' soothed Tabitha. 'And it's those we're here to talk about, not your lovely clothes. They really *are* lovely, though. Customers will be clamouring to meet you, Mr Watson.'

'Do you think so? So we're going to do a show then?'

'Oh, I think so.'

'When we last spoke, you mentioned that you were booked up here until the autumn,' Jenna reminded her.

'Oh, yes, I'm booked up *here*. But who says we have to do the show here?'

Jenna sat forward.

'You have another venue in mind?'

'Correct me if I'm wrong, darling, but you have a glorious great mansion house in the country, don't you? Why not have an exhibition there?'

'In *Bledburn*?'

She looked wildly at Jason, who laughed.

'I've done exhibitions in Bledburn before,' he said. 'Down the garages by the flats mainly. With spray paints. Dead classy, it were.'

'But you mean we should show his work at Harville Hall,' Jenna said. 'Would the London art world be interested? Shouldn't we keep things here in London?'

'I don't see why. Imagine how fascinated people would

be to visit the home of the Starmaker herself. I think it would double our clientele at a stroke. At least.'

'Oh, Tabitha, I think it's a brilliant idea but I'm not sure . . .'

Jenna's gaze sought Jason's again.

'We like our privacy,' she said, as if pleading with him to back her up.

'It's just for one night,' he said unhelpfully.

'But the place is a wreck. We're in the throes of renovation and, so far, only the kitchen and half a bedroom are anywhere close to presentable.'

'How romantic,' said Tabitha, bulldozing through Jenna's objections. 'A half-ruined mansion. Absolutely perfect for an art installation.'

'And there's my frieze in the attic,' Jason piped up. 'That can't be shown anywhere else anyway.'

'A frieze in the attic!' Tabitha's eyes lit up over the rim of her tumbler. 'How wonderful. You must let me come up and see it for myself.'

'Of course, you're welcome to visit,' said Jenna, feeling more flappable than she would like. 'And then you'll see the state of the place. Honestly, Tab, apart from the kitchen, it needs rewiring, for a start.'

'Candlelight,' said Tabitha dramatically.

'And *damp*,' said Jenna. 'Not good for the canvases, I'd imagine.'

'Oh. No.' Tabitha's onslaught was temporarily halted. 'That's not good. But you're getting it sorted out, I should imagine?'

'Well, yes. Got people coming in next week. All the same . . .'

'Well, there you go then. Honestly, the décor doesn't

matter a bit. The shabbier the better, in fact. It's the pictures we want people to be looking at. The pictures . . . and you.'

'I'm not for sale,' said Jenna with a laugh.

'No, but you're my major selling point. An evening with Jenna Diamond.'

'Myatt.'

'Jenna Myatt Diamond. In her gracious new home.'

Jason huffed. 'With a pissy little art show on the side?'

'I'm sorry, Mr Watson,' said Tabitha, sounding quite earnest. 'You are what will bring them back. But Jenna is what will bring them *in*. I'm afraid we all need to use what resources we have in a crowded marketplace. And Jenna is an absolutely prime resource.'

'Everyone's for sale,' snarked Jason.

'Yes, Mr Watson,' said Tabitha primly. 'Indirectly, perhaps, but there it is.'

'Call me Jason, for God's sake. The only people who ever called me Mr Watson were sarcastic teachers at school.'

Tabitha smiled at him, warmly this time.

'You're an extraordinary artist,' she told him.

'Thanks.'

'I'm very excited at the prospect of exhibiting you. I think this will be an event, perhaps an historic event. I want to make sure it's everything it can possibly be. For your sake, Jason, and for Jenna's. And, yes, for mine.'

'I really think,' Jenna said after a pause, 'we'd be better off renting somewhere here in London. Somewhere offbeat and a bit different, sure. But not my home.'

Tabitha sighed. 'Well, I can't force you to agree, of course. Whatever you'll do, there'll be media interest. But you'll create a real sensation if you'd only go along with me. I thought we could always rely on you for that, Jenna. You always played the press so well, so intuitively.'

'On a professional level, I do think you're right. It's the very thing I'd suggest, if I were you,' said Jenna unhappily. 'But . . . when it's my life . . . it's different . . .'

'Ah,' said Tabitha. 'There's the rub.'

'What timescale are we looking at?' Jason spoke up, and it was so unexpected that everyone just stared for a moment.

'Oh. Well. I don't know. That could be up to you, of course. Another advantage – you exhibit when *you're* ready.'

'I'm ready now,' said Jason. 'But the house isn't. But I think it's a good idea. If I'm going to put myself out there, I want to do it in Bledburn first. I want the big shots to see where I'm from, to drive through the estate on the way to the show. I'm up for it. Jen?'

Jenna was so taken aback by this that she found herself nodding like a dog in the back of a car window.

'You really think so?' she said.

'Yeah. Why not?'

'Well . . . What about our privacy?'

'We aren't inviting anyone to move in, are we?'

She pondered.

'No. Well. Looks like I'm outvoted. Harville Hall it is.'

Tabitha called for champagne and the art show, and Jason's launch into the art world, was enthusiastically-toasted, especially by Jason, who seemed to have accepted that he would need to develop a taste for expensive fizz from now on.

'So, August thirty-first,' said Jenna, once they were

out taking some air on the roof garden of Tabitha's building. 'That doesn't give us long. We need to at least strip all the walls downstairs. Then there's . . .'

'Jen. We don't need to do anything. We don't want to live in an art gallery. The exhibition is about the art. It's not about the fucking plastering.'

She turned from the little Japanese-style fountain she'd been admiring.

'You're very forceful today, aren't you?' she said, smiling. 'Full of opinions suddenly.'

'Yeah, well, maybe I've started to see that all this might work out,' he said. 'Maybe I'm starting to take myself seriously.'

Jenna came to join him at the wall, looking out over Mayfair.

'That's good,' she said. 'That's really good. Because you should take yourself seriously. As long as you keep your sense of humour, though, because you'll go mad without it in this business.'

'I'm not going to change,' he said. 'Just because I'm wearing this poncey suit doesn't mean I'm going to start talking like Lawrence Harville.'

'Perish the thought.'

'What's that?'

He pointed down to the Shepherd Market area, at the little huddle of exclusive shops and restaurants that clustered around it.

'Shepherd Market. Some good restaurants, if you fancy eating out later.'

'No, I mean that shop. That one, all black and gold, next to the one with the little lollipop tree outside the door.'

'Oh.' Jenna squinted, then sucked in a breath. 'My God. A sex shop! In Mayfair!' She leant over the wall, looking harder. 'I bet it's a ferociously expensive one. None of your cheap plastic tat for the locals here.'

Jason nudged her hip with his.

'Remember what I was saying about dressing you up? Tit for tat,' he whispered.

'You don't mean . . .'

'Why not? I'm curious. I want a nose round inside. Come on.'

They bade Tabitha farewell and made the short journey to Shepherd Market. The shop was called Le Cinq à Sept, which made Jenna think its clientele was probably very rich men shopping for their mistresses. It gave out an air of the heady and illicit from the very start.

The window wasn't blacked out, nor was it filled with mannequins in flashy scarlet and black latex, but it was of smoked glass and the display was discreet and tasteful – mainly piles of pretty boxes and well-wrapped parcels with the odd silver-backed hairbrush or marabou slipper here and there, to give the air of an artfully disarranged boudoir.

'Is anyone watching us?' asked Jenna nervously, looking about her, but the area was quiet enough in this post-lunch hour, being off the main tourist drag.

'Not a soul,' said Jason. His face was a little flushed from the champagne and his eyes were glittering with excited purpose. 'Come on. Let's go in.'

He put a hand on Jenna's shoulder and escorted her into the shop. A bell jingled in an old-fashioned way that somehow made Jenna feel she was walking into another world, and, in a way, it was.

Quiet classical music played into a room that could have been any fashionable boutique. It was cool after the hot London street, and soothing to the eye after the bleached pavements they had walked to get here.

A linen-suited woman at a counter near the back simply nodded and returned to the catalogue she was browsing.

'This is nothing like that shop Mia used to work in,' remarked Jason, looking around him. 'That were wall-to-wall dildoes.'

'Jason!' Jenna flashed a look at the counter. The woman feigned not to have heard.

'What? I'm in a sex shop. It's OK to talk about the kind of stuff you'd buy from a sex shop, in a sex shop.'

'It's a . . . oh, forget it.'

Jenna had stepped towards one of the rails, fascinated by the sheer, gauzy flim-flammery that floated from the hangers.

'This is just gorgeous,' she whispered, fingering the peach and lilac silk underwear set that was first to hand. 'You'd hardly know you were wearing it though.'

'I don't suppose you can try before you buy,' said Jason regretfully.

The assistant coughed gently then, when Jenna looked over, said, 'We do have a fitting room, and some samples you can try on in various sizes.'

'Thank you,' said Jenna, turning abruptly back to the rail.

'Not tempted?' Jason smirked, then coughed himself when he caught sight of a tiny little price tag attached to the bra strap with silk ribbon. 'Fuck me,' he whispered loudly. 'How much?'

'This is high end designer stuff,' Jenna whispered back. 'Look at the brand.'

The label of a well-known fashion house was sewn – exquisitely – into one of the shoulder straps.

'Oh yeah, I've heard of them,' said Jason.

'And the quality – I mean, just feel it. Like gossamer.'

'It's nice, but . . .'

'And I've got money,' she said. 'So . . .'

He turned to her and unleashed the full bright force of his teeth.

'You want these, don't you?'

Jenna had just seen an accessory that went with the set – a pair of beautiful, elegant, ribbon-laced cuffs. Perfect for aesthetically-pleasing bondage with a touch of luxury. The thought of Jason tying those ribbons together to keep her hands restrained while he did whatever he wanted to her . . .

'I think I do,' she said.

'Don't just go for the first thing you see,' he chided. 'There's a shop full of this stuff. Take a good look around.'

'But I've fallen in love with these already,' she said. 'I definitely want them. I'm going to try them on, but I might try some other things too.'

'OK, well, how about you choose one set and I choose another?'

'Deal.'

They browsed through more racks of the frilly and flirtatious before arriving at a section that seemed to enliven Jason's interest. The lingerie in this area was black and sinful-looking with all kinds of bits missing or added on.

He picked a bra that was hardly worthy of the name off a hanger. It was made of black PVC, less shiny than latex but with a subtle kind of sparkle that added a touch of class. The cups soon made it clear that that was an illusion, though. They were barely there – quarter cups that would expose the nipples. There were straps above to create the frame of a full-cupped bra, with strips of gauzy lace travelling up either side of the nipples, but these would act not as skin-coverers but as borders to enhance the display. In short, it was one very rude garment and Jenna blushed just to look at it.

'What do you think of this?' he said, in a very low voice, since they were now quite near the assistant.

'Doesn't leave much to the imagination,' she breathed.

'Yeah, well, I use my imagination every day when I paint,' he said. 'I might want to give it a rest in the bedroom.' He looked from the bra to Jenna's chest. 'Mind you, my imagination's working pretty hard right now. Picturing you in this.'

The quiet depth of his voice, coupled with the implication of his words, sent a shot straight through her. How could he talk like this in public? Well, in front of a third party, anyway. It was designed to confuse and humiliate her. And to arouse her.

He fingered the matching knickers, brief enough from the front view, with a triangular PVC panel in the centre, bordered by an elasticated lace detail. The sides were of fine black mesh, but when Jason looked at the back, it was almost non-existent. The wearer's bottom would be almost completely bare, save for a little gathered mesh frame around the cheeks.

'Oh, yes, these would work,' he said, with a snuffle of amusement. 'They'd work very well.'

Jenna felt a dampness in her own, less exotic, knickers, and she squirmed to think of how this daring pair would feel on and around her skin.

'Work for what?' she whispered. 'Not for sensible every day wear, that's for sure.'

'Yeah, this isn't M&S, in case you hadn't noticed. Sensible knickers aren't what we're after here.'

'So are those your favourites? Are they going in the basket?'

'They're definitely on my list for trying on.'

The assistant cleared her throat.

'Can I help you at all?' she said.

'We want to try some of these on,' said Jason. 'But first I want a scout round the back room. What's in there?'

'That's where we display some of our more intimate items,' said the woman.

More intimate? Jenna looked in puzzlement at the array of frankly obscene underwear around her and wondered how on earth that was possible.

'Pleasure enhancers,' the woman added, seeming to note Jenna's bemusement.

'Ah,' said Jenna, cottoning on.

'Oh, I'm always in the market for pleasure enhancement,' said Jason, winking.

Jenna cringed but followed Jason into the back room without catching the assistant's eye.

'Wow,' she said, once through what she thought of as a kind of magic portal. 'This is so unlike that other sex shop I went to that time.'

And it was. That other sex shop had been a glaring assault on her ocular faculties: shelf after shelf of brightly coloured plastic and garish packaging.

Here, everything was muted and tasteful. The materials were polished metals or smooth minerals. Marble, crystal, aluminium. It looked almost more like a showroom for executive gadgets or the gift shop on a fossil-rich section of the coast than a place where sex toys were on sale.

'No way is this a butt plug,' said Jason, picking up a beautiful decorated china implement that wouldn't be out of place on some mantelpiece in a stately home.

'I hope it's sturdier than it looks,' she commented, trying not to think about the thing shattering into fragments during use. 'What on earth . . .?'

She picked up a flogger with a comfortably ergonomic rubberised handle and ran her fingers through the strands.

'It actually feels like hair,' she said. 'Like human hair. My hair.'

Jason tried it out himself.

'Couldn't hurt much,' he commented. 'Nice idea though. This is more like it.'

He handled a paddle of such high quality leather that Jenna felt intoxicated just breathing in its scent. The surface was tooled with a cut-out pattern of flowers that would, she imagined, make a very pretty transfer on to the skin.

'I could tattoo you,' he said. 'Paint you. I'd like to make my own version of one of these, to my own design.'

'Perhaps you could do that,' said Jenna. 'Get in touch with whoever makes these and see if they'd let you.'

'I fucking would, you know. You think I'm joking, don't you?'

'I'd never dare think that,' said Jenna.

'I'm going to ask that woman out front.'

Before she could stop him, he was heading purpose-fully back to the front of the shop, leather paddle in hand.

'Excuse me,' he sang out, coming to a halt by the desk.

Jenna stopped abruptly, a foot or so behind him, trying to look as unobtrusive as possible.

'Yes, sir?'

There was a tell-tale little pause during which Jenna surmised that being addressed so respectfully in a shop had flummoxed Jason.

'I was wondering,' he said, recovering himself, 'who makes these paddles?'

She took it from him and examined it with obvious pleasure.

'Ah, these are beautiful, aren't they? Handcrafted by an expert. He has a little workshop south of the river. He's exclusive to us, you know. You won't find his imple-ments anywhere else.'

'Unless I went to the workshop,' suggested Jason. 'I'd like to contact him, if you've got his details. Got a propo-sition for him.'

The assistant was clearly surprised.

'He trades under the name The South Bank Tannery, but he's called John Lindo. I can call him for you, if you want. What sort of thing did you want to discuss with him?'

'A commission,' said Jason.

'Oh, well, I daresay he might be interested. Let me call him for you.'

She looked up the number on her mobile phone and began to dial.

Jenna watched all this, too curious to remember to be aghast, and also seriously impressed with Jason's confident and rather suave manner. He was full of surprises.

'Hello, Mr Lindo? It's Caro here, from Cinq à Sept – the Mayfair branch. Yes, lovely, thank you. How are you? Oh good. No, no problems at all, but I have a customer in the shop who would like to talk to you, if you wouldn't mind. Don't worry, it's not a complaint. Yes. Fine. I'll put him on then.'

She handed the phone to Jason.

'Hi,' he said, turning to wink at Jenna, who shrank back even further. She felt critically exposed by what was going on, as if the shop assistant were now a voyeuristic third party in their relationship. She knew their tastes in underwear, and, much worse than that, she knew that Jason liked to give her bottom a good spanking. She squirmed a little at the thought and pretended to take an interest in a rack of babydoll nighties.

Jason's voice floated over to her, settling among the clouds of lace and ribbons.

'I was looking at one of your paddles in the shop and I'm really impressed by the design and the workmanship. Yeah. So I was wondering if you'd make one especially for me, if I came up with a design of my own. Yeah? That'd be great. How about tomorrow? Jen?'

She came reluctantly back into the group, hearing her name.

'What are we doing tomorrow? Got any meetings or owt?'

'One, in the morning. Should be finished by lunchtime.

And I was going to pop into the office, just to be friendly and make sure everything's ticking over.'

'Right. Yeah, how about tomorrow afternoon then? Three sounds good. Where are you, exactly? Will do. Cheers. Oh, yeah, sorry, it's Watson. Jason. See you then, then.'

He handed the phone back to Caro, who uttered a few polite words before ending the call.

'Well, that seemed to go well,' she said. 'Do you want this?' She proffered the paddle.

'Yeah, I think I do,' said Jason, taking it and slapping it into the palm of his hand. 'And there's some stuff we'd like to try on.'

'Of course. Just let me find our samples. Do you know your size?'

This was addressed to Jenna, who mumbled the answers. She was far from her efficient, professional self in here, and Jason seemed to enjoy the contrast, smiling at her and ruffling her hair.

'You've gone all shy,' he said, as the assistant disappeared behind a curtain that presumably concealed a stock cupboard.

'I'm not used to broadcasting the details of my private life in shops,' she replied, smoothing her hair back down with an irritable hand. 'I'm dying of embarrassment here.'

'It's only Caro. She won't tell anyone,' said Jason. 'That's what these posh shops are all about, isn't it? Good service. Keeping the customer's secrets.'

'I suppose so. I bloody well hope so. The last thing I want is us on the front page *again* with some sordid S&M sex scandal.'

'Do you think it's sordid? What we get up to?'

'No, I don't, but I know what the tabloids would make of it.'

Caro reappeared with some open boxes trailing fountains of tissue paper.

'These are the ones you were looking at, I think,' she said. 'Our changing room is just at the very back of the shop, behind that shelf of bondage harnesses.'

Hearing the words 'bondage harnesses' coming from the rather school-mistressy lips of Caro made Jenna want to giggle, but she restrained herself.

'Thank you,' she said, grateful that Caro had not mentioned her fame or made any appearance of recognising her at all. Perhaps she didn't. Strange thought.

The changing room had silk-lined walls, soft lighting and a beautiful oval pier glass in which to study one's gussied-up body.

Jason entered behind Jenna and put his hands on her shoulders, reaching down to unbutton her blouse from the top.

Jenna watched his progress in the mirror, watched his strong, sure hands work at the buttons, watched her skin emerge from the cream silk shell.

He slid the shirt off her, revealing her skin, subtly sheened from the expensive moisturiser she used. She watched him bury his nose in her neck and breathe her in, ending the inhalation with a low groan of desire.

She felt his fingers at the fastening of her trousers now, and then they crumpled down, sliding past her thighs and knees to heap at her ankles.

She stepped out of them, along with her shoes, and looked at herself, framed by Jason's arms, in her pretty but unexciting pale pink lace underset.

'You look so prim and proper,' said Jason with a smirk. 'But I think we're about to change all that.'

He unhooked Jenna's bra and made a meal of removing it, but he didn't try to touch or cup her breasts, which surprised her.

Apparently he picked up on this, because he said, 'I'm not going to get too carried away too soon. I want to see you in these little numbers first.'

'Are you really going to get a bespoke paddle made by that guy?' she asked, her mind still half on the telephone conversation.

'If he's up for it. Why not?'

'It's just . . . It seems so . . . The potential for him to go to the press.'

'Oh, Jen, don't be paranoid. He won't if we ask him not to. And it'd look bad on him. Might affect his business if his clients feel he can't keep a secret.'

'I suppose so. I don't have to go, do I?'

'Of course you do! I'm not going alone. Get those knickers off – her outside'll be thinking we're shagging in here if we don't get a move on.'

She looked at herself, naked in the mirror, with Jason at her shoulder. She barely recognised herself. It wasn't that her body or face had changed, though her hair was less styled and her make-up barely there, compared with her days of LA glory. No, there was something in her eye – a vulnerability, maybe, or an uncertainty – that made her look younger. Every day she spent with Jason seemed to bring a new challenge, a new thing to learn about herself. She seemed to be reassessing her entire self, and the meaning of her life.

No wonder she looked a bit scared.

When was the last time she had given control to another person?

Never.

And now, here was Jason, making decisions over her head, getting her to do things she had never dreamed of doing. Would she have done these things for Deano? She really wasn't sure.

'OK,' she said, trying to strike a confident note. 'This is me. Dress me up.'

Jason took the flirty lilac and apricot silk set first. The knickers were relatively tame in the front, with their scanty triangle of lilac silk surrounded by pale apricot lace, but at the back they were almost non-existent; just a pair of elastic straps on either side, travelling diagonally up her bottom cheeks from the crevice between her thighs. Essentially, they were crotchless and would provide no barrier at all to even the least assertive of lovers. And Jason was far from being that.

'Whoa, baby,' he said appreciatively. 'This is what I like to see. Knickers that aren't really knickers. You can wear them any time you like.'

She posed in them, making the adhesive hygiene strips inside rustle.

'And the bra,' prompted Jason, handing it over.

The matching bra had peephole slits over the nipples that could be tied shut with two little flaps of lilac silk ribbon. Jenna knotted them shut, feeling the delicious naughtiness of it so that her nipples hardened and brushed the material. Oh God, it was turning her on. She couldn't possibly walk about with this thing on underneath her normal clothes – she'd be permanently hot and bothered, not to mention feeling the backlessness of the knickers at the same time.

She imagined them under a close-fitting elasticated dress and the idea made her gush between her legs. She'd never understood the appeal of tarty underwear, thinking it was made only to appeal to men, but now she was starting to think otherwise. She felt as if she might positively burst with sexuality and it was a strangely empowering sensation.

Jason hooked a finger into the loop of one of the bows and untied it, revealing her nipple, as it pecked cheekily through the parted silk.

'We're having these,' he said decisively. He took the nipple between his fingers and Jenna watched him roll it, then do the same with her other breast. He pressed himself into her from behind, and his new suit of fine black cloth covered her bare skin in the most pleasing manner. It was much better than the rough denim she was used to. She wanted to rub herself up and down against it, especially when she recognised a hard bulge pushing at her bottom.

'We shouldn't do this,' she gasped, but the furtive frottage was going to both of their heads, and shoulds and shouldn'ts were sliding slowly off the agenda with every laboured breath they took.

'No,' he said, suddenly pulling back. 'Not till I've seen you in the other set, anyway. Take those off.'

The lump in his trousers was rudely evident, and Jenna grinned at it in the mirror as she bent to remove her knickers.

'You won't want to be taking that back out into the street with you,' she said.

He looked down and then caught her gaze with his, straight and cool.

'Trust me, I won't be,' he said.

She dropped her jaw.

'What do you . . .?'

'Carry on,' he said. 'Here.'

She exchanged the scrap of pastel-coloured silk for the PVC quarter-cup bra. This certainly crossed the line between cheeky and downright rude. Her nipples stood proud over the PVC curve that failed to contain more than an inch or so of her lower breasts. The lacy strapping that described the outline of a real bra framed them beautifully and very overtly. It was crazy, thought Jenna, how a few bits of material could transform one from innocent to very, very guilty. Naked, her body was something to be looked at, admired, perhaps gloated over – but in this, it was something to be fucked. There were no two ways about it.

'You look proper dirty.' Jason voiced the same thought in his own inimitable fashion. 'Put the knickers on before I have to jump you here and now.'

She pulled on the matching pair. The feel of PVC over her pubis, even with the hygiene strip, was almost overwhelming. The gathered elastic at the edge of the mesh, signalling that a large portion of her bottom was bare, sent another strong rush of arousal through her. Again, there was no doubt that these knickers were to be worn to be spanked in and then fucked. She couldn't escape from that reality, especially when she caught the look in Jason's eyes. In his head, he was doing those things to her right now.

Evidently his body was keen to catch up with his

head, for he strode forward and trapped her in his arms, pushing his erection down towards the apex of her thighs.

He moved one hand to the fastening of his suit trousers and Jenna hissed in panic.

'We can't. Not here.'

'Why the fuck not? Who's gonna know?'

'These clothes – they're the samples. They aren't the ones we're actually buying. We can't . . . we should return them in the same condition they were given to us . . .'

Jason sighed, then Jenna watched a slow smile dawn on his stormy face.

'Fair enough,' he said. 'Get on your knees, then.'

'What?'

'Do I have to raise my voice so Caro hears us? You heard.'

Jenna stared at him, seeing that he continued with the unfastening of his new trousers.

'You mean . . .?'

He winked.

'I think you know what I mean.' He nodded sharply downwards. 'Go on then. In front of the mirror.'

Jenna laughed with disbelief, then, without thinking further, she sank down to her knees. The changing room was carpeted, which was a relief. From the corner of her eye she could see herself in profile in the mirror. Her nipples pointed towards Jason like arrows and the smooth curve of her bare bum in its black mesh surroundings was clearly visible.

She put her hands on his thighs for purchase, bent forwards and found the tip of his cock with her lips. What a sight this was to see in the mirror. She couldn't resist darting little glances over to it, enjoying the sight of herself looking whorish and sinful much more than she would ever have expected to.

Jason's hand in her hair made her sigh, her breath wafting over his erection.

'Suck it,' he whispered. 'Go on. And watch yourself while you do it.'

She watched his long, smooth length disappear inside her mouth then appear as a bulge in her cheek from time to time. She made her breasts jiggle and her nipples brush against his trousers, then pushed out her bottom extravagantly, fascinated by how outrageous she could make herself look. What a show she was putting on – for Jason and herself, but she imagined other people watching as well. What if Caro had CCTV?

The thought startled her and she stopped sucking for a moment and took a quick eye tour of the ceiling corners.

'What's up? Keep at it,' chided Jason.

Reassured that there was no such hazard in the room, she went back to work. Imaginary watchers added to the thrill, but real ones . . . not so much.

She lapped and sucked at him while he began to thrust gently into the back of her throat.

'Call this a bra?' he muttered, his voice low and guttural. The hand that wasn't rooted in her hair came down to pat the side of her breast before seizing and twisting a nipple. Her cry choked in the back of her throat, consumed by his thrusting thickness.

'You wore this because you want to be treated this way, didn't you? It's a cocksucker's bra, and you suck cock like a pro, babe. A pro. Oh.'

The final syllable was stretched out into a sudden

urgent moan. Jenna waited for the burst of bitter liquid
to hit the back of her throat. It came. She swallowed and
made a deep purr of satisfaction at a job well done.

Once he was licked clean and tucked back into his
trousers, she tried to smooth down her disarranged hair.
This was an easy task compared with trying to calm
down the riot in her naughty knickers. *Not fair*, they
seemed to protest. *Why does he get his and you don't?*

Sometimes that's life, she said to herself. Besides, if
they were to count up orgasms between them, she would
be the outright winner. He always made sure she came
at least twice in any single encounter, to his once. Perhaps
it wasn't so unfair.

She removed the provocative garments and dressed
again in her London-on-a-hot-day silk shirt and chinos.
Were there any traces on her face of what her mouth
had been doing? Not after she had reapplied lipstick and
dabbed at her shiny forehead with a tissue. A spritz of
watermelon-scented cologne finished the cover up job.
Fresh as a daisy once more. No sign of that filthy tart
who'd been down on her knees with a man's cock in her
mouth, nipples and arse on full display to whomever
might fancy getting a good eyeful of them.

Which of those women was the real Jenna?

She couldn't work it out.

'So we're buying the lot then?' said Jason laconically,
leaning on the door and watching her transform into
Business Jenna once more.

'I think so,' she said. 'Don't you?'

'What do you think? We should come here again. At
least, it would be "again" for me.' He smirked.

'You're awful,' she said perfunctorily, turning from the

mirror and heading for the door, sample underwear in hand.

'You aren't,' he said, taking hold of her shoulder and stilling her for a long, tongue-heavy kiss. 'You're fucking awesome.'

'I try my best.'

They paid for their purchases, Jenna doing her utmost to look Caro in the eye and give the impression of a woman who hadn't just performed a blow job in a sex shop back room. It seemed to work. Caro remained her discreetly professional self and expressed a hope they might return as they made for the door with their boxes and bags.

'You ever thought of opening a shop outside London?' Jason asked Caro, turning at the door.

Jenna huffed, wanting to be out of the place now, but she waited.

'Well, I don't know, it's something we might consider if the right place becomes available. Perhaps Bath or Edinburgh.'

'Nah, they're not the right place. Think about Bledburn.' He tapped his nose. 'It's up and coming, you know.'

Jenna grabbed his wrist and manhandled him through the door.

'You idiot,' she said. 'As if she's even *heard* of Bledburn.'

'If she hasn't now, she soon will,' he said. 'After our show.'

Jenna began to hurry along the street, keen to reach the safe and shaded sanctuary of the hotel before anyone pointed at her.

Once they were in the marble lobby, she turned to Jason and raised her eyebrows.

'So you're keen on the idea now?' she said. 'You're happy to bring yourself to the world?'

'Yeah, why not?' he said laconically. 'Seems a shame to deprive the world of me.'

'What's changed your mind? You were so . . . guarded before.'

'I know you believed in me, but that gallery woman must know good stuff when she sees it. If she thinks I can cut the mustard, well.'

'Yes.' Jenna felt a hard stone of anxiety crumble at the base of her stomach. 'Yes, she knows exactly what she's talking about. And she feels the same way about you I do.'

Jason bent his lips to her ear at that.

'Really?' he murmured. '*Exactly* the same?'

'Not that,' she whispered fiercely. 'Don't be stupid.'

'Stupid, am I? You don't think your posh mate would go down on me in a sex shop then?'

'Shut up!'

'You're pushing your luck, madam,' he said, still pouring low, gravelly words into her ear. 'Don't forget what I've got in these bags.' He held up the shiny carriers that could have come from Harvey Nichols or any expensive boutique.

The shop's name was scrawled across in a stylish black font, surrounded by entwined hearts and roses.

'Don't go tipping it out all over the floor,' she begged in an agonised whisper. 'Come on. I'm going for the lift before you do something that makes tomorrow's *Daily Mail*.'

They attracted plenty of attention as they strode across the shiny, sparkly floor to the lifts. Jason in a sharp suit was a feast for the eyes, and Jenna noticed how the female – and many of the male – guests checked him out as they passed. They almost ignored her, in fact, which she found amusing and also a little alarming.

She quelled a brattish urge to call 'Don't you know who I am?', putting her energies into calling the elevator instead.

Once safely inside, and having jettisoned three other guests at lower floors than their own penthouse, Jason held the bags out to Jenna.

'So, Ms Myatt,' he said. 'Which one of these are you going to play with first?'

'What do you mean?'

'Well, all that back there in the shop was very nice for me. But you didn't get no satisfaction, did you? I think we ought to sort you out. Fair's fair.'

Jenna saw her cheeks flame red in the mirrored wall behind Jason.

'I don't know,' she said. 'Everyone fancies you in that suit. Did you notice?'

'Do they?' he said, and she was touched by his lack of vanity. 'I wasn't looking. Too busy watching your arse.'

'They were jealous of me.'

'They'd have good cause, if they knew what you were about to get.'

The lift stopped and the doors slid open.

'Come on, then,' said Jason, with a filthy wink. 'Chop chop.' He patted her bottom, chivvying her out on to the top floor.

Once in the suite, Jason handed her the bags.

'Go and get changed, then. Your choice. I'll be waiting in the bedroom.'

'OK,' said Jenna, infected by his lustful enthusiasm.
'Oh – and Jason.'

'Mm hmm?'

'Keep the suit on.'

'Deal.'

In the bathroom, Jenna unwrapped the precious arti-
cles from their pale tissue paper and tried to decide what
kind of mood she was in. Playful pastels or serious PVC
kink? As she rummaged, she found something they hadn't
tried on in the store – the exquisite ribbon-tied gauntlets
that matched the lilac and peach set. This made up her
mind for her, and she put on the bra with its bows over
the nipples, and the knickers that sheared away to nothing
behind before tying on the sweet silken cuffs at each
wrist.

Posing in the mirror, she was happy with what she
saw, although she *must* remember to call in on Luca, her
London hairstylist, before they went back to Bledburn.
There was a glow about her that owed nothing to any
hi tech foundation or skin polish. Her eyes were bright
and dewy in a way that reminded her of her teenage
photographs.

'Forever and ever?' She mouthed the words at the
mirror, then put her hand over her face.

She removed it and gave herself a stern glare.

'You're getting swept away,' she said. 'Don't question
it. Don't put a label on it. Just enjoy yourself.'

She thrust out her chest, making the ribbon bows
strain over her nipples, then turned around to admire
her back view, the double elastic straps crossing her
bottom cheeks in cheeky diagonals that described a V
shape with the base right between her legs.

Then she held out her wrists in a pose of mock surrender.

'Tie me, tease me,' she whispered.

She had no doubt that Jason would oblige.

He had been lying on the bed, casting lazy eyes at the canopy above, but he shot up into a sitting position when he saw her.

For a few moments, he said nothing, just sat there with a slack jaw.

'Will I do?' she said, holding out her cuffed wrists towards him.

'Come here,' he growled in reply, reaching for her.

When he was able to snatch her fingertips, he pulled her roughly on the bed, having her fall in a heap on his lap.

Long minutes of grappling, wrestling and snogging ensued, rumpling the bed far beyond its original impeccable neatness. Jenna felt herself coveted, immobilised and arm-locked into helplessness until she lay caught up in Jason's body, feeling the deliciously expensive fabric of his suit all over her bare skin.

'Did you want something?' she whispered pertly, once his tongue was back in his own mouth.

'You fucking bet I do,' he said. 'Thought you'd drained me dry in the shop but . . .' He thrust his hips, making her feel the steel of his erection. 'Apparently not.'

Ah, the advantages of taking a younger lover, thought Jenna. Plenty of encores.

'I'm just wondering which of the hundreds of possible ways I want to have you,' he said. 'On your front, on your back, on your knees, against the wall . . . the list goes on.' He kissed her again, scouring the inside of her mouth with his roving tongue. 'But I think . . .'

He disentangled himself from her and rolled her on to her front, swiftly tying the two sets of ribbons on her cuffs together, then looping them around a bar on the wrought-iron headboard. She lay on her belly, arms above her head, able to move her legs, but not to any real purpose as she was tethered in place.

Jason, behind her, put an arm beneath her and lifted her on to all fours. With her wrists tied low, she had to keep her head down. She could picture herself, with her bottom jutting out in its tight elastic strapping and her spine sloping down. Jason pulled her legs well apart until she felt her lower lips divide and open, the tiny strip of peach silk that called itself a gusset slipping inside.

'Mm,' he said, running his fingertips up and down her inner thighs. 'So you want me to keep my suit on? Why's that then?'

'Because you make my mouth water in it,' she said. 'You make me want to pin you down and ride you until you pass out.'

'But I'm not the one that's pinned down here,' he said. 'That would be you.'

Without warning, he held her by her thighs and swooped down to push and probe his tongue inside her spread pussy lips. She quivered and yelped with shock, but soon sighed into the melting delight of it.

She had to accept it; she was tied and at his mercy. There was nothing for it but to let him do his worst. His worst seemed a lot like his best from this position. The slight sandpaperiness of his chin and cheeks stimulated her tender skin and she craved more of it, wanting to luxuriate in that friction. He buried his face deeper while she tried to push back, giving herself to him as if she were the gift of an exotic feast.

He was certainly eager to sample her, flicking his tongue back and forth over her clitoris until she was on the very edge of crying out, then withdrawing and pushing his fingers inside her instead.

In the meantime, his mouth was busy on her bottom, delivering luscious, sucking kisses to her soft round curves. Her sensitised skin could hardly bear all the intermingling sensations, especially when his free hand crept up her belly and untied the little ribbons that covered her nipples. Now they were free to be rubbed and pinched, along with everything else that was happening. Her senses swirled into mindlessness. All that mattered was the building of her climax.

And it was coming – it was coming faster and faster, threatening to overwhelm her from the inside out.

It was so close, it was *there* . . . And then it wasn't.

Jason removed his hands and his mouth and gave her one loud smack on her rump, waiting for her moan of protest to end before saying, 'Thought I'd make it that easy for you, did you? I don't think so, sweetheart. I want to get every penny of value out of your new gear.'

The next thing Jenna knew, Jason was lying with his head between her legs, looking up into the soaked strip of silk. He inhaled deeply, as if breathing her in, but he didn't touch her. All he did was let out his breath slowly, so that it fanned her pussy lips and clit, all of which would have begged for his attention if only they could.

She made a sobbing sound, hoping it would make him take pity, but he didn't.

'Keep still,' he said, when she tried to lower herself towards his face.

She huffed and tried again, but her reward was another sound smack to her bottom, so she decided to do as she was told.

'Please,' she whispered instead.

Another slow, warm breath circulated around her private parts.

Jason's arms came up underneath her, his hands finding her nipples once more. He pattered his fingertips lightly on their swollen tips, then stroked, keeping up his slow, concentrated breathing between her thighs. It was so slight and yet so horribly arousing that she bucked again. Mistake. He left her nipples and brought his open palm down on her bottom again and again, six hard spanks this time.

'Keep. Still,' he said, accompanying the order with two more percussive slaps.

'How long?' she wailed.

'How long what? How long is a piece of string?'

'Nooo. How long do I have to wait for . . .?'

'For this?' He put his hands on her hips and lifted his face quickly to her lower lips, pushing his tongue inside her knickers for a deep, full stroke of her clitoris.

'Yes,' she whispered, whimpering with disappointment when he dropped his head back down to the bed.

'I don't know. I haven't decided yet. I like you like this, all quivery and wet and desperate and tied up. Oh! I know.'

He shuffled himself quickly off the bed, to Jenna's considerable anguish. She couldn't see what he was doing, her cheek pressed to the duvet, but she could hear the rustle of bags and tissue paper and she thought he must be getting the other underwear set out, for some reason. Or . . . oh no. The *other* thing.

'Time for some artwork,' he crowed.

'Not too hard,' she said hurriedly.

'Oh, not in the mood?' He paused, putting a hand on her bottom with what seemed to her like hesitation.

'I wouldn't say that,' she said. 'Just . . . not too hard. That's all.'

'I want to see the picture it makes.'

'So do I. Hard enough for that, then. But my skin feels sensitive and I'm not sure how much I can take.'

'That's OK, babe. Just let me know when enough's enough.'

'I will.'

Perhaps this exchange affected Jason's confidence because the first stroke was a mere whisper, a sweet little brush that didn't even snap.

'Oh, it tickles,' she said, wriggling so she strained in her ribbon tethers.

'I think I'd have to do it harder,' he said apologetically. 'To make a mark.'

'That's all right,' she said, suddenly brave. 'Go for it.'

This was followed by a much more jarring blow, causing her to lurch forward and suck in a breath.

'You did say,' reproached Jason. 'Are you OK? Ooh, that looks good.'

'Is it pretty?' she gasped.

'Really pretty. If I can do a few more, I'll let you look at it in the mirror after.'

'Deal.'

She braced herself and breathed through the succeeding strokes, easing herself into the headspace that allowed her to accept them without rancour. Yes, now this was feeling good, the slow burn building between her already throbbing pussy lips.

Another seven or eight smacks of the strap ensued before Jason laid it aside and went to stand further behind her, a connoisseur admiring a masterwork.

'Really nice,' he said. 'I can't wait to meet this bloke. I'm going to work on my design tonight.'

'Can I . . .?'

'Yeah. Hold on.'

He came around to untie her and took her over to the full-length mirror on the wardrobe door. Over her shoulder, she saw a lacy pattern on her buttocks, bright red and creamy white, a kinky tattoo.

'It really works,' she said with some surprise.

'It's good, isn't it? You have to be dead careful where the strap lands though. Need a good eye.'

'Well, you've got that, haven't you, da Vinci?'

He smiled at her reflection, revelling in the compliment.

'OK, enough of the artistry,' he said. 'Back to basics. Get back on that bed, as you were, and spread those legs. You're in for it now.'

And she was. She took everything he had to give her, tightening her muscles around his thick, thrusting length. She imagined his eyes on her patterned rear, gorging on his handiwork. He ran his thumbs over her bottom cheeks, exploring their texture and heat, the sensation adding to everything else that rioted inside her.

It was a hot, hard coupling, ramming her towards the wrought-iron headboard, exercising every muscle she possessed and a few that were still in development. He made her come twice before he was ready to unload, by which time her knees had given way and he was having to keep her upright on all fours with an arm beneath her ribs. She floundered like a rag doll, helpless to do anything but take what she was given.

Afterwards, they lay in salty languor, on damp sheets. Jenna's thoughts were half-formed, little scraps floating by like the spots before her eyes.

'I'd go there again,' said Jason. 'That shop, I mean.'

Jenna laughed an exhausted laugh.

'I think what just happened constitutes a rave review,' she said.

'London's all right, really, isn't it? It's not like I expected it to be.'

'No? And what was that?'

'I dunno. Like you see in films. Red buses and those soldiers in furry hats and that. It's more like a real place, though, but bigger.'

'You really are a Bledburn boy, aren't you?'

'Through and through. Never had any choice in the matter. But I'm starting to see that there's a hell of a lot more to see and do.'

'There certainly is. And your talent will take you wherever you want to go.'

He paused, staring up at the ceiling with depthless dark eyes.

'It's not just my talent, though, is it?' he said. 'I've always had that. It's you.'

'What do you mean?'

'My talent never got me anywhere until you came along. It's not that I'm ungrateful or anything, don't think that, but it doesn't seem right. It doesn't seem right that you can't get anywhere on what you've got unless some person with a big list of contacts notices you.'

'Well, I see what you're saying, but it's the way of the world. There are lots of good artists out there, but we need filters, or we'd be overwhelmed with them.'

'But there are probably loads and loads of people just as good as me who'll never even make it this far. It just doesn't seem right,' he repeated.

'I do get that, Jason,' she said after a while. 'And perhaps, once your name is made, you can do something to help those people. But until then, we have to work on getting *you* to the top of the pile.' She stroked his cheek. 'Where you belong,' she whispered.

He sat up, suddenly enthused. 'That's what I'll do,' he said. 'If I get famous and all that. I'll set something up to find kids like I was, from dead end towns, heading into dead end lives. Catch them before it all goes to shit, like it so nearly did with me.'

Jenna struggled up beside him and laid her head on his shoulder.

'You're a good man, Jason Watson,' she said. 'And I love you.'

'It's mutual, babe. Anyway, where's that diary? I've got a feeling it's about to get to the dirty bit.'

'There isn't going to be a dirty bit,' said Jenna with a peal of laughter. 'It's written by a Miss Prim and Proper Victorian governess, you idiot. She may allude to some "slight discomfort" on her wedding night or something, but that's as far as it'll go.'

'Don't be so sure. She seems like a bit of a goer to me.'

Jenna shook her head, but she tottered on shaky legs to the drawer that held the diary and brought it back for a spot of bedtime reading.

Chapter Eight

February 21st

A month has passed since Lord Harville proposed to me, and I must apologise most profusely for being so errant in maintaining this journal, but there has been so much to do, to say, dear Lord, so much to think! Too much for me at times, I swear.

I try my best to continue to regard my altered status as exceptional good fortune but, alas, on some days it does not strike me that way.

What girl is luckier than I? I have caught a rich and titled man. Many women of much better birth and station do not do half as well. He is a little older than I, but certainly a fine figure of a man and many would consider him handsome.

Am I one of those many? Yes, I think I am. I do feel a great access of sentiment when he turns his eyes upon me, and in those glances I can forget all the difficulties that pertain to our attachment.

Yes, there are many difficulties. We announced our

engagement and set a date for the wedding of March 10th, but very few congratulations have been spoken.

Even my parents recoiled at the news, assuming straight away that I had allowed him to seduce me and was now in a shameful condition. In vain have I tried to convince them otherwise – I suppose I can only wait until time proves my cause.

The family of his first wife have refused their invitation to attend the wedding – imagine having no wish to meet the woman who will be mother to their own grandchildren! It is quite unnatural!

The servants seem to have made the same assumption as my parents, for none will talk to me, though perhaps it is jealousy that fuels their animosity.

Worst of all, though, are the girls. Maria and Susannah have been little beasts since they found out. They refuse to attend to their lessons and they whisper among themselves without cease, even as I try to teach them.

A few days of this broke my will to remain calm and I lost my temper with them, telling them in no uncertain terms that the marriage would go ahead with their approval or without it.

Maria spoke to me then directly for the first time since the announcement.

'We think you are a witch, and you have Papa under your wicked spell. Release him or we will tell the police and have you burnt at the stake.'

I laughed, not from mirth but incredulity at their ignorance.

'You goose,' I said. 'Nobody is burnt at the stake any

more and nobody believes in witches. We live in an age of enlightenment and science.'

'People like you have duped the world,' said Maria. 'But we are wise to your scheme. You mean to marry Papa and have some brat of a boy to take our inheritance from us.'

When I told Lord Harville of her words, he railed against them so fiercely that I feared for the girls.

He warned them that they must knuckle down and accept me as their new mother, or he would disinherit them both entirely and send them away to earn their own livings. What a threat to make to such young girls! But he would not be moved.

It certainly ended the accusations of witchcraft, although their demeanour remains sullen and hostile.

What is to be done? I only wish to befriend them but they turn their faces from me with every advance. I try to take their part with their father, but he says only that they must learn obedience and he will not indulge such behaviour.

I made bold to ask him if he loved them, and he was angry with me then – as angry as I have ever seen him.

I knew then that I love him truly, for the thought that all might be done with between us was more than I could bear. And he is so affectionate, so youthful, when we are alone. He even carved our initials on a tree trunk in the wooded part of the garden.

Jenna looked up at Jason. 'I saw them,' she said, catching her breath with excitement. 'I saw their initials.'

'In the garden? Go on. I'm still waiting for the dirty bit.'

'I'm waiting for Lord Harville to stop being such a bastard to his children.'

'You'll be waiting a long time, I reckon.'

Jenna sighed, feeling that he was right.

'He's a stereotypical Victorian patriarch all right. Anyway. Back to the romantic gestures.'

I wear a sovereign that he gave me on a ribbon around my neck.

'I saw that too,' cried Jenna. 'I found it, by that tree. No ribbon, but there was a hole in the sovereign that it could have gone through. Oh my goodness. What an amazing thing.'

'Might be worth a bob or two,' said Jason.

'I'm thinking more of the historical value. Perhaps I should give it to Lawrence Harville, as a family heirloom or something.'

'You must be joking. You don't go near that bastard ever again, do you hear me?'

'I don't want to,' said Jenna. 'I'd give it to his solicitor or something. I just feel that it probably ought to stay in the family.'

'We don't know that she *is* family yet,' objected Jason. 'They haven't got married. No kids.'

Jenna took the hint and read on.

I despair of ever winning the girls round. It seems all I have to look forward to is their bare toleration of me and nothing more. It breaks my heart to think of it, for we could be such dear friends if they would only relent.

'Can't really blame them,' said Jason. 'They've only known the woman five minutes. Why's Harville in such a hurry?'

'I imagine he wants a male heir,' said Jenna dryly.

'They were mad for them back then. You'd think Frances would cotton on.'

'Too blinded by it all, I suppose. It does blow your mind a bit when somebody so far above you takes notice of you. I should know.'

'Oh, Jason.' A kiss broke into the conversation. 'I felt like that,' said Jenna, breaking off. 'The first time somebody really famous called to invite me for brunch. No thought of why or what they might want from me. Just "Oh my God, so and so invited me for brunch, no way!".' She laughed.

'Who was it?'

'I never kiss and tell,' said Jenna primly. 'And in that case I didn't kiss either. Let's just say it's a very famous, iconic British recording artiste, known for his chameleonic changes of style and his arachnids from another planet in the solar system. And he's just as gorgeous in real life.' She sighed.

'You've lost me,' said Jason. 'Tone down the long words, yeah?'

But she knew he knew who she meant, and they shared a complicit smile.

'So, come on, turn the page.'

She turned it, as lightly as she could to avoid getting fingermarks on the dry paper.

March 3rd
    Such a terrible turn of events, I hardly know how to describe it.
    David went up to town three days ago, to buy things for the wedding next week. I so wanted to accompany him but he insisted I stay here with the girls – he

thought our close confinement together without him might encourage them to place some trust in me, even perhaps some confidence.

But it has not, far from it.

They have disobeyed my every instruction and, for the most part, hidden around the house and garden so that I scarcely know where they are or even that they are not lost or hurt. I am sure the servants assist them in this, for I saw the slyest look on Eliza's face when I asked her if she had seen the young Misses.

But 'Oh no, ma'am, not I' is all I can obtain from their false lips.

Yesterday I became so perplexed with it all that I chased them about the house, determined that they should come and spend the afternoon with me in the sitting room and that we should finally make a peace treaty, but the impudent pair ran into my own bedroom! The very idea of it!

I will own that I was very angry by the time I joined them in there, and I had a number of cross words for them. When I found them hiding in my wardrobe, I was furious and I made to haul them out of it, but in a trice the pair of them had me in there. They shut the door and, before I could rush out and apprehend them, they had locked me in my room.

I heard the key turning and their laughter, and I could do nothing but throw myself on to the bed and cry. I did not even bang on the door or call a servant to let me out. My sense of failure was too acute, too painful to admit any witness.

What is to be done? How can I continue in this house, when I am hated by its daughters and held in

contempt by its servants? David is not enough, even if
he does love me. I want to beg him to send them away,
to give the staff notice, and to begin our married life
as a fresh start, with all of these people gone from it.

'Well,' said Jenna, drawing breath. 'Those girls are
certainly *very* naughty, but to want to cut them out of
their father's life . . .?'

'She's upset. So would I be. Why didn't he take her
with him?' Jason said, shaking his head. 'He might have
known leaving them all together was asking for trouble.'

'Perhaps he hasn't gone to arrange wedding things,'
hazarded Jenna. 'Perhaps he has a mistress and he's
visiting her. Or he's addicted to the gaming tables. Or
– could be all sorts of things.'

'The Harvilles like their secrets,' Jason agreed.
'Skeletons in the closet – literally.' He shuddered.

'Do you think it's Frances? The body you found? God,
what a thought. Poor woman.'

'She should have run from Harville Hall as soon as
she got out of that room. If she did get out of it. Read
on, then. I want to know if she does.'

I will insist that the girls are sent to school the moment
he returns from London. That will give them something
to think about.

Yesterday I was shut in here, and here I remain. I
have waited in vain for some servant to come up with
supper and release me, but nobody has been. I heard
the usual evening sounds of the house – the dinner
gong, the girls running up and down the stairs, some

distant clattering from the kitchen. But nobody came to release me.

Once darkness had fallen, I knocked on the door, called for help, tried to open the window but the drop is too much and I would break a bone.

Eventually it became clear that I must resign myself to spending the night in captivity. At least I had the means to wash and change my clothes, even though I was faint with hunger. I lay on the bed and must have drifted off to sleep some time before midnight.

When I awoke, in the light of dawn, suffering much from hunger, I noticed that there was a dark patch on the wallpaper. Drawing closer, I perceived that somebody had written upon it in a dark charcoal. 'Help me,' it said.

One of those infernal girls must have come in and done it while I was asleep. I know that this is the most likely explanation, yet it chilled me to the bone and I confess that I am now so miserable and distressed that I want nothing more than to leave this place and go back to Mama and Papa and our genteel poverty.

If I am ever released from here before I fall prey to the inevitable consequences of privation, that is. I know David will be back tomorrow, but I do not know how long a body can survive without water. I will try to call to the servants again. I can do no more.

'Deario, poor Frances,' said Jenna. 'She must have been very afraid.'

'At least they feed you in prison,' said Jason.

'What *were* the servants thinking of, to leave her there like that?'

'Perhaps the kids wouldn't hand over the key.'

'Little monsters,' said Jenna. 'They must have felt desperate, to do this, though.'

'So, does she get out?' hinted Jason. 'Or is she the skeleton, hidden there after dying of starvation or something?'

Lord help me

I am lost

I send you my prayers

The last will and testament of Miss Frances Manning, being of sound mind. Am I of sound mind? And I have nothing to bequeath, save my engagement ring, which is for David. May he have joy of it, and know that I would have been a good and true wife, given the chance.

February 23rd

Thank heavens. He has returned and I am free.

When I awoke yesterday, there was a bat in the clothes drawer. It flew straight out into my face when I opened it to remove my underwear. I must have screamed fit to bring the house down but still nobody came.

Another cruel trick, designed to make me think I am haunted. They will not defeat me. I will not succumb.

Finally, one of the maids released me this morning. I think they knew that David would be back later and feared the consequences of his finding me imprisoned.

'Where are the girls?' I demanded to know, but Eliza shook her head and would not say. 'For the love of God, bring me food and water,' I said. 'For I am fit to faint. How could you let them use me thus? How?'

*She shook her head and disappeared. I called after
her that I would be telling David all that had passed.*

*When he arrived, oh, the relief of it. The sound of
his carriage was the sweetest music. I ran out to greet
him, ahead of the servants who lined up in the porch.
Of the girls, there was still no sign.*

*'Oh, thank heavens you are back,' I cried, and only
then did I break down into a torrent of grief. I had been
withholding it for hours, perhaps in the knowledge that
nobody would care overmuch if I did collapse. But I knew
my David would tend to me and hold me close.*

*At least, I thought he would. Instead, he seemed put
out by my tears and begged me to contain myself.*

*'Whatever could the matter be, Fan?' he asked, and
he sounded cross. 'And where are the girls?'*

*'I do not know for they have not shown their faces
since they shut me in my room and locked the door.'*

'They did what?'

*'Come inside, dearest, and I will tell you. Oh dear.
I trust you had a good journey? And London was to
your liking?'*

*'You are babbling, Frances. Come inside. At least let
a man put aside his luggage and take off his hat before
assailing him with all this preposterousness.'*

*In the drawing room with his whisky poured and
his top waistcoat button undone, I told him all that had
happened in his absence and he was not pleased to hear
any of it.*

*He called for the girls and lo! they appeared, most
impeccably turned out with ribbons in their ringlets and
snowy white pinafores – quite unlike the grubby urchins
I had last seen.*

'Now, now, you two,' he said without preamble, cutting into their prepared speech to welcome him home. 'What's this I hear about shutting Miss Manning in her room and locking her up?'

They, the pair of slyboots, gave each other the most startled look – quite convincing it was, too – and swore on their lives that they had no idea what he was talking about.

'Now, do not try to play the innocents with me. I will have the servants in. They will be able to give me the truth of the matter.' He turned to me, frowning. 'Surely a servant would have come looking for you?'

'They were in on it,' I said. 'It was a conspiracy.'

He stared. 'Frances, please have a care. What you say cannot reasonably be the case. My girls, regrettably, yes, I can imagine it. But the servants?'

Maria and Susannah stared at me as if butter wouldn't melt. Oh, I could have risen to my feet and . . . But somehow I restrained myself.

'Call them,' I said desperately. 'Question them. They cannot lie outright to you, their master.'

He rang the bell and asked that all the servants of the house be brought to the drawing room. Maria and Susannah stepped daintily aside as they trooped in and ranged themselves in a deferential row before us.

'I have heard some most disquieting news,' opened David. 'Miss Manning tells me that, for the duration of my stay in London, she has been locked inside her bedchamber without sustenance. Can this possibly be true? Whitear?'

Whitear, the butler, stepped forward.

'I am not aware of such a situation, my Lord,' he

said. 'But I seldom have dealings with Miss Manning. Perhaps Eliza is the best person to ask?'

He turned to the parlour maid, who has been openly scornful of me from the day of my arrival.

'Of course this is not true,' she said, and I gasped. 'How can you speak such monstrous falsehood?'

David looked gravely at all of us, his gaze resting finally on me. I looked in his eyes for some proof of his belief in me, but I could not find what I sought.

'My love, I think I will send Josh for the doctor. You do seem extremely overwrought. Perhaps it is the excitement of the wedding?'

The smirks on the Misses' faces were almost enough to drive me to violence.

'But they are lying,' I cried, rising to my feet. 'Eliza, can you look me in the eye and repeat what you have said? Can your conscience allow it? I do not know what those girls have done to buy your loyalty to their evil tricks, but think of how you will be served in the hereafter if you persist in this wickedness?'

'That's quite enough, Frances,' said David, quite sharply. 'Staff, you are dismissed. Girls, you may go to your room. Josh, do not leave straight away - go and call on Dr Middleton and explain that he is needed urgently.'

Left alone with David, I could barely breathe, let alone speak, such was my outrage.

'I tell you, they locked me in,' I insisted.

'Are you sure the door handle was not merely stiff?'

'I was shut in for two days, and not a soul came to my aid. I ate nothing, nor did I drink.'

'My dear, you strike me as feverish. Dr Middleton will soon see to this.'

'But David . . .'

'Enough! I will not hear another word of this. Must I listen to my own children maligned in my own house? No. Take some brandy, Frances, and do try to calm yourself. Your demeanour is most unbecoming of a future Lady Harville.'

I could stand no more of this and I resorted once more to tears — but this time of anger and frustration rather than the aftermath of my ordeal.

David left the room, muttering, and did not return until the bell rang, signalling the doctor's arrival.

The doctor declared that I had a mild fever and should rest.

'In your experience,' David said, 'does fever bring on delirium?'

'It can do, but the lady's fever is mild.'

'Perhaps it is on the wane,' suggested David.

'Perhaps. But, if so, I wonder that I was not called before?'

'Forgive me, doctor. I was out of town and did not know of the young lady's indisposition.'

'If I have a fever,' I blurted, tired of being spoken of as if I were not there, 'it is because I have spent two days locked in a room without food or water.'

'You see, the delirium persists,' said David sadly.

'Oh dear,' said Dr Middleton. 'That is a great shame.'

They went outside the room and conferred with one another.

When they came back, they spoke to me, so convincingly and with such persuasive art, that I begin to feel that perhaps it was all some kind of fever dream. I know I have the testimony of this diary, but can I truly say

that I was in my right mind when I wrote those words?
I no longer know.

'Bloody hell,' said Jenna. 'She's been masterfully gaslighted by a pair of pre-pubescent girls.'

'She's been what?'

'Gaslighted. Made to doubt herself and what really happened to her. I think she really was locked in that room. What do you think?'

'I don't know. Perhaps she really is a bit wrong upstairs.'

Jenna shook her head. 'I don't think so. She writes so clearly. There's no hint of disturbance, although the behaviour of the girls is obviously getting to her.'

'*Really* getting to her,' Jason added. 'Plus the sudden proposal thing. It could throw you off course. And the doctor reckons she's ill too.'

'I still think she's been played.'

'By kids?'

'And the staff. I don't know. The girls have something to gain if they can stop the wedding. They're obviously enraged at the thought of losing their inheritance. The staff . . . I'm not so sure. Perhaps they just feel for the girls, or they're loyal to the first Lady Harville in a kind of Mrs Danvers way.'

'Mrs who?'

'You haven't read *Rebecca*?'

'No, but I might have shagged her, back in the day.'

'Oh, stop it. It's a book, a gothic drama in which the second wife of a rich man is made very uncomfortable by the housekeeper, who remains obsessed with the dead first wife.'

'What, like, in a lesbian kind of way?'

'Most likely. I mean, the book was written a long time ago so they wouldn't have made that kind of thing explicit, but you don't have to read far between the lines.'

'Ah, shame. There could have been some hot girl-on-girl scenes.'

Jenna sighed.

'I can see I'm going to have to educate you.'

'Ooh, please do.'

He smooched into the curve of her neck and shoulder, rapacious still, despite their comprehensive earlier exertions.

'On the subject of great literature and general knowledge,' said Jenna sternly. 'You don't need much education as far as . . . hanky panky . . . goes.'

He laughed.

'Hanky panky? Nobody calls it that.'

She giggled with him. 'It is a bit daft,' she agreed. 'Not as bad as rumpy pumpy, though. That one's enough to turn you right off.'

Jason tapped the diary page.

'So do you think the wedding's off? He thinks she's nuts, she thinks he's a bastard who deliberately didn't listen to her. Not very well suited, are they?'

'Not a match made in heaven, no.' Jenna sighed. 'I'm rather hoping the next entry will tell us she decided to go back home after all. But then, that leaves us with our mystery body in the cellar, and us none the wiser.'

'Perhaps it's better not to know,' said Jason. 'Not as if we can do anything about it, is it?'

'No. True. Poor Frances.'

'Come on. One more page.'

March 10th

My wedding day at last! Though why I say at last, I cannot tell, for our engagement has been a brief affair. David saw no cause to wait and neither did I. I could only wish for a more pleasant day – we have blustering gales and showers of hail. Thankfully my trip to the church will be made in a closed carriage.

My parents arrived last night, with Mary. I had hoped the girls might make a friend of her, but they have kept to their rooms and the nursery, refusing to even come down to the drawing room to make the acquaintance of their soon-to-be relatives. David promises that he will send them to school once we are wed. I should not look forward to it so, but I do.

I had some high words with Mama when we were able to find some time to ourselves – I was able to assure her most forcibly that there is no shameful reason for my precipitate marriage. It was simply Harville's wish.

'He is a great catch,' she said, but there was some doubt underlying her words.

'But you do not approve?'

'Oh, not at all, how could I disapprove of your making such a fine future out of such poor material? You will be comfortable for the rest of your days, my dear.'

Still that doubt plagued her tone. I pressed her further.

'Does he love you, do you think, Fan?' she said at last.

'He is sincere in his affections, I am sure,' I replied, as hotly as I could.

'His daughters . . . You say they are difficult?'

I sighed.

'Difficult indeed. But Lord Harville knows that I have tried my best with them, and he promises me they will be sent away to school.'

'I could never send Mary away, especially so young. The younger one is not yet nine, I believe.'

'It is different for people in society, Mama.'

'I know that. I suppose your own children, especially if they are sons, will grow up far from you.'

I did not care to think of it.

'We will not cross that bridge before we come to it,' I said, and then the men entered from the dining room, having smoked and drunk their fill.

I wish she had not voiced her doubts about David's strength of affection for me. It has planted the seed in my own mind, and I slept but poorly. I shall be a haunted-looking bride, with dark circled eyes and dull skin. David may change his mind at the altar, and then we are all back where we began – my family, penniless, with no prospects of improvement.

But I must try to work wonders, with Mama's help and Mary's probable hindrance! Eliza, the maid, has been told to assist us, but I do not want her sly, sullen face anywhere near me on this morning of mornings, and I sent her off to see to the girls.

The next time I write in this book, I shall be a married woman!

'I think her mum's got it right,' said Jason. 'He doesn't love her, just wants more kids, and by more kids I mean a boy.'

'I agree. Poor Frances – she knows it too, although she doesn't want to admit it. I suppose all the business of the lock-in was never mentioned again? She makes no reference to it at all. Though Harville has agreed to send the girls away as some kind of compensation, I suppose.'

'He wants his boys. He's got no use for the girls any more.'

'Honestly, how did they live with themselves?'

Jenna put the book aside crossly.

'Parents abandoning children still goes on,' said Jason softly. 'It wasn't just them Victorians.'

'No, I didn't mean that – I was talking about Lord . . . Oh, love. You must wonder all the time who your dad was. Is. Is or was.'

'Ah, no, not really.' He put his head on the pillow and gazed up at the subtly spotlit ceiling. 'I'm over all that now.'

'But you wondered?'

'Of course, when I was younger. I mean, it didn't mark me out or anything. Half my mates never saw their dads. But most of them knew who the bugger was, at least. They had a photo, or a teddy bear from before they split, or something. I had nothing.'

'And your mum never gave you a clue?'

'Oh, forget it, she was hopeless. Every time she got pissed she'd be hinting that he was some kind of big deal, then she'd sober up and change her mind and tell me it could be one of half a dozen blokes. She always had some bloke on the side, usually a married one. She wasn't very popular with the other mums, to say the least.'

'She said something after you got out of jail. Something about how it would all come out one day,' recalled Jenna.

'She was tanked up, Jen. I'm sick of hearing it. Anyway, I don't care if my father was Mickey fucking Mouse. He's irrelevant. He's nobody. He's nothing.'

'I doubt he was Mickey Mouse,' said Jenna gently, stroking his forehead. 'You haven't got the ears.'

'No, but I didn't inherit my talents from my mum. So perhaps it was Banksy. What do you reckon?'

'That would be the publicity coup of the decade.'

She lay down beside him, suddenly overwhelmed with fatigue. It had been a long, hot, busy, interesting day.

'Maybe he'll come out of the woodwork once I'm famous, like,' said Jason. 'Wanting his cut. He can fuck off.'

'You've made up your mind you're going to be, then?' said Jenna. 'Famous, I mean.'

'If it happens, it happens. I don't care about fame, but I want to paint for my living, no matter what. I want to be with you, and I want to earn it. I'm not going to be any rich woman's pet poodle.'

Jenna laughed tiredly.

'You're anything but that.'

'More like a tiger, eh?' he said, turning his face to her with a lascivious wink.

'Not tonight, Josephine. I'm exhausted. And tomorrow you learn how to walk the walk and talk the talk.'

Chapter Nine

Jason looked up at the handsome red-brick building in the heart of South Kensington and said, 'They like flowers here, then.'

'Oh yes,' said Jenna, motioning him up the steps. 'They do courses in flower arranging here. Incredibly expensive, but meant to be very good.'

'That's not what I'm here for, I take it?'

'Of course not.'

'So . . . what *am* I here for?'

They had reached the top step. A large brass plaque, so shiny they could almost see their reflections without any distortion, revealed the building's function.

'Margery Mountjoy College of Etiquette.'

'What the fuck's a college of etiquette?'

He pronounced it 'etikwet'.

'Good manners,' said Jenna. 'But it's more than that. It's about being able to go through life mixing with all classes of people without any of them laughing at you. I took a course here after Deano's first album went platinum. Money well spent.'

'Really? Margery Mountjoy was the one that sucked the Bledburn accent out of you, was she?'

'Well, not her exactly. She died decades ago. But this was where I came to transform myself into a London "It" person. It worked for me, and I think it'll work for you.'

'What if I don't want to be a London "It" person? Whatever that is.'

'Jason, don't be obtuse. It's just a little schooling in how to make people feel at their ease with you.'

'Sounds more like it's a schooling in how to have airs and graces.'

'Oh, God, you sound like my mother! That's what she was like. "What's wrong with Bledburn ways? They'll turn you into a snob." But I'm not a snob, am I?'

'Well . . .'

She thought he was teasing. She hoped he was.

She pushed the double doors with determination, leading them into a large, luxurious, marble-floored lobby area.

'Hundreds of people take courses here every year and come out raving about the place,' she said.

'I'd rather just come out raving. I could enjoy a good rave right now. Good weather for it too.'

'Oh, stop it. You're just trying to wind me up.'

'Would I?'

They stopped at a reception desk, presided over by a very well-dressed and very fragrant lady with a tight updo.

'Welcome to Margery Mountjoy,' said the lady, with a winning smile. 'What can I do to help you?'

'Hello, I'm Jenna Myatt and I've booked a session with Georgina.'

'Let me check the record – ah, yes. So you have. Please take a seat and she'll be with you very shortly. I'll just ring to let her know you're here.'

'You see,' whispered Jenna, as they seated themselves on a cream leather couch bookended by luscious green plants. On the coffee table in front of them was a fan-shape of glossy magazines. 'Perfect manners. Makes you feel welcome and important straight away.'

'I dunno about that,' said Jason. 'I think it's a bit creepy.'

'Don't be so silly. It's just a question of confidence, and being comfortable around people. I don't feel that you really are, not yet. This will help you.'

'You don't think I'm confident?'

'I think you're cocky, which isn't the same thing. It comes from a chip on your shoulder. It's aggressive, when you need to be assertive. I don't want that to come over when you're trying to make your name. It'll alienate people you need on your side.'

His jaw dropped. 'Now she tells me! You think I'm a chippy, aggressive bastard. Well, thank you so much.'

He was about to get up and leave, when a very thin middle-aged woman with a helmet of shiny black hair and an immaculate Chanel suit stepped out of the lift and made a beeline for the couch.

'Ah,' she said, her thin magenta mouth curving upwards into a smile. 'Ms Myatt. And Mr Watson. You're in very good time. Hello, I'm Georgina May.'

She held out a hand, which Jenna took first.

Jason folded his arms and looked at the ceiling, then, when nudged by Jenna, stood up to shake Georgina's hand.

'I'll have coffee brought up,' she said. 'Unless you'd prefer tea?'

'Coffee's good,' said Jenna.

'Or beer,' said Jason hopefully.

Georgina laughed politely but her mouth settled straight back into its magenta line and she called to the receptionist to bring coffee up.

Georgina's office was more like the drawing room of a stately home, on a slightly smaller and more comfortable scale. Beautiful works of art lined the walls and the furniture all looked antique.

'Jenna – do you mind if I call you Jenna?'

'Please do.'

'I believe you're an alumnus of ours.'

'That's right. I came here, oh, it must be thirteen years ago. Maybe fourteen. And I was taught by Tiggy Henderson.'

'Ah, dear Tiggy. She has retired, but she keeps in touch. Exhibits her roses all over the country.'

'Yes, I remember she was proud of her roses.'

'And I'm sure she'd be proud of you. You brought a lot of business our way, when you were working in London, I'm told.'

'Oh, yes, you did wonderful work with a lot of my clients.'

'Thank you. And now you have made another booking with us.'

Georgina looked pointedly at Jason, who was slumping in his chair like a teenager who'd been told he couldn't borrow his parents' car.

'Yes,' said Jenna, trying not to feel embarrassed by Jason's extremely negative body language. 'This is Jason.

He's a very talented artist who is shortly to have his first gallery exhibition. But he's not at all familiar with the art world, or the world away from the small town he comes from.'

'I can say all this for myself, you know,' he said, coming to hostile life.

'Please do,' said Georgina, smiling again.

'I'm from the same place she is,' he said, jerking a thumb at Jenna. 'Same estate, even. This accent is the same as what she once had. But she's better than all that now apparently.'

'Don't you think you are?' said Jenna.

'There are good people living there,' he said fiercely. 'Don't tar everyone with the same brush.'

'You aren't here for elocution,' Georgina cut in, welcoming the receptionist with the coffee tray with a smile and a wave at the table. 'Nobody has any plans to change your accent.'

This winded Jason.

'Oh,' he said, looking at Jenna with uncertainty. 'Don't they?'

'No,' Jenna confirmed. 'Look, you are you, and I want you to stay that way. All this is about, as I've said, is confidence. Knowing your way around the world outside Bledburn. Making friends. Making sure people are interested in you for the right reasons.'

'Precisely,' said Georgina, pouring from the cafetière.

'So no rain in Spain stuff?' he said, looking between the two women.

'No rain in Spain stuff,' said Georgina, smiling up at him. 'I promise.'

'So what, then?'

'We're going to role-play some social situations, and you'll learn some very basic body language techniques for looking and sounding confident. Oddly enough, the more confident people think you are, the more at their ease *they* are with you. And the more people warm to you, the better disposed they'll be towards your work. Does that make sense?'

'So, me minding my Ps and Qs will get people to pay for my paintings? Is that what you're saying?'

'Something like that.'

'What about the wild men of rock 'n' roll? People still buy their records. Deano Diamond, for instance.' He gave Jenna a hard look.

'Deano's wild man image was pretty carefully cultivated,' admitted Jenna. 'If he ever trashed a hotel room, we'd always signed a contract with the hotel, promising in advance to pay for all the damage. That interview where he swore at the reporter and made that speech about Iraq? Staged.'

'You are fucking kidding me?' Jason's eyes almost popped.

'No, I'm afraid not. Deano's as mild-mannered as they come, when he isn't performing for the cameras. Sorry.'

'Perhaps that's something to work on,' suggested Georgina. 'Less of the fucking. It's OK on a late-night show but wouldn't go down well on *Newsround*.'

'I'm not going to be on *Newsround*.'

'Are you sure about that?'

'I'm going to be on *Newsround*?' Jason seemed delighted by the idea.

'It's possible,' said Jenna. 'We need to make sure you

have broad appeal. An inspiration for the children as well as an *enfant terrible* for the art world.'

'A tall order,' noted Georgina. 'But we can try. Now, let's start with posture, shall we? Would you mind standing up?'

Jason put down his coffee cup and rose to his feet.

'You don't quite know what to do with all your height, do you?' said Georgina, after looking him up and down for a while. 'You're slouching. Do you feel awkward, being the tallest person in the room most of the time?'

He shrugged. 'Dunno. I never really think about it. But yeah, as a teenager I felt a bit weird about it. It all happened too quick. I was a squeaky shortarse one day and this great big thing the next.'

'So you shot up and weren't really sure what to do with all the extra bits of arm and leg?' suggested Georgina.

'Yeah.'

'And since then, you've compensated for your height by slouching, slumping your shoulders, bowing your head? Well, I've got good news for you, Mr Watson. You can stand tall. You just need to get into some good habits.'

He was already putting back his shoulders, a little stung, it seemed, by Georgina's description of his stance. He unbent his knees, straightened his spine, thrust up his chin.

'There, now we can see all of you,' she said. 'But you're very stiff. The trick is to find a way of standing and moving that shows off your figure to best advantage, without looking as if you're on a parade ground. Do you play any sports, Mr Watson?'

'Call me Jason,' he said. 'And no. I do some gym stuff now and again, if I can be arsed.'

'Gym stuff's all well and good, but I'm thinking about whether you ought to take up cricket.'

'Cricket?' he scoffed. 'That's a posh boys' game.'

'Don't let your prejudices blind you,' cautioned Georgina. 'Besides, I thought Nottinghamshire had a very good cricket team.'

'I wouldn't know.'

'There is a cricket club in Bledburn,' said Jenna. 'Over on the other side of town from the estate. By the lakes.'

'Well, then, perhaps you could think of joining? You see, cricket is all about good posture. Using every part of your body, making sure you know what you're doing with your arms and legs. I do recommend it, especially for you. Your height will be handy for spin bowling. Give it a try.'

'I might,' he grunted.

'Now, let's work on your expression and body language. I'm going to go through a number of role-play situations with you. Number one, you are at a gallery exhibition of your work, and I'm a stranger approaching you to talk about it. Bear in mind, I could be a potential buyer or a journalist or just an interested art student. I could even be a woman trying to get you into bed! You don't know who I am, or what my agenda is. So. Are you ready?'

'I think so.' He picked up his coffee then put it down. 'Not really. I feel like a dick. It's not natural.'

'No,' agreed Georgina patiently. 'It's not. But pretend. Go and look at one of my paintings and I'll come up behind you.'

He walked, in an exaggeratedly swaggering fashion, up to a portrait of a rich Georgian man in a powdered wig.

Jenna wanted to laugh at his over-zealous examination of it – he wasn't from the 'less is more' school of acting.

'Oh, are you the artist?' cried Georgina, slinking up to his shoulder.

'What if I am?'

She stopped short, hands on hips.

'Oh, well, I'm sorry I asked!' she exclaimed. 'Jason, that was so unnecessarily aggressive. All but the most thick-skinned would have slunk away, feeling rejected.'

'Perhaps that's what I want,' said Jason. 'Who wants to be pestered at their own party?'

'Well, if that's the way you see it . . .' Georgina turned to Jenna, her eyebrows aloft.

Jenna tried to smooth matters over.

'But we want buyers, don't we? And you won't know any of them until they introduce themselves. I know nicey-nicey isn't in your nature, and that's why we're practising it. Just give it a go, please? For me?'

Jason sighed. 'For you,' he said. 'I was just . . . Well, if people are really interested, they'll work on you, won't they? If they really like my stuff, they won't be put off if I'm a little bit mardy.'

'Mardy?' Georgina furrowed her brow, as if exposed to a foreign language.

'Bad tempered,' Jenna translated. 'Jason, you can be as mardy as you like when you're a millionaire in your own right. Until then . . .'

'OK, OK, I get the picture,' he grouched.

'Good,' approved Georgina. 'We'll run through it again, shall we? Now. Are you the artist?'

'Why, yes, madam, as a matter of fact, I am,' said Jason, in an exaggerated interpretation of Dramatic Toff.

'Oh, for heaven's sake,' said an exasperated Jenna. 'Now you're just taking the mickey. Can you please *try*?'

'What?' said Jason. 'I thought that was what you wanted.'

'What we want,' said Georgina, laying a hand on his forearm, 'is for you to be yourself, but with a cherry on top. And the cherry is good manners and charm.'

Now it was Jason's turn to look as if he needed an interpreter. He turned his rather hurt gaze to Jenna.

'Are my manners that bad?'

'No, but they need polish,' she reassured him. 'That's all it is. Polish.'

'Well, I give up,' said Jason. 'Tell me what to say then. What should I do when a random stranger comes up and starts asking me questions?'

'Well,' said Georgina, 'to the question "are you the artist?" a simple "yes, I am" would suffice. Then the ball's in your questioner's court. You can either wait for them to continue the conversation, or, if you suspect they might be a buyer or somebody who can further your career, you can add something yourself – something about the paintings, about yourself, about how excited or nervous you're feeling. It's really up to you. But the key is to be calm, to be confident, to be engaging, to be attractive.'

Jason shrugged, still clearly uncomfortable with the situation.

'OK then,' he said. 'Give it another go, I suppose.'

'I will.' Georgina cleared her throat. 'Are you the artist?'

'Yes.'

There was a slight pause. Georgina was forced into continuing the conversation.

'This is stunning work,' she said. 'I so admire your technique. I wonder, can you tell me a little bit about how you came to develop it?'

'Er.' Jason stalled, obviously thinking about how best to answer. 'Well, that's quite a difficult question. It sort of developed itself. I mean, I never had lessons or nothing. Just kind of took in everything I saw and tried things out until I was happy with them.'

'You're self-taught, then? How extraordinary. Do you have any particular influences?'

'Well, uh, I like those *Where's Wally* books.'

There was a pause.

'Are you . . . pulling my leg?' Georgina asked faintly, turning to Jenna. 'Is he?'

Jenna grinned.

'I think he might be serious.'

'I *am* serious,' said Jason. 'I got one as a kid and I looked at it for hours, every night in bed. Then when I started school they had some in the book corner. I wouldn't let the other kids near 'em. They were mine, as far as I was concerned. Used to get into bother for it, kept in at playtime. But that was good, cos it meant I got to look at them even more. Do you know them?'

'I'm not familiar, I don't think.' Georgina's smile was as professionally charming as ever, but Jenna got the distinct impression that a kind of shocked fascination at her new client was underlying it.

'You should get one. They're like all these different landscapes and backgrounds with tons of people all over them and you have to find this particular little guy in amongst it all. The detail is amazing. I tried to memorise them. When I was a bit older, I used to copy them, hours and hours it took. Then, when I was even older, and I'd looked at a few more art books and got to know a few more different styles, I had this idea. I'd do *Where's Wally*, but in my own style, and with my own voice. I mean, not a *voice*, cos it's a picture, but do you know what I mean?'

Georgina's smile was genuine now, Jenna thought. She was really impressed, drawn in by Jason's sudden flowering of passion and enthusiasm when he spoke of his work. The grumpy so and so of a few minutes back seemed to have disappeared.

'I think I do,' she said. 'The books were your original inspiration, and you've taken that and made it your own.'

'Yeah. Cos I wanted to say something with my art, not just "can you find this little dude?" Good though that was. I wanted to say something about my world, where I live, what I see.'

Georgina nodded and turned to Jenna.

'I do think you must retain this unpretentiousness of his. It has a real charm of its own. It would be a shame to lose that.'

Jenna nodded.

Jason scowled.

'Were you listening to me?' he demanded. 'I'm pouring out my heart here and you're just . . . Well, I thought you were supposed to be the expert on manners. It seems a bit rude to talk about me as if I'm not here.'

Georgina was instantly contrite.

'Of course, you're absolutely right. Do excuse me. I'm not used to having a client *and* a referrer at a session together. It's rather made me unsure which of you I should be addressing. But of course, it must be both, to the detriment of neither.'

'Right,' said Jason, flicking a look at Jenna.

'What I meant to say, Jason,' Georgina continued, 'was that, once you embark on a discussion of your work, you don't need any kind of polish at all. And that's as it should be. You need to sound as sincere as you are. What we're dealing with is small talk. So may I try another scenario with you?'

'All right.'

'You're at a reception or drinks party of some kind. Jenna here introduces you to a friend of hers. I will play the friend.'

The three players convened in the centre of the room, pretending their coffee cups were champagne coupes.

'Jenna, how marvellous to see you again,' cried Georgina, air-kissing with a will.

'Georgina, it's been such a long time. And you're looking fabulous. I'd like to introduce you to Jason Watson – you may have heard of him? He's one of our foremost Young British Artists. Jason – Georgina May. Georgina – Jason.'

Georgina gave Jason a significant look down to his free hand.

He seemed to cotton on all at once, and thrust the hand abruptly towards Georgina.

'Yes, but a little stiff,' she said. 'Try again. Just make it look easy and natural.'

His second attempt was more to Georgina's liking, and she took his hand and shook it.

'What's all that kissing thing though?' he wanted to know. 'Do I have to do that?'

'It's more for established friends,' said Georgina. 'Especially female friends. If you don't know the woman well, it's best to stick to a handshake.'

'Good. Because it'd make me feel a right ponce.'

Georgina's smile was tight at the corners.

'Shall we make some more polite conversation?' she suggested, launching into her next gambit without waiting for consensus. 'Oh, yes, of course I've read all about you in the arts pages,' she said. 'I tried to get tickets for your show but, dear me – gold dust!' She smiled with practised warmth.

'Oh. That's a shame,' said Jason awkwardly. 'Maybe next time I can get you on the guest list.'

'That would be wonderful. I hear this marvellous new talent was a discovery of yours, Jenna, is that right?'

'Absolutely,' said Jenna. 'And I thank my lucky stars our paths crossed.'

'So . . .' There was a glint in Georgina's eye that made Jenna suddenly wary. 'How did that happen then?'

Oh, she knew, of course, Jenna thought, annoyed at the sudden burst of heat on her face. Everybody did – everybody who read the papers or took the slightest notice of tabloid gossip.

'I was kipping in her attic,' Jason said matter-of-factly. 'Dossing, like. She found me there, and saw my paintings on the wall.'

'You were homeless?'

'Do I have to go through the whole story?' He turned to Jenna. 'I mean, everyone knows. It were in all the papers.'

'I'm sorry,' said Georgina. 'But I knew that your situation was . . . unusual. I thought it best that you should be prepared for people's perhaps excessive curiosity. Sometimes, when a story is as juicy as yours, people can forget your right to a private life.'

'Juicy,' said Jason contemplatively. 'Yeah. It's that all right.'

'People may well pretend to know less than they actually do, just to hear it from the horse's mouth, so to speak,' said Georgina. 'And perhaps get a nice titbit that hasn't been in the papers, to gossip over with their friends.'

'Can't I just tell them to fuck off, if that's their game?' said Jason.

Georgina laughed nervously.

'Well, it's your prerogative, of course, but it might not work to your advantage. I'd like to offer you some other options.'

'Like what?'

'You can simply point out that the story has been in all the newspapers, if they want to go and refer to Google. That should be enough to silence any overly zealous questioners. You can laugh it off. You can simply change the subject. Any of these will steer the conversation away from more intimate waters. Would you like to try it?'

Jason shrugged. 'OK.'

'Oh yes,' said Georgina, 'weren't you on the run from the police?'

'Yeah, with your mum,' said Jason.

Jenna snorted with laughter.

'Maybe that's going a bit far,' she suggested.

'What? It's a joke!'

'Again,' said Georgina, 'a somewhat aggressive one.'

The session continued in this vein, with Jason trying

to conform, then bursting out with some or other little act of provocation when it all became too wearing.

Jenna was not sure the experiment was a complete success but, after all, these skills were best learned in the practice and she could hardly expect him to go from snippy to suave in the space of two hours. It would all come in time.

Leaving the building with her nerves slightly frayed, Jenna descended the steps in front of Jason, trying not to be the one to speak first. If she did, she would only sound patronising, or frustrated with him.

She waited instead for him to offer the first word.

'Well, that was charming,' he sneered, at pavement level, while Jenna looked vaguely up the road in search of the chauffeured car they had hired for the day.

'Yes, Georgina is one of the best in her field,' she replied levelly, ignoring the sarcasm.

'And what a field it is. Turning people into smooth bullshitters.'

'Oh, Jason, that isn't it. Stop being so defensive. I'm only trying . . .'

She gave up, climbing into the car as it pulled into the kerb beside them.

Jason got into the back seat beside her.

'Trying to what? Make me into something I'm not?'

'No. Making you into the best you can be. You're going to need to stop taking everything so personally, if you want to succeed. Good manners are just a bit of oil for the wheels, that's all. You can apply it as necessary, and be your horrible self all the rest of the time.'

That elicited a reluctant smile.

'I like being my horrible self,' he said. 'It's me.'

Jenna squeezed his knee.

'I wouldn't want you any other way. I just want to make life easier for you, if this all comes off. Fame can be very disorientating, especially if it's overnight. I want you to be prepared; to have a little stash of PR weapons at your disposal.'

'Oh, well, if it's weapons, I want a samurai sword.'

'Think of it that way,' said Jenna with a smile. 'Think of these little phrases and mannerisms as your armoury. They keep people from hurting you.'

'Talking of hurting . . .' said Jason, leaning suddenly forward and instructing the chauffeur to drive them to an address south of the river.

'Oh . . .' said Jenna, remembering.

Jason smiled his first genuine smile since arriving at the charm school.

'You've had me performing like a show pony all morning,' he said. 'Now it's my turn.'

'Oh God, you aren't going to . . .?'

'A deal's a deal. I take a hit from you, you take a hit from me. And this one is going to be very artistic.'

The car dropped them off by Borough Market, where they went in search of lunch before the fateful appointment.

Jenna was all for hiding inside one of the plethora of upmarket restaurants in the area, but Jason baulked, drawn in by the fascinating sights and smells of the market. They ended up buying a bag of some kind of Balkan delicacy Jenna had never tasted before – spinach and feta pastry parcels served with a poached egg and beetroot hummus – and took them to a bench by the river to eat al fresco.

'Nobody's recognised you,' Jason teased, opening the paper bag. 'You're disappointed, aren't you?'

'Not at all. And I'm pretty sure I *was* recognised. It's just that people around here are too cool to make a fuss about celebs. The Market's often crawling with them.'

Jason took a bite from his pastry, looking over the river to the dome of St Paul's.

'It's all right here,' he said. 'I never thought there'd be bits like this. I thought it'd all be horse guards and . . . I dunno. Big Ben.'

'There's so much to London. Much more than you could take in in a whole year. I missed it, when I was in LA.'

'Do you miss LA?'

'No. Well, it's summer. Ask me again in six months and my answer might be different. But on the whole – no.'

'You don't miss that life?'

She turned to Jason. 'You know, sitting here, by the river, eating gorgeous food with a gorgeous man, knowing that I have a project to sink my teeth into and so much to look forward to . . . Well, what do you think?'

He swallowed at that, and looked away for a moment.

'You feel like that?' he said quietly.

'Yes. After years of just running to keep up with myself, I feel I'm doing what I want, at last. And loving it.'

'I've never had anything to look forward to before,' said Jason. 'I mean, a feeling that there's a point to it all. It's weird.' He flashed her a sudden, heart-stopping smile. 'It's nice. Tell me it's real.'

She put a hand on his.

'It's real.'

They shared a brief but heartfelt kiss, then finished the remains of their lunch.

'I hope you're sitting comfortably on that bench,' said Jason, his mood skipping along with the sunbeams from emotional to teasing. 'Cos you won't be, later on.'

'What do you mean? We're going to meet that craftsman, aren't we? That's all.'

'Is it?' said Jason, eyeing her roguishly. 'Is it all?'

'What are you saying?'

'Come on. Let's go and find him.' He pulled her up, dropped their bag of rubbish into the nearest bin, and began to run with her across the cobbles, into the heart of the district of restored warehouses that loomed around the market.

Jenna was aware of the attention they were drawing, and she dreaded it in her heart, yet she felt so joyous and free at the same time that it didn't seem to matter as much as it might. This was like being young again, like taking a picnic to the fields with Deano and running down to the river, stripping off, swimming in its shallow sparkle. And why shouldn't she feel young? She was only thirty-five, damn it, not an old timer. To hell with being on top and in control and mature and sensible all the bloody time.

He whirled her around a corner, into a dark alleyway between warehouses, and pushed her up against the wall before descending upon her with all the passion and abandonment she had come to know from him.

'Mmm, babe,' he drawled, releasing her ravished mouth. 'I want him to see that lipstick smeared all over your face and know you've just been snogged half to death.'

Jenna started to ask why, but Jason resumed the kiss with all the energy and thoroughness of somebody who trained at it for several hours a day.

'Because this time,' he whispered, answering the question she had never had the chance to pose, '*I* want to be seen to be the client. Not you. I want to be the one who has the idea, and you to be the one who goes along with it.'

'A reversal of what we did at the charm school?'

'Yeah, if you want to put it that way.'

'You want to save your pride.'

'Perhaps I do.'

Jenna hid her face in his shoulder.

'I was going to ask if you could see this bloke alone. Let me go back to the hotel and meet you there.'

'Not a chance. You're coming with me. I want this guy to know exactly who I'm designing my masterpiece for.'

She made a strangled little sound of pained shame, then capitulated.

'I suppose you'll be unbearable forever if I don't?'

'I suppose I will.'

'Come on then. Let's find him.'

John Lindo's workshop wasn't far from Borough Market. It was in a street of thriving pubs and delicatessens, in a building that looked as if it had once been stables. Behind it, trains rumbled almost without cease, coming in and out of nearby London Bridge station.

Jason was the one to knock on the door for this appointment. It was opened by a mild-looking middle-aged man in heavy apron and gloves.

Jason introduced himself and the man smiled, recalling the appointment.

'Ah yes. You called yesterday from Cinq à Sept. Do come in.'

Inside, the space was large and airy, all the light coming from front wall windows high up near the ceiling. A variety of workbenches and machinery stood on one side of the floor, while on the other was a fairly comfortable arrangement of old sofas and chairs with a makeshift kitchen occupying the corner.

Lindo led Jenna and Jason to this side of the room, heading over to the sink to fill the kettle.

Jenna couldn't help but notice that the wall was rather interestingly decorated with all kinds of spanking implements hanging from nails. It made her scalp prickle and she tried to look away from the threatening leather and wood, but it was all around her, inescapable.

'So you bought one of my pieces?' Lindo said, turning to them again, having put the kettle on.

'Yeah,' said Jason. 'A leather one, but I see you do wood as well.'

'I do. Those are the materials I work with most, but I'll turn my hand to most things. I've done some work in plastics too. How did you find it?'

'How . . .? Well, it was in the shop.'

Lindo smiled, shaking his head.

'No, I mean, have you given your new purchase a go?'

'Oh, right, I see.' Jason grinned, turning taunting eyes to Jenna. 'Yes. It was just the job.'

Jenna cringed inwardly. Not that Jason had mentioned which way around the thing was done. For all Lindo knew, it could have been Jenna with the whip hand.

'That's good to hear,' said Lindo. 'Now, I have ordinary teabags, or I can offer some fruit and herbal teas.'

'Ordinary for me,' said Jason, while Jenna opted for blackcurrant and ginseng.

'So,' Lindo pursued, pouring the drinks. 'Do you think it was better or worse than other examples you might have used before?'

'Well, I'd say it was better,' said Jason. 'Because not only did it do the job, it was pretty as well.'

Lindo nodded and handed the mugs of tea to his guests before seating himself opposite them.

'That's my intention,' he said. 'I wanted to create something fearful and yet also beautiful. Something for the aesthetes among us. Of course, many of those who share our fetish are quite happy with a bog-standard belt or a wooden spoon, but I always thought the experience could be so much fuller, with the right implement.'

'Yeah,' said Jason, clearly excited by the discussion. 'I get you. That's why I came to you. When I saw your stuff in that shop, I felt like I understood what you were doing and really appreciated it.'

'It's kind of you to say so.'

Jenna, sitting a little bit back from this mutual appreciation society, felt a desperate nag of embarrassment within her. Hearing what she and Jason had done referred to as a fetish had shocked her, for some reason. Had she really travelled so far towards the margins of society? Perhaps it was the beginning of a steep slope, and if so, where would it end?

Like the discreet lady in the shop, she was confident Lindo would not go blabbing their sex secrets all over town. Nonetheless, she felt something like fear at the thought of allowing a third party to know what she and Jason did behind closed doors.

They had started discussing the technicalities of transferring Lindo's designs on to the wood or leather, and Jenna drifted into a nightmare vision of all this getting into the papers. What would it be like, to have something so intimate splashed all over the headlines? How would she ever be able to face anybody again?

'Excuse me,' said Lindo, breaking into her unpleasant imaginings. 'But you look awfully worried. Are you all right, Ms . . .?'

Ah, was he pretending or did he genuinely not know who she was?

'Myatt,' she said, with a small but grateful smile. 'But please, call me Jenna.'

She took a sip of her tea.

'Are you feeling quite all right?' Lindo repeated the question.

'Oh, yes, I'm fine. Just . . . a little nervous.'

'Och, well, you've nothing to be nervous about.'

Jenna noticed for the first time his soft Scottish accent.

'I suppose it feels a bit strange to be talking about this kind of thing with a stranger, eh?'

She nodded.

'Well, don't you worry. Nothing that happens inside this place ever gets outside. I'm talking about orders, clients, conversations – nothing. I have a client list some of the papers would love to take a look at – plenty of famous names on there. But I'll never tell. Why would I? I'd lose good business. And if you're worried about me thinking you're strange and unnatural . . .' He laughed heartily. 'Well, I'd be a bit of a hypocrite. My wife likes to test my new designs out on me.'

Jenna smiled, suddenly very much more at her ease,

now she knew that she and Lindo were both the submissive parties in their relationships. There was no need to feel embarrassed after all – or no more than Lindo did, anyway.

'Yes,' he continued, 'I started this business on her suggestion. I made a little paddle with a rose carved into it as an anniversary present, and she was so taken with it she suggested I try to sell my work. I was surprised at how quickly it took off. There's quite a market out there.'

'I love your designs,' said Jason eagerly. 'But I was wondering if you'd consider making me a paddle that I'd designed? I'm an artist myself, and I'm always looking for new ways to work. But I wouldn't have a clue about all the machinery craftsman side of it.'

Lindo nodded, intrigued by the suggestion.

'Well, whyever not?' he said. 'Do you have a particular design in mind?'

Jason grabbed a folded piece of A4 paper from his inside jacket pocket.

'I was doing a few doodles last night. Not sure if any of them are any good . . .'

Lindo examined the page, while Jenna tried her best to peek at it. She hadn't seen Jason doing these sketches – perhaps she had been asleep at the time.

She watched as Jason jabbed a finger at one.

'Maybe that one? Do you think it would work?'

Lindo replied with a slow nod, then flashed a smile at Jenna and handed her the paper.

'What do you think? Which is your favourite? It's your skin, after all.'

A clutch of little pencil sketches adorned the page, in varying degrees of elaborateness. The one that drew her eye was one of the simplest: a large heart shape with the letter J cut out of it.

'Would this one be simple to make?' she asked, showing it to Lindo. 'It looks like the easiest – none of the curly-wurly patterns on the others.'

'Well, I can do curly-wurly patterns,' said Lindo with a smile. 'It's not a problem. But you like that one?'

'I kind of like the idea of what it would look like . . . after use,' she said, coughing slightly to cover her blushes. Now she knew all three of them were thinking of her bum, with a red heart on each cheek and a white letter J in the middle. One for Jason, one for Jenna.

'Yeah,' said Jason, with low-toned satisfaction. 'That would look peachy.'

'Well, that would be no trouble at all,' said Lindo briskly. 'I can turn one out for you now. Were you thinking wood or leather? Or something else?'

'I'd go for leather. I just like the feel of it more,' said Jason. 'I suppose that's more work for you, though? Stitching and that?'

'No more work at all. Wood requires a lot of sanding and smoothing. Come over to the workshop side and we can make a start.'

Jenna and Jason watched transfixed as Lindo demonstrated how to cut and fashion the leather into a serviceable spanking implement. At times, Jason was allowed to perform an operation or two, which he set to with a will.

'I'd like to get into this,' he said, looking up from machining stitches around the edge of the paddle. 'Craftsmanship, like. I think I'd be good at it. I always bunked off textiles lessons at school cos I thought it'd be all embroidery and shit. But this is really good.'

'You have the knack, I think,' said Lindo, watching with approval.

Jenna had to admit she was enjoying watching Jason at work. Those skilled, sensitive, strong hands had more than one talent. They gave pleasure, they gave pain and they created so much that was beautiful. Perhaps she ought to get them insured. Come to think of it, that would make a good press release . . .

She came back to earth when Jason, having buffed the leather to a high shine, slapped the finished product into his palm.

'I like it,' he said. 'Nice weight, feels solid but flexible too.'

'Yes, I get a lot of testimonials from customers saying the same thing,' said Lindo. 'They're beautiful to look at, but also they pack a high quality sting.'

Jenna bit her lip at that. A high quality sting, indeed. At least she wouldn't be letting any old cheap rubbish tan her behind.

'I can't wait to see the result,' said Jason, sucking a quick breath in between his teeth and looking at Jenna.

She looked away.

Lindo cleared his throat discreetly.

'Well, you know, I do have a little loft upstairs if you'd like some privacy . . .'

Jason's beaming smile left Jenna in no doubt that he was going to take Lindo up on his offer.

She looked at the door.

'Shouldn't we . . .?'

'Don't forget,' said Jason softly, coming to stand next to her. 'I performed like a puppet for you all morning. Fair's fair.'

He was right. The bargain had been made. Jenna could only hope Lindo's loft was a bit more spacious than the changing room at Cinq à Sept yesterday. She seemed to be making a habit of getting up to rude things on business premises lately.

Jason held out his hand. Jenna took it.

Lindo chuckled and led them over to a little door at the back of the room that opened onto a diagonal ladder staircase.

'Up you go, then,' he said. 'I'll nip to the shop next door and get some of their nice biscuits. And perhaps a bottle of wine to share? You'll both have earned a drink, I think.'

He turned and left them at the foot of the ladder, Jenna heaving a sigh of relief at his discretion. Now she wouldn't be fretting about how much noise they were making.

All the same, her heart was bumping all over her ribs like a pinball as she followed Jason up the ladder.

Reaching the top, her mouth dropped open and she gasped.

The place was kitted out like some kind of professional spanking parlour.

'Fuck me,' said Jason, obviously impressed. 'Check it out.'

There were hooks in the roof and metal rings attached to all the support posts, for the chaining of miscreants. Rack upon rack of different implements lined the low walls. The floor was furnished with chairs and stepstools and strange little folding items for arranging your victims upon. In the centre was an honest-to-goodness spanking bench, in padded leather, with cuffs attached.

Jason began to tinker with this, finding that it could be moved on hinges into all kinds of different configurations.

'Clever,' he said. 'I wonder if he makes these too. We could buy one.'

Jenna bit back a dry remark about how easy he seemed to find spending her money. Probably not the wisest thing to say, under the circumstances.

Instead, she merely said 'Hmm' and watched him adjust the bench until it was to his liking.

'OK, then,' he proclaimed, turning to grin at her. 'Care to hop on board?'

'You want me to get on that thing?'

She was dubious, mainly because of the cuffs. What if she got stuck in them?

'Why not? Try it for size.'

'OK, but don't do those cuffs up.'

Jason pouted. 'I thought you were into bondage.'

'I'm into bondage in my own home,' she emphasised.

He shrugged. 'Up to you. But come on. This paddle won't test itself. I need your arse, good and high.'

He slapped it into his hand, and the leathery sound, together with his words, galvanised her. She couldn't resist Jason when he was in forceful mode. Within seconds she was prone on the spanking bench, draped across its padded upholstery with her smart skirt straining over her rear curves.

It was surprisingly comfortable and she settled into her pose, gripping the sides above her head and keeping her feet together.

There was a window just above them, set into the

roof, and she heard the patter of pigeons crossing it, and their billing and cooing, which added to her feeling of reassurance in a strange way.

Jason seemed bent on stripping away that sense of comfort, though, along with other things. He unzipped her skirt and began lowering it over her hips. Jenna was immediately aware of being in a strange place, belonging to a strange man who might return from the shop at any moment.

'Lindo . . .' she quavered.

'He won't come up. He's left us to it. And besides, how can I test this out over clothes? The design won't show up.'

'Couldn't we do it back at the hotel?'

'Relax, Jen. They don't have all this kind of kit back at the hotel, do they?' He slapped the leather cushioning just above Jenna's head. 'Unless they've got a secret dungeon in the basement. That'd be cool. I wonder if there are hotels that do that. We could open one. Make Harville Hall into a resort for kinky bastards. What do you reckon?'

'Jason . . . Could you just get on with whatever you're going to do?'

'Whatever the lady desires,' he said theatrically, pulling the skirt right down to Jenna's knees. 'Something to think about, though.'

'Something to think about and then say "no way",' retorted Jenna.

Jason laughed. Still laughing, he smacked his palm down hard on her knicker-clad bottom so that she squealed in surprise.

'Is that the way to talk to me, when you're flat out

on a spanking bench and I'm carrying a big old leather paddle?' he asked lightly.

'Probably not,' she conceded.

'Right.' He pulled down her knickers.

It was very warm in the loft room with the glaring London sun penetrating the single-glazing of the roof window. Jenna felt that her thighs were already sweating, whether with heat or apprehension or something else she couldn't be sure.

Her light cotton top stuck to her back and her palms were slippery against the leather. Why wouldn't he just get on with it?

Without preamble, he did. The paddle snapped down on her already-warm bottom, causing her to arch her back and lift herself slightly off the bench.

'Get down or I'll have to cuff you,' said Jason gruffly.

'You surprised me!'

'Don't be daft. You're on a spanking bench with your bare bum in the air. What do you think is going to happen?'

She reached behind to rub the sore spot on her right cheek.

'Eh, and none of that, madam!' Jason was indignant. 'Or the cuffs definitely go on.'

He laid the paddle on her fingers and she removed them like a shot, reverting to her previous pose.

'Are you going to be long?' she whined. 'I'm worried about being overheard . . .'

'Well, I'm not,' said Jason. 'I couldn't care less who listens in. And I'll be as long as it takes.'

'As long as it takes for what?'

'As long as it takes for me to work off feeling like a

right twonk all morning with your mate Georgina. Could be a long old session, Jen.'

'I was only trying to help,' Jenna wailed.

'Yeah, and so am I.'

The paddle cracked down again, on the other side.

'Therapy,' whispered Jason.

Jenna resigned herself to accepting whatever he had in mind for her. If she stayed still and took it quietly, perhaps it would be over sooner. Surely it was too hot for him to put much effort into it, anyway.

But the sun's ferocity didn't seem to affect him at all. He gave her bottom a thorough workout, laying the paddle rhythmically and regularly in the same two spots on her right and left cheeks until she felt she couldn't stand it. She tried to shift her behind around, to coax him into striking a different area of her skin, but he was resolute.

'Don't spoil the pattern, Jen,' he scolded. 'There's a cane up there on the wall I might try otherwise.'

Er, no thanks.

She tightened her grip on the bench, her knuckles whitening with the effort.

It was harder than she remembered to take this pain. Surely yesterday, with the filigree patterned paddle, had been a breeze in comparison? This time it was too hot, and Jason's rhythm was too unvarying. The same spot, over and over, and now he was getting faster as well, his confidence in full glory.

'Oh please,' she mewled, ready to throw herself sideways off the bench.

He stopped, and she was grateful for his tender mercies until she realised that he was finished anyway.

'That should do nicely,' he said, crouching low over her bottom so that she could feel his breath, adding to the fierce heat already radiating from it. 'It's gorgeous, Jen. Two perfect hearts with the letter J in each. Only thing missing is a 4 in the middle. If they designed a butt plug with a number 4 for the base . . .'

'Oh, for God's sake.' She couldn't help an aghast little laugh. Why had she thought it was a good idea to get involved with a highly creative person?

'What? It would look amazing. Don't you reckon? J 4 J all the way across your arse. A human canvas.'

'I'm already one of those,' she said, shifting uncomfortably to try and dissipate some of the stinging heat. The movement only emphasised how sticky-wet she was between her thighs. 'Take a photo. I want to see what it looks like.'

'Oh right. Sure.'

He snapped her cheeks and brought the phone round under her nose. She admired the pretty patterns of red and white, and the well-toned skin on which they were printed. Despite her lack of a home gym and trainer, she wasn't doing too badly on the yoga and jogging round the garden regime. Or maybe it was the sex. Yes, come to think of it, she was getting every bit as good a workout as she ever had done.

'Come on, that butt plug idea was good,' wheedled Jason. 'Don't reject it out of hand.'

'Perhaps you could Photoshop it in?' she suggested.

He crouched beside her, stroking along her spine, his lips by her ear.

'Perhaps that decision should be mine, hmm?'

She clenched her buttocks.

'I think we should pay another visit to that little shop,' he continued. 'I could make the number four myself. I just need something to attach it to.'

'I think we ought to get back to Bledburn. We've done everything we came to London for.'

Jason chuckled and kissed her neck.

'I don't see you moving off that bench, love. You seem to be taking root there.'

'It's surprisingly comfortable,' she admitted. 'And I'm too hot and sore to think about moving just yet.'

'You're hot all right.' His lips found their way to her mouth.

She lay, dazed and floppy and layered with perspiration, lazily accepting his kiss, his tongue, his greedy hands all over her.

By the time he climbed over her, straddling her on the bench, and slid his uncovered cock inside her, she had forgotten everything except how her sex ached and throbbed for him. Their surroundings, their timetable, their possible company downstairs had all disappeared and she was conscious of nothing but her body and his, and the urgent need for them to meet.

His weight on her increased her temperature and made her stickier than ever, but she couldn't have cared less. The place could have been consumed in a fireball and she'd still have nothing on her mind but the guilty, blissful feeling of him inside her, working at her, building up the friction until she had no recourse but to dissolve into her orgasm.

She lay, flattened and content beneath him, waiting for him to fill her with his own climax, longing for nothing more now than to sleep in his arms.

But of course, they would not be able to do that.

Jason withdrew and got to his feet again mere moments after pumping his seed into her, pulling on his pants and suit trousers with a hurried air.

'Thought I heard the door go,' he said as she peeled a cheek from the leather bench to level an unfocused gaze on him.

She blinked and tried to bring her exhausted brain and body back to life.

'Are you sure?'

'Yeah. Lindo's back. Come on.'

He laughed fondly and kissed her forehead, apparently amused by how out of it she was.

'Do I have to carry you?'

'You might.'

But she managed to remove her dead weight limbs from the bench, sinking first to her knees on the planking floor before gathering enough energy to pull up her knickers and skirt. Her shirt was now virtually transparent, the white dobby cotton sticking to her curves in a very unkempt manner. As for her hair . . .

Still kneeling, she dragged her handbag over by its strap and took out her brush and mirror. She couldn't get it quite back into her usual chic style, but she could at least stop it from looking as if it was plastered to her head. And her make-up . . .

Emergency blotting and reapplication was necessary, during which Jason paced the room, looking out of the yellowing roof glass at the thick skies outside.

'You're going downstairs into a workshop, not along the red carpet,' he scolded, teetering at the top of the ladder. 'Come on, for fuck's sake.'

'He's going to know,' she said with certainty, snapping her compact shut.

'Well, of course he is. Look what we brought up here.' Jason waved the paddle at her.

'I don't think I can face him.'

'Don't be daft. Come on.'

He came across to take her by the elbow and propel her towards the ladder.

'The bench,' she panicked, breaking away and scrabbling inside her handbag for the mini-pack of baby wipes she kept.

Jason waited, rolling his eyes, while she wiped down the leather, desperate to free it of any lingering traces of what had passed.

'Now are you ready?' he asked, long-sufferingly.

'Bad manners to leave bodily fluids on other people's furniture,' she replied primly.

'Georgina must have forgotten to mention it,' said Jason with a sardonic smile. 'Perhaps you ought to tell her. Next lesson.'

She jabbed him between his shoulder blades as he reached the ladder in front of her.

'Yeah, I will,' she said.

She was relieved that Jason entered the main workshop floor first. He would have to deal with whatever was found there.

Lindo was sitting in the rest area, reading the paper.

He folded it up, smiling, as his company revealed itself.

'Ah,' he said. 'I've poured you each a glass of wine. Got a lovely, cold, crisp white, as it seems to be the weather for it. Or perhaps I should have gone for fizz?'

He looked at Jenna, who realised that he was referring

to her fame, making the assumption that she lived a champagne lifestyle. He certainly did recognise her then.

She overrode her little impulse of dismay by making a beeline for the wine and saying, 'Oh, no, a nice cold white sounds perfect. Thank you.'

'So then?' said Lindo, with a delicate throat-clearing sound, once everyone was seated with a glass.

Jenna and Jason exchanged a glance.

'Do we have a verdict?'

Jason put the paddle down on the table.

'Class,' he said.

Jenna looked down at the pale liquid in her glass.

'Did it perform as you hoped?'

'Yeah, it did. Just the result I was looking for.'

'That's excellent. And . . . were you favourably impressed too?'

Jenna forced herself to meet his smile.

'It was good,' she said.

'The first time with a new implement is always exciting for me,' said Lindo. 'And when it's one I've made myself . . . well . . . that's a thrill beyond describing. To feel your own work turned against you. What a unique feeling.'

'It must be,' said Jason.

Jenna was curious now.

'Does your wife ever tell you what to make?'

Lindo's eyes took on a dreamy quality.

'Sometimes,' he said. 'Though she never goes into detail. But some mornings she might ask me if I have a lot of work on, and if the answer's no, she'll place an order. She might say, "I need a good, thick strap for my collection, one that will make a proper red stripe." Or the other day she asked for "a thin-handled whip that will leave marks". I made both, and there have been others.'

'What's your favourite?' asked Jenna impulsively. 'And your least favourite?'

'Well, I can take quite a lot of pain, so I'd say my favourite was the cane. It really hits the spot when I want more than sensation play. My least favourite – oh, I don't have one. I love them all. Every single one has its good points. Yourself?'

Jenna had not expected the question to be turned back on her.

'Oh. Well. There's a lot I haven't tried. I don't think I'd like any of those thin, whippy things. For pleasure, I like one of those light flogger things. They don't really hurt.'

'Ah, you see, for me, that would be a disappointment,' said Lindo. 'What about you, Mr Watson?'

'I like 'em all,' said Jason equably, after swallowing a mouthful of wine. 'Paddles are good cos she squirms so much. I like to see a good squirm. But, yeah, we've got a few others to try out yet, before I pick a favourite.'

'Lucky you,' said Lindo. 'I sometimes wish I could go back to the days when it was all new and I had no idea what to expect. These days, we work like a well-oiled machine, but there's something about that genuine anxiety of the first few sessions . . . Ah. I do miss it.'

'How long have you and your wife been together?' asked Jenna.

'Twenty-two years,' said Lindo. 'It wasn't our kink that brought us together – it took a few years for that to come out. What a piece of luck when it did.'

'It must happen the other way too,' mused Jenna. 'Two

people who love to be the one in control getting together, for instance, or two submissives.'

'If they love each other, I suppose it doesn't matter,' said Lindo, shrugging.

'If they love each other,' echoed Jenna. For the first time in days, she found herself thinking of Deano. Perhaps that was their problem. They had been too alike. If she had asked him to be more dominant in the bedroom, what might he have said?

She couldn't imagine it. How, then, could she say she knew him well?

'Well, then,' said Jason, draining his glass with a cavalier flourish and banging it on the table. 'Cheers, mate. I've really enjoyed this afternoon. Learnt a lot. Might open my own workshop.'

'Oh, I don't want competition,' said Lindo, smiling.

'Nah, just for my own personal use,' he said with a wink. 'You can keep your customers.'

Jenna was glad to get out, back into the sweaty jumble of London. She'd had the feeling that Lindo was constantly on the verge of revealing too much information and she didn't want Jason to feel obliged to join in.

'Nice bloke,' said Jason, as she called for the car.

'Good craftsman,' she said.

'Yeah. Like me. What do you think? Shall I start knocking my own stuff up? I'd like to do that. I mean, painting is great, but I love all that hammering and sawing and stuff. Made me feel proper manly, you know?'

She laughed. 'You don't need a hammer and nails to prove *that*, my darling.'

'Not to you,' he said, digging her in the ribs. 'But to myself.'

'You seem obsessed with proving yourself just now,' she observed. 'It's OK to take things slowly. You don't have to do everything at once.'

He leant back against the wall, exhaling into the clammy air.

'If not now, then when?' he said, turning his eyes to her. 'I've dossed about for too long. Feel like I need to make up for lost time. And there's so much to prove. Prove I'm an artist, prove I'm a decent bloke, prove I'm a *man*.'

Jenna laughed. 'Who doesn't think you're a man? It seems pretty clear to me.'

'To you, babe,' he said, reaching out to tickle the back of her damp neck. 'In the bedroom, yeah. But I mean outside the bedroom. In the other places where it counts. In the house, in the street, at the bank.'

'Ah, money again. It will come,' she said seriously. 'It might take its time at first, but it *will*. In the meantime, if you like, you can consider everything I pay for as a loan. I know you'll pay it back. I believe in you.'

'Yeah, you do, don't you? Weird.'

'Not weird.' She laid her head on his shoulder. 'Perhaps if I do it hard enough, you'll start to believe in yourself.'

Chapter Ten

Later on, in the bedroom at the hotel, the diary came out again.

The air conditioning was switched to blissfully cool and they lay in a post-shower sprawl, Jenna in a silk robe and Jason in boxers, appreciating each other's scented skin.

'Tell you what, we haven't read about the wedding night yet,' Jason prompted. 'I want to know if Harville's a dirty perv. I bet he is.'

'I don't know why you're so insistent a middle-class Victorian lady is going to want to write porn,' said Jenna, tutting.

But she took the book from the bedside drawer and turned to where they had left off – the morning of the wedding.

March 11th

I write these lines as Lady Harville. My name has changed, but that is not all. So much has changed, in the time it took for our hands and hearts to be joined for all time, that I can scarcely catalogue it.

I have risen in station to a place of elevation I never dreamed I could occupy. A humble governess, the daughter of a failed businessman, I now prepare to conduct the rest of my life as a lady of quality. The penniless girl may now order whatever she desires without second thought. I have leapt from mutton pudding to veal à la Béarnaise; from calico to silk. I may not feel it yet, but in name and in fortune, I am now an aristocrat.

I have changed also, from single young woman to wife, and what a momentous change that is. I have been accustomed to pleasing only myself, but now I must please another, and put his wishes at the forefront of my awareness. It will not be easy to make this alteration in my very heart, but I am sure I will strive to do my duty and make my husband the happiest man I can.

Another change, and one of which I am apprehensive, is my transit from governess to mother. How will I ever replace the parent those girls remember so fondly and so sadly? I fear they will never take me into their hearts and I will remain always outside their sphere of confidence, branded an outsider and hated for it. I have pledged, all the same, most solemnly, to do my best for Maria and Susannah, in hopes that the day will come when we might be dear friends.

Another delicate distinction is that between servant and served. The staff still look upon me coldly but they must know that to do so for much longer will result in their being replaced — for I will not hesitate to insist that they seek another place, if they cannot treat their mistress with the respect she deserves.

Finally, another change, a most private one, and one

I blush to mention. But I intend to be fearlessly honest
here in my diary, and so I must not gloss over it.

'Now we're getting to the good bit,' said Jason, putting
his chin on Jenna's shoulder to better view the book's
contents.

'Anyone'd think you were sex-starved,' said Jenna dryly.
'Which we both know not to be the case.'

'Yeah, but it's interesting in all this oldy-worldy
language. I want to know how she describes it. I bet she
cops out and says something sketchy like "it was like
opening up to the sun", or something. Girls can never
call a spade a spade.'

'Don't be sexist. Anyway, let's see, shall we?'

I awake a new person, a woman experienced in the
duties of marriage. When I came into this bed, I was a
mere girl, trembling in ignorance of what awaited me.
I had heard that, to get a child, a husband must 'couple
with' his wife in some way, but I had no fixed idea of
what such coupling might entail.

Now I know it, and what knowledge! David came
to me, his eyes burning with a strange light that made
me shiver. He would not let me keep on the beautiful
nightdress from Paris I had made especially for my
trousseau. Instead, he made plain that he wished to see
me unclothed and unadorned. I nearly burned up with
the shame of it, for none has seen me naked since I was
a small child, and I had hoped to evade any such embar-
rassing necessity. But my mother had advised me to
follow his lead in all respects – the only advice she gave
– and so I clung to this tenet as if it would save my life.

After all, he had been married before and knew what he was about.

He sat down in a chair across the room and made me stand before him and remove my nightgown there. I wanted to cross my arms, to cover myself, but he told me, quite calmly and gently, that this would not be permitted.

He told me I was beautiful, that such a beautiful body should never be covered, but exhibited in its glory, for the delight of he who possessed it.

This was a strange thought, to think of my own flesh and skin as belonging to another. Yet it is how my Lord is pleased to view our union, and I suppose all men are so. He told me I must cease thinking of my body as my own and clothe and adorn it always to his taste, in the full knowledge that he would only look at me with the thought of removing all such clothing and adornment in the bedchamber.

'He seems a bit intense,' commented Jenna.

'Knew it. What did I tell you? Raging pervert.'

Jason nodded sagely.

'It's so weird,' continued Jenna, 'to think that most girls from what would be called good families had absolutely no clue about sex. I can't imagine growing up like that.'

'The boys all worked it out from what they got up to at those public schools, I bet,' said Jason.

'You could be right. I hope none of them took quite the same approach with their brides, though . . . Ouch.'

'Reminds me,' drawled Jason into her ear, 'I've got plans for your arse, woman.'

'Not tonight you haven't,' said Jenna primly.

'How about the night of the exhibition? Since you're
going to make me work for that . . . you can have a little
something of your own to work towards. I think that's
fair.'

'We'll see,' said Jenna, biting the inside of her cheek.

'Not "we'll see". The answer I'm looking for is "Yes,
sir, if that's what you want, sir." Come on, then. Say it.'

He held both Jenna's elbows in a tight grip, waiting
for her words.

'"Yes, sir, if that's what you want, sir,"' she parroted
sulkily. 'Now can we get on with this? It looks as if you're
right and she really is going to treat us to a bit of Victorian
erotica. So have some manners and listen.'

Jason loosened his grip, satisfied with her answer.

'Go on then.'

*For me, who has been accustomed to view a body as
a treacherous, weak thing – a wicked vessel for the more
noble element of the soul – it was so unaccountable to
hear such words that I scarcely knew where to look.*

*Luckily, my husband had some suggestions on that
score. He urged me to look at myself in the pier glass.*

*I was reluctant to do so, for I have never allowed my
gaze to linger over my nakedness, but I had no recourse
but to obey. I listened as he spoke in lustful, sometimes
crude, terms of what he and I both saw. He ordered me
to hold and touch those parts of myself I dare not name,
let alone repeat the strange names he had for them. He
saw that I was on the verge of shameful tears, and told
me that this was a gift to me and that I must put away
all my silly girlish ideas about modesty and propriety and*

accept that a wife's role is to be wanton in the bedchamber, and to accept the pleasure her husband seeks to give. Thus it is useless to be coy about the body. He would teach me to enjoy myself, to bring my buried needs and desires to the surface and indulge each one of them.

I told him I would do my duty, and he laughed, loud and long.

'Duty will be the least of it,' he said. 'Now bring yourself to me.'

I stood at his feet and he stood also, exploring all that I had with his fingers. If I protested, or made any sound at all, he sealed my mouth with a kiss. Such a kiss – he put his tongue between my lips. It felt so immoral, so disgusting – and yet, I hate to recall, I found it pleasurable in some deep way I cannot bring myself to examine.

Even when he probed between my legs, the kiss was enough to lighten my head and let everything pass. Everything was permitted to him. I had only to open myself.

He told me this, several times, in a low whisper, before laying me on the bed.

I watched, my eyes half-open, for I feared his wrath if he closed them, while he undressed himself beside the bed. What a time it took. He had so many different things to remove. Cufflinks, cuffs, tie pin, neckcloth . . . The list went on. With each act of divestiture, I saw a little more of him.

Everything I saw was impressive, from his strong wrists to his broad shoulders. When the neck of his shirt fell open, I wanted to gasp at the delicious sight of his unwrapped throat and the glimpse of a chest that seemed to have dark hairs upon it. I had not realised men's

*chests could have hair upon them. I have only seen the
pale little chests of the boys in the streets of Nottingham
in summer as they play under the pump.*

*His shirt and undershirt removed, I saw a great
many more of these dark wiry curls, descending low to
his middle and then moving downwards, more downy
and soft now, from his navel. How powerful he seemed
without his clothes – more so than with them, though
in a different way. The man of property in his swallow
tail coat and silk top hat was become the elemental man,
the essence of masculinity.*

*But I did shut my eyes when he came to remove his
lower garments.*

*He did not chide me for doing so, but he noticed, and
his chuckle was low and amused.*

*'What, do you think if you shut your eyes you will be
safe from what I have here?' he said. 'Indeed you will not.
You might as well open them, and know what peril it is
you face, rather than be left to your imaginings. No doubt
they are lurid enough. Come, Frances. What do you fear?'*

*'It is not fear,' I told him. 'It is . . . I cannot say. I
do not wish to look upon it.'*

*I felt him kneel upon the bed beside me, the mattress
weighted to one side.*

*'You will do more than look upon it,' he said, more
roughly. He took hold of my chin with a finger and
thumb, pressing them into my jawbone. 'You will find
much of your married life subject to its whims. Look
upon it, Frances. Look upon your master.'*

Jason laughed.
'Fucking hell,' he said. 'The man's off his head.'

'So, you wouldn't say that kind of thing?' said Jenna slyly.

'It's different if I say that kind of stuff. I know you're up for it. This poor cow hasn't got a clue.'

'He could be a bit more sensitive,' Jenna agreed. 'But then, that's Victorians for you, probably.'

'Harvilles, more like.'

'Yeah, that wouldn't surprise me. Harvilles.'

Jenna sighed, thinking of her own narrow escape with a scion of that ilk.

'I don't know if I dare read on,' she said.

'I'll do it,' Jason offered. 'I've got used to that curly writing now.'

'Oh, go on then. But don't laugh in the middle of a sentence. Poor Frances. She deserves a bit of sympathy.'

'No, I'm with you there. She does. OK then.' Jason cleared his throat and read on.

'*I opened my eyes, but what I saw was not what I had pictured. Nothing like the small appendage sported by Michelangelo's David. This was a longer, thicker thing, curving upwards like a hunting horn . . .*'

'You promised you wouldn't laugh,' Jenna reproached.

'No, but "hunting horn"! I wonder if she wanted to blow it.'

'Don't be horrible.'

'Sorry. I'll try to control myself, OK?'

It was certainly almost twice the length of my hand, and it looked primitive and fierce, rising from its nest of downy dark hair as it did. I could look at it for only a second or so before lifting my eyes to his.

They glowed with satisfaction. His smile was wide and bright.

'Touch it, Frances,' he said. 'Put your fingers around it and feel its spirit.'

Its spirit, if such it possessed, was warm, firm, and yet also soft. In my hand, it felt like something I could bend, but I did not dare try.

My husband was satisfied with my quick obedience. He rewarded me with kisses, and not just upon my face. His mouth roamed the length and breadth of my body, his breath hot and fast and broken by growls at times. He was like a wolf, come to feast upon its prey. I should never have imagined him so, from his behaviour in the drawing room. Are all men thus? I suppose I shall never know.

He left no part of me untouched by hand or mouth, even when I tried to shut my legs to his attentions. He would not have it, and made me lie in such an abandoned pose that I felt sinful in the extreme.

At length his wanderings seemed to come to their end, and he crouched above me, close enough for his hair to brush my skin.

'You know what I must do?' he breathed, and I shook my head. 'The best I can do is show you. But be warned. There will be some pain, some blood.'

'Some . . . blood?'

I felt a bolt of panic rise in my throat and I tried to push him off, but he held me in place, shaking his head.

'No, Frances, no. You should have been told. Your mother?'

'She said nothing of blood.'

'It will be only very little. And it will not last long. The pain will soon ease and then all will be much easier.'

'You are sure of this?'

He stroked my face.

'I am quite sure. Hold tight to my shoulders. I will be as quick as I am able.'

Yes he was quick. And it did hurt. And there was blood. But none of these three things made the strongest impression on me. Much stronger, staying with me in my mind, was the sense of violation and of terrible degradation that I felt. Pain was nothing in comparison. Blood could be washed clean. But this feeling of having been burrowed into and invaded could not leave me.

It is not as a wife should feel, is it? I dare not confess it to David, for he will know that I am not what he expected when he married.

'You look ill,' he said, roughly, unsympathetically, when he had finished and released me.

'Oh, I am not ill,' I said, though my nether regions throbbed and I could feel the warm trickle of the blood upon my thigh.

'Then what's amiss? I'll fetch a cloth.'

He went to the nightstand and returned with a damp flannel, with which he dabbed at my sticky skin.

'Nothing is amiss,' I said, but my voice was high and forced. My breathing was not natural – sometime during the indignity, my breath had become caught in my throat, and I could not seem to correct it.

'You might try and look it, then,' he groused. He saw something in my face and his next words were gentler. 'I promise you, the worst is past. Now that this hurdle is crossed, you will find that pleasure is easier to achieve.'

'Will I?'

I could not imagine it. I lay down and shut my eyes, hoping he would think me asleep.

He lay back down beside me and made me open my eyes, pulling the lower lids down with his thumb on my cheek.

'Do not pretend with me, Fan,' he whispered. 'I will not have pretence.'

'I am tired.'

'You try to hide from me. But I am not the regular kind of man, who is happy to stumble on blindly, ignoring the distance between him and his wife. I will not have distance, or hiding, or any of those things that make a marriage slowly die. I will have you, in all honesty, as naked spiritually as you are bodily. I will own you and you will rejoice in my ownership.'

He sounded like a preacher, but what was he preaching?

I did not want to be preached to.

Is it wrong of me to wish I could step backwards in time?

For all the fortune and wealth and position I have achieved, I cannot help thinking that something else has been lost – something I can never retrieve.

'Oh, that poor girl,' said Jenna as Jason shut the book.

'What? It'll probably get better. Or it probably would, if she hadn't married him. Stupid decision in the first place, though, marrying a Harville.'

'Yes, well, I think you'll find all this predated the trouble at the pit,' said Jenna.

'The disaster had already happened, though,' he pointed out. 'She never mentioned that.'

'It was thirty years earlier. She wasn't local.'

'I suppose.' Jason lay back. 'I do feel sorry for her. But then, your first time's always shit, isn't it?'

'I don't know. Was yours?'

Jason gave her a droll upwards look.

'Do you really want to hear about that?'

'Go on. How old were you?'

'Not old enough. Still at school, just.'

'I hope you were legal.'

He grimaced.

'Can't remember. Roughly. On the border.'

'And was it with Mia?' Jenna hesitated to bring up the name, but she thought there was no point brushing Jason's past under the carpet, really. It was part of who he was, when it came down to it.

'Yeah. Mia. We were at that stage. Little notes to each other, drawn-on tattoos on each other's arms. Kissing in the kiddie park while all our mates made sick noises.'

'I can't see you as a mushy lad,' said Jenna, wishing – not for the first time – that she could have known Jason earlier, saved him from some of what he had had to go through.

'Not so much mushy as rampantly horny,' he said with a cheeky grin. 'Couldn't keep my hands off.'

'Some things don't change then.'

'No, and they aren't about to either.'

He rolled over, pinning her down so suddenly that she squealed.

'Got it?' he said, coaxing her into a long, tongue-heavy kiss.

'I think so,' she said, emerging blearily. 'Were you nervous? The first time?'

'A cross between nervous and raring to go,' he said.

'I was worried about hurting her. She was all right though. She was more up for it than I was. She was no shrinking Fanny Harville. She knew what was what, that girl. What about you?'

'What about me?'

'Your first time?'

Jenna wished she hadn't brought up the subject. It all seemed such a long time ago now, and yet, when she shut her eyes, she could be there.

She could be there in the tent, at that little illegal free festival in a field in Lincolnshire, smelling of wood-smoke, hearing the thud and wail of the different sound systems outside.

A little blurred around the edges from cider and the fragrant smoke of the joints Deano's friends were sharing outside, she lay down on the sleeping bag and let her mind whirl. They would think she was a lightweight. She had wanted to stay up with the others, to prove that she could rave around a campfire all night long, but the truth was, she couldn't. She'd need to work on her stamina. All that marching through miles of fields with a huge rucksack, followed by dancing like a lunatic and blowing whistles, had broken her.

Or so she thought, until a voice spoke at the flysheet.

'You aren't going to sleep already are you, Jen?'

She opened her eyes and smiled. Deano's hair gel had given up the ghost, and his blond spikes were flopping down. His eyeliner was smudged, but that seemed to suit him, making his unearthly, almost silver-blue eyes gleam more brightly than ever. He was the most gorgeous boy in town, and he wanted her. It was crazy.

'You feeling OK?'

'Yeah. Just dog tired. That hike earlier on killed me.'

'Aw, no,' he said, in a high, cartoon-character voice, crawling up beside her on the sleeping bag and pawing at her shoulder. 'Please don't die, Jenna Wren. What would I do for my smoochies?'

He lay beside her and she let her tired eyes focus on his face, earnest now for a change. He had been manic enough all day.

'You'd do all right,' she whispered. 'Plenty of girls after you.'

'Not like you,' he said. 'You're special.'

'So are you.'

He didn't deny it. He knew it was true – enough people had told him so. But it was the first time Jenna had heard it, and she savoured the exquisite feeling.

'Do you really think so?'

'I can show you.'

And that was where it had started, though she had been hoping for this, and dreaming of it, and imagining how it would be, all the way up in the minibus and all the way across those endless fields. It had been the only thing that had kept her going. If she didn't make it to the festival, she didn't get to sleep with Deano.

She had planned it in her mind so perfectly that any little deviation from her fantasies threw her. He didn't take as long to get her in the mood as Imaginary-Deano had, and he was surprisingly less confident than she had thought. She still managed to get a free hand to her canvas rucksack, to scrabble about in there for the pack of condoms, before it was too late.

'What's this?' he said, when she pressed the foil square into his palm.

'Er, take a wild guess.'

'I thought you were on the Pill?'

His slightly ungracious reaction to this didn't stay with her, though, and neither did his unceremonious rush to bolt through her maidenhead. She put the bits that weren't perfect out of her mind and pulled together the good bits over the gaps until her memory was sewn up in a pattern she liked.

Only now, nearly twenty years later, did it occur to her with a minor shock that this was not the true pattern. She had deliberately chosen to forget certain aspects of it – aspects that might have acted as a warning.

Afterwards, when she had felt at her most vulnerable, tender and shining from what had just passed between them, he had pulled up his jeans and grunted something about going outside for a smoke.

Why had she forgotten that? It had made her cry at the time.

But then, when he had come back in, two hours later, he had spooned her and kissed her and told her she knew how much he loved her, didn't she?

Yes.

She had told herself, yes.

And he had loved her. It had been love. There was no way hindsight was going to rewrite that precious time of her life; she wouldn't allow it. That rush of young love – that first opening up to one person, in the hope that such happiness could last a whole life – had an almost sacred quality to her. She had enshrined it and preserved it like a holy relic.

Did Deano feel the same? Or was it all just water under the bridge now, irrelevant? She felt such a sharp pang that she had to turn away from Jason in case he saw it in her face.

'Bad memory?' he asked sympathetically, putting a hand on her shoulder.

'No, not bad, exactly. Just . . .' She tried a laugh. Not very convincing. 'It was such a long time ago.'

'What was it like in the Dark Ages?' quipped Jason. 'Did blokes know about the clitoris back then?'

He seemed to realise that his levity of tone was a misjudgement.

'Hey,' he said, more gently, when she didn't reply. 'Jen. Talk to me.'

'Sorry,' she whispered, then she cleared her throat and turned back to him with a determined effort to chase away the . . . regrets? Whatever the feelings were. 'Just for a moment, it felt as if I was back there, back in the tent.'

'The tent?' Jason smiled at her. 'I can't see you doing the camping thing.'

She smiled back.

'No, not these days. Maybe glamping? That looks all right. But all that hammering pegs into the ground and communal shower blocks – ugh! Mind you, we didn't even have those, where we were. It was a festival.'

'What, Glastonbury, you mean?'

'No, less official than that. An illegal one, in the middle of nowhere. The band were headlining – their first gig outside the local pub scene.'

'Cool.'

'Yes.' She let him stroke her hair. 'I was pretty cool, in those days. I had attitude and passion, and a rock star boyfriend. Aspiring rock star boyfriend, I should say.'

'He aspired right on up there,' commented Jason. 'Anyway, you've still got attitude and passion.'

'You've got more.'

'Aw, hey.'

He kissed her.

'Do you miss the rock star boyfriend, then?' he asked, his eyes suddenly darkening.

'Oh, Jase.' She sighed, leaving the exhalation as a place-holder for the answer she couldn't quite formulate.

'You do?'

'I missed him while I was with him,' she said.

'Eh?' His screwed-up forehead made her smile.

'I mean . . . even while we were still together, I started missing what we'd had. Because he changed. We had five glorious, gorgeous years, and then it all began to fall apart. Not the career – both our careers were rocketing to the stars by then. But little things – too subtle to notice at first.'

'So your first time was good, then?'

'It was OK.' Jenna shook her head at Jason's insistence on keeping the conversation on its original rails. 'It wasn't the divine rapture I expected, but it was probably better than a lot of first times. And the times after that were better. Better and better.'

'I don't really want to know about that,' said Jason, a tad sourly.

Jenna hummed a few bars of 'Jealous Guy', and he held her closer.

'Yeah, I am a bit jealous, so what? It's natural. He had you for years and years and he was an ungrateful bastard. I wish I'd been around then, that's all.'

'I wish you had. Although it might have been a bit

complicated. But then, so was everything. I suppose what's making me feel a bit blue is the idea that perhaps even those first five lovely years weren't as good as I thought they were.'

'No?'

'I was carried along on this amazing electric current of love and lust and success and stardom. It was so exciting, neither of us stopped to draw breath. We were so in love with the *idea* of us that we never really examined the reality. Do you see what I mean?'

'In love with love? Mia and I were a bit like that. Like she wanted everything to be romantic all the time. It was exhausting. But when I wanted some real love from her – some support, some understanding – she went all quiet on me.'

'Yes, sort of like that, I guess. And with us, it was all magnified by the media coverage. So much "golden couple of rock" stuff. You really wanted to believe the hype. It became internalised. Deano and I were tied together by all sorts of things, but love was only one of them. Perhaps only a small one. We were playing a part, as well as having a relationship.'

'Pressure,' said Jason.

'Yes, and I think Deano felt it more keenly than me, because he's more naturally selfish. I'm not trying to be horrible, by the way. It's just the way he is. I think it started to feel like a prison to him, and he wanted to break free. Even though he still cared for me, in his way.'

'In his way?'

'Yeah, well, like I just said, he was selfish. I got glandular fever when I was twenty-one and, instead of staying with me, he went off to holiday on some Hollywood actor's private yacht for a month while I was in hospital trying not to succumb to liver failure.'

'What a tosser.'

'Yes, but I really didn't see it that way at the time. I chose not to. I was upset, of course, but I told myself that he was doing it for his career. Networking. And that hanging around a hospital in London wasn't going to achieve anything for us.'

'Jen. Fucking hell. I'd have stayed with you.'

'Would you?'

'Of course. What do you take me for?'

She nestled her head deeper into the crook of his arm.

'A keeper,' she said.

'Didn't you think you deserved better?'

'I didn't think of it like that. I've told you. I was so invested in keeping our perfect showbiz couple thing going that I lied to myself constantly. Even when pics came out in the *News of the World* of him rubbing sun lotion on this famous model, I refused to accept it. The girl was topless, for fuck's sake! It was so obvious. I got about a hundred calls that day, asking for my reaction to the story. I made a statement in the end, from my hospital bed. "Deano's entitled to have female friends, and to take holidays whenever and with whomever he likes. Neither of us owns the other." And I really believed that.'

'Bloody hell, he had it made, didn't he? Jammy fucker.'

'As long as it was true love in my head, and in the papers, I could ignore pretty much anything.'

'Wow. I wonder how many other showbiz relationships are like that.'

'Oh, you'd be surprised,' she said with a hollow laugh.

'He kept up the champagne lifestyle, and then it turned into a cocaine and girls lifestyle and then one day I just woke up and knew he didn't love me any more.'

'It must have been a shock.'

'Yeah. It was seven years ago. We limped on for seven more years, more for PR than anything else. Seven stupid pointless lonely years.'

'You didn't want to leave him?'

'I didn't see the point. I didn't think I'd ever want anyone else, and I was still his manager. I concentrated on building a profile for myself instead – hence *Talent Team*. It was all a big distraction from the gaping void in the centre of my life.'

'Quite a good distraction,' offered Jason. 'International megastardom. Better than knitting, right?'

She laughed and kissed his neck.

'Thank God for you is all I can say. I really never expected . . .' Her voice cracked and he cuddled her tight.

'It's all better now,' he said. 'You left in the end. You did the right thing.'

'Yes, ironically it was my distraction technique that caused the final rift. He *hated* that I was getting as famous as him. It made him start behaving like an absolute wanker – trying to humiliate me by parading girlfriends in front of the media. In the end I had to file for divorce, or lose all the respect I'd built up in the industry.'

'You did right.'

'Funnily enough, as soon as the papers were served, he started behaving like the old Deano again. Funny, friendly, warm. I think it was just such a relief for us both, to be out from under that weird microscope. We get on quite well now – when we have to.'

'You mean he's been in touch with you since you came back to Bledburn?' Jason sat up, eyeing Jenna with some alarm.

She bit her lip. She should really have told him.

'Only a couple of phone calls,' she said. 'When you were arrested and all that awful stuff was going on. He called to offer his support. He was very nice about it. A bit narky when he found out about you, though . . .'

'Was he, by fucking Jove?'

'Jason, calm down. It's OK. We're not about to get back together. The situation was extreme that's all. Since then, all our communication has been through our lawyers. Come on. Hold me again. I was enjoying it.'

Jason shuffled back down into his former cradling position, but Jenna could feel his restlessness and the uneven rhythm of his heart.

'What if you get famous?' she said softly. 'Really famous, like Deano? Do you think it'll change you?'

'You're already trying to change me,' he pointed out. 'You and that Georgina one.'

'I'm not trying to change you,' she said long-sufferingly. 'As I've already explained. Polishing is not the same as refashioning.'

'Polishing,' he snorted. 'Makes me sound like a bloody sideboard.'

'Refining, then.'

'Refining? Like oil. Don't you prefer me crude, then?' He winked and pinched her thigh.

'What a wag you are, sir. But how do you think you'd react to fame, seriously?'

He was quiet for a few moments.

'Always thought I'd quite like to bling it up,' he said.

'You know. Get a massive place with a pool, loads of fast cars, women, dress up like a pimp. But I seem to have got the luxury lifestyle before the fame, somehow, so . . . I don't know.'

Jenna snuffled with amusement. 'I'm trying to picture you in the white fur coat and all the jewellery. Really can't. You just aren't LA.'

'Oh, aren't I? Thanks for that. Guess I'll stay in Bleddy then, shall I?'

'No, I mean, you're too down to earth for all that La-La stuff. They wouldn't know what to make of you.'

'I don't care what anyone makes of me. If I'm famous, it's for my paintings. They can stick to making something of them. I don't want all the magazine lifestyle crap. I just want my painting and my Jen.'

She sighed happily, wriggling against him.

'Don't ever change,' she whispered.

'I don't plan on it.'

Chapter Eleven

When Jenna and Jason returned to Harville Hall, they found Kayley in the kitchen. This wasn't a great surprise to them, as she'd been cat-sitting Bowyer in their absence and so had a key and licence to spend time in the house if she wanted.

'Hey up, how's our boy?' asked Jason, slipping out through the French doors and calling the cat in.

'He's been fine,' said Kayley. 'Caught some mice out the back there. There must be nests and nests of 'em. That garden's gone wild since . . .'

She trailed off.

Jenna recalled the tale Kayley had told of her history at the house – the wild parties with Lawrence Harville, ultimately resulting in his blackmailing her to lie about the false charges against Jason.

The residual stirrings of her loathing of the previous homeowner dealt her a stab in the heart, accompanied by a little wave of resentment at Kayley. The latter was soon chased away by the much better memory of how she had come clean and saved the day in the end.

'Jason's made a start on it,' said Jenna. 'But it'll take time.'

'Yeah. I'll put the kettle on, eh? How was London?'

'Good.' Jenna put her handbag on the table and took the weight off her weary driving feet. She missed the days of having a driver. Having staff. Perhaps once this sabbatical was over she'd hire more, make an employment programme out of it for Bledburnians in need of a job. 'I've got some news actually. I'm going to need your capable assistance.'

'Well, you know I'm here for you. Since I got the push from the Youth Service, I'm free to help with whatever.'

'I told you I'd retain you. I'm putting you on a salary from the end of this month.'

'Really?' Kayley turned around from the kitchen counter, her eyes shining. 'I mean, it's too good of you, considering . . .'

'All's well that ends well,' said Jenna. 'Let's leave all that behind us and just get on with things.'

'Fine by me. So what's the big news?'

'Jason's going to have an exhibition. Here.'

'What, like, in Bledburn?'

'In the Hall. Right here. Before I finish the renovations.'

Kayley clattered more than was necessary in the setting out of the teacups.

'Oh my God, that's amazing. When?'

'We haven't set a date yet, but I don't see the point in hanging about. Jason's got more than enough work to show, and as long as the pre-publicity's good, we should expect plenty of viewers.'

'I should reckon so! Folk'll give their right arm to
see inside your house.'

'Well, quite. It's a bit annoying to think that people
will be more interested in what kind of bedding I use
than Jason's art, but that's the world we live in, isn't it?'

'Sad but true. So you'll want me to do what?'

'Prepare a press release for the *Bledburn Gazette*.
Organise a printer for some posters. Source a caterer.
I've got my gallery-owning friend Tabitha for advice
– I'll give you her number. She'll have plenty of ideas.
The show is officially hosted by her gallery, so you'll
need to mention that on all the advertising . . .' Jenna
trailed off, noticing that Kayley was looking rather
beleaguered.

'It's a big job,' she said. 'I don't want to muck it up.'

'You won't. I'm here – I'll be involved as well. And so
will Tabitha. And, in the end, the only person who can
really muck it up is Jason, if he suddenly decides not to
do it.'

'Not to do what?'

Jason reappeared at the French windows, Bowyer
purring in his arms.

'The show. I'm just telling Kayley.'

'Oh, yeah. Milk, no sugar, ta.'

He let Bowyer pad away on the granite tiling, looking
for a cooler spot to curl up than the arid garden, and sat
down beside Jenna.

Kayley brought the tea over and sat down opposite
them.

'You'd better start sifting through your work,' Jenna
said to Jason. 'Decide which pictures you want to exhibit.'

He nodded.

'I can't get my head round it,' he said to Kayley. 'Who would have thought I'd ever be in this situation?'

She smiled ruefully back.

'Life's thrown us all a few surprises lately,' she said.

Jenna felt the truth of this deep in her heart.

'Good surprises, mainly,' she added.

They chatted about the gallery, and some of their London experiences (barring the racier ones) until Kayley had finished her tea and was ready to go home.

'Tomorrow we'll make a start on our publicity,' Jenna told her, showing her out. 'I promise you, by the end of this summer, Jason will be a star.'

Jason, standing behind Jenna, put his hands on her shoulders.

'What do you mean, "will be"?' he joked. 'I've already made all the front pages.'

'For all the wrong reasons,' said Jenna severely, shutting the door. She turned around to face him, putting her hands around his neck. 'But not this time. This time, the reasons will be right.'

They woke up one bright morning a week or so later, to hear Bowyer scratching at the door and mewing plaintively.

Jenna put the pillow over her head while Jason laughed softly and rose from the bed, splendidly naked, to sort out some feline breakfast in the kitchen.

Jenna, awaiting his return, ran through a mental checklist of the day's tasks. Finish painting the bedroom ceiling. Cut back some more of the out of control rose bushes. Get the poster design to the printer. Negotiate with one of the classier glossies to cover the event. God, it was all so much like when she was at work that she wondered how she dared call it a sabbatical.

At least she didn't have to go into any office, she thought. She could do it all naked if she really wanted to. She threw aside her summer-weight duvet and sat up, looking down at her body.

God, it was getting obvious she wasn't working out very much. She did yoga, and stuck to a Pilates routine when she remembered, but most of her exercise these days came from sex. And very good exercise it was, too, but she could still use some toning around the upper arms. Jason would complain, of course. He said he liked her with a bit of curve. Especially her bum.

She rolled over and tried to twist her neck around to observe that part of her. Useless. She'd have to look in the mirror.

She hopped out of bed and examined her back view in the freestanding full-length mirror she'd had delivered a few days ago. She was quite satisfied with it, smiling dreamily as she thought of all the ways Jason had to enjoy what she offered.

She patted it with one hand, enjoying the firmness under her palm and the slight resistance. How was it that Jason's hand felt so different from her own? What was it that he did, to make that contact so sensual, and so shocking?

She tried a smack. The sound was piquant, but the sensation was nothing like what she experienced from her lover. All the same, a patch of faint pink blushed into being. It was pretty. She worked on deepening the colour, but she couldn't bring herself to hit hard enough.

'How does he do it?' she asked herself aloud.

'I can show you if you want.'

Jason leant into the room, hands on the top of the door frame, grinning a wide, louche grin.

Jenna spun around, hands over her mouth.

'How long have you been there?' she said, once she'd caught her breath.

'Long enough,' he teased.

'You shouldn't spy.'

'What are you going to do about it?'

He swaggered into the room, impressively for a man who was completely naked and joined her at the mirror.

'You can't intimidate me,' she said, but she was already breaking into a flirtatious smile, sensing the beginning of playtime.

'Who said anything about intimidating you?' he said, arriving behind her and putting his hands on her arms. 'You said you wanted to know how I did it. Did what?'

He kissed her ear as she squirmed, unwilling to give an answer.

'Go on,' he whispered. His voice tickled her ear.

She watched him in the mirror, enjoying the sight of his height at her shoulder.

'I like this mirror,' she said, as a diversionary tactic.

'So do I. But you're trying to dodge the question. How do I do . . . what?'

'I was wondering how you managed to make the impression that you do on my . . . skin.'

'On your . . . skin,' he mimicked. 'What, this skin here?' He nipped at her neck.

'No, I mean . . . You saw what I was doing. Why are you even asking?'

'Cos it's fun to watch you trying to get out of saying stuff, of course.'

She watched transfixed as his hands moved to her breasts, cupping them. How giant his hands looked, and how red and stiff her nipples became in them.

'This skin?' he whispered, tweaking the swollen nubs.

'No! I meant . . . for God's sake.' She pushed her bare bottom back into him so that his hardening cock slipped into its crease. 'This!'

'Oh, I like that,' he said, holding her there and grinding himself into her. 'That feels good. Would you like to take it further?'

She tensed.

'Not like that, not yet,' she whispered.

'Then when, babe? Because I've been waiting a long time for your arse.'

'When I'm ready.'

'Perhaps we ought to start getting you ready.' He slid a hand down, opening her cheeks, giving himself more space to explore the area with the tip of his engorged cock.

Jenna was simultaneously turned on and horrified by herself. How could she find such rude treatment pleasurable? But she did. She felt her juices begin to flow in earnest, just imagining Jason pinning her down and making her take it there.

He mustn't know, though. What would he think of her?

'I don't know,' she said huskily, 'if I'll ever be ready for that.'

'Are you sure?'

She realised suddenly that she was unconsciously

rotating her hips in tiny movements, inviting him closer and deeper. Whatever her mouth said, her body seemed determined to disagree.

'I think you're readier than you let on,' said Jason. He kept up his pressure for a little bit longer, then released her.

She wanted to kick herself for the disappointment she felt.

'OK then,' he said briskly. 'Spanking masterclass. Let's get a chair and you can watch in the mirror.'

'What?'

'You asked me how I did it. I'm going to show you.'

He dragged over her armless velvet dressing table chair and sat himself down in it.

'Come on then,' he said, slapping his bare thigh. 'Let's have you.'

Jenna giggled and shook her head, but she knew this wouldn't wash for long.

'Oh, for God's sake,' she huffed, obeying after her moment of token resistance.

'Look at yourself in the mirror now,' ordered Jason.

Jenna glanced at the mirror and wanted to wail. She looked so extremely undignified, with her hair hanging over her face, her legs waving in the air and her bottom high and well-presented on Jason's lap.

'What do you think?' he said.

'I look really awful,' she said.

'You don't. You look great. What you need to do is get the right posture. So if you straighten your legs and put your feet on the floor – yeah. See. That looks kind of elegant, especially if you keep them like that while I spank you. Tenner says you can't though.'

It was an improvement, she had to admit. Her legs looked endless and shapely, and her bottom a luscious rounded peak. She gripped the frill that ran around the bottom of the chair in both fists in order to anchor herself in position.

'Tenner, eh?'

'Is the bet on?'

'All right. Ten pounds to you if I kick my legs.'

'Done. And you will be. Right, watch your bum in the mirror and see how quickly I can get it red.'

He began to spank her, lightly at first, so she could watch with pure fascination, unmixed with discomfort, and see how erotic the sight was. Jason's hand, falling again and again on her defenceless cheeks, together with the look of intense but pleasurable concentration on his face was a powerful combination. Even more than usual, she was quickly worked up to a state of keen arousal.

'I'm starting slow,' he said. 'You can already see how I'm doing it differently to what you were, when you thought you were alone. You were holding back right at the last second, because you can't hurt yourself. I don't hold back. That's the only difference really.'

Now he really wasn't holding back. The opening warm-up was over and his hand fell heavily on her wobbling flesh. She wanted to kick her legs, but she concentrated hard on keeping them straight and diagonal, putting all of herself into her thigh and calf muscles, so that they ached along with the sting of her behind. This dissipation of pain worked for a while, and she felt strong at being able to take what Jason gave and still hold on to her dignity.

But dignity made a swift exit when he upped his heft

to level three. Her bottom, already stained a rose petal pink, soon crimsoned. Her feet waggled at first, her ankles rotating, then they were lifted clear of the floor for a good kick.

'Told ya,' crowed Jason. 'Ten easy ones for me. I'm going to give you ten with the paddle to celebrate.'

'Oh, you . . .' But she didn't continue. She didn't want anything else added.

'Stand up. Back to the mirror. Look over your shoulder at your arse while I fetch the paddle. It might look red now, but believe me, it'll be redder by the time I finish with you.'

She pressed her thighs together, feeling the heat between them as she observed the deep red hue of her bottom. But there was more to come. She allowed herself to enjoy the fullness of the quiver that ran through her at the thought. Then she imagined what she saw in the mirror on the front page of a tabloid, in glorious technicolour. The idea of it squeezed a breath from her. She was already famous for her love life. But they didn't know the half of it. If they did . . .

Jason breezed back, paddle in hand. He took her in his arms, kissing her, while he rested the paddle against her bum cheeks. It felt deliciously cool there for a moment. Just a moment, though – until he started patting it on her hot spots.

'Right then,' he whispered. 'Bend over, right over, with your hands on your ankles, so you can see through your legs. And look at the mirror.'

'Thank God for yoga,' said Jenna dryly, adopting the suggested pose. 'I'd never be able to hold this position otherwise.'

She looked through her legs at the mirror, seeing her face, flushed, and with hair hanging down to the floor. She had to strain her eyes a bit to see as far up as her bottom, but she could do it if she tried. Most shaming of all was how this position opened her up so that her pussy lips were wide and nothing was hidden from view.

Jason understood the awkwardness of the stance and he stood close with a hand on her spine to keep her steady.

He was quick and firm with the paddle, laying on five hard strokes to each side, moving lower with each one so that strokes nine and ten were squarely on the tops of her thighs.

Each smack made Jenna yelp and let go of her ankles, but she recovered herself swiftly each time, with the help of Jason's hand on her back.

'And that,' he said, with one extra stroke for luck, 'is what happens when you challenge me.'

'I didn't,' she whimpered, letting go of her ankles to succumb to the overwhelming temptation to rub her sore bottom.

'Well, sort of. Anyway, there's your answer. I'll take my tenner after you've said thank you.'

'Thank you?'

'When I say "said" thank you, I'm thinking more of a show of gratitude. A show of gratitude on the bed with you on all fours. Am I clear?'

He patted her bottom and she thrust out her lower lip for a second before smiling and hurling herself on to the bed.

They were both too aroused for the sex to last long.

A minute or so of low moans and 'oh yeahs' from Jason, and the two of them collapsed, sated and sweaty, on to the duvet.

'Only one thing could have improved that start to the day,' said Jason, once words returned to him.

'Oh? And what's that?'

'Getting inside your sweet, tight little arse.'

He reached around to cup and squeeze it.

'After all,' he said, 'it belongs to me.'

'Does it now?' Jenna wanted to argue, but in her heart, she couldn't. She wanted to give him this gift.

'You know it does.' He kissed her parched lips. 'So tell me, babe. Is it on the cards?'

'I never say never,' she said lightly.

'Never's a long time to be looking at your hot, smacked bum without being able to have it.'

'OK,' she said. 'Here's the deal. We work up to it, little by little, and if I'm ready by the day of the private view, you can do it that night.'

'Are you serious? My own private view, after the private view?'

'If you want to put it like that. But we'll work up to it, remember. I'm not going into it cold.'

'Cold is the last thing you'll be,' promised Jason. 'Don't worry. I'll stock up on lube and stuff. You'll be good and ready by the time the show comes round. You might even want it sooner.' He winked.

'Don't hold your breath. It's a big idea to get used to. I'm not as grossed out by the thought as I used to be, though.' She didn't add that she was secretly highly aroused by it. Best to let him think she was nervous, so that he took it as slowly and gently as possible.

'You won't regret it,' he said, drawing her into ecstatic kisses of gratitude.

Withdrawing, sleepy-eyed again despite their having only recently woken up, he said, 'Speaking of regrets.'

'Oh? What? What are you regretting?' Jenna's eyes opened wide from the near-slumber into which she was so pleasantly falling.

'Not me. I've got no regrets, believe me.' He kissed her again. 'I was thinking of our ghost mate. Her from a hundred and fifty years ago. I'm going to be listening out for funny noises again tonight, now that I know a bit about her. We still don't know how she ended up as a pile of bones in the cellar.'

'Well, I don't suppose *that'll* be in her diary, unless the killer adds an entry of their own.'

'No, but there'll be clues. I mean, already she's got a weirdo husband, two stepdaughters who hate her guts and none of the servants are very friendly either.'

'I thought Lawrence Harville said it was a suicide.'

'Well, if it is, the diary'll let us know, yeah? She'll sound all depressed and start talking about ending it all, I suppose. Give us a look. Did you unpack it?'

'I think so.' Jenna reached an arm over to the bedside table and scrabbled in the drawer until she found the fabric bag in which she kept the book.

'So we'd got to the wedding night?' she said, trying to chase away the blur in her brain and remember their last reading.

'Yeah, and he was a bit weird and she felt weird about it too,' contributed Jason.

'So that was March . . .' She flipped through the pages. 'Oh. Nothing now until May. Here.'

May 3rd

I had resolved to keep this diary no longer. As a married woman, I thought it behoved me to make my husband my confidant and recipient of my deepest thoughts and feelings.

But there are things I cannot tell him – that he is deaf to – and so, with reluctance, I take up my pen once more.

I have done what I consider my best to please him and be a good wife. I have always been patient and considerate of him and the burden of responsibility he carries. I am highly sensible of my good fortune in being chosen as his bride.

But I can no longer remain silent on the subject of his daughters. My daughters, as I suppose I must call them. But their behaviour prevents it. I cannot see them as children of mine at all, for they are so filled with hate and spite that I make it my study to avoid them whenever possible.

They have cut up my dresses, filled my escritoire with worms and snails from the garden, emptied my scent bottle and refilled it with spirit vinegar. Yet I have shielded them on each occasion, telling myself that they are overset by the sudden change in domestic circumstances and are to be more pitied than censured.

Yesterday, however, I could no longer contain myself.

The day being sunny, I took myself into the garden with my needlework while D kept to his study, as he so often does. I had ordered a little tisane and some light sponge cake from the kitchen and the girls offered – unusually, but I took it as progress – to bring it up for me.

I promised them cake if they were kind enough to do this, and they went to the kitchen with a great show of enthusiasm. Before they left, Susannah even called me 'Mother'. 'We should be pleased to, Mother.' I was as happy as I have ever been in these weeks since my marriage, wondering if at last the difficult days were past and we could look forward to peace and family unity hereafter.

You will perhaps have already grasped that this was not to be so.

The tray was brought out with great care and ceremony, the prettiest china plate used for the cake. My tisane, in its delicate bone cup, looked a little paler than I was accustomed to, but I supposed the infusion may have been more than usually hurried by the girls in their excitement.

They sat with me at the wrought iron table, watching eagerly as I divided up the cake and poured them pink lemonade from a jug they had asked to be made up whilst on their errand.

Then, as I raised my own cup to my lips, their eyes were avid, almost gleaming, and I felt suddenly rather disturbed.

'What is it, girls?' I asked.

They shrugged and looked impatient.

'Take your tea,' urged Maria. 'Do not mind us.'

I raised the cup once more, but before it met my lips, I became aware that it smelled quite unlike my customary herbal blend. In fact, the smell was strong, and familiar, but for a moment I could not place it.

When I did, I dashed the cup down in horror.

The girls' faces fell.

'Why do you not drink?' asked Maria belligerently.

'Oh, you little monsters, is it really possible . . .?' I could not believe two well-bred little girls were capable of such a thing at first, but their guilty demeanours confirmed my worst suspicions.

'We have done nothing wrong!' they protested.

'Nothing wrong? You see nothing wrong in . . . in . . . what you have done?'

I had risen to my feet and my voice was sufficiently raised to draw the attention of my husband, who joined us on the patio with evident displeasure.

'What have my daughters done?' he growled. 'Of what do they stand accused?'

'My love, I can hardly say the words. It is too repulsive. Too indecent. Too altogether shocking.'

'We have done nothing,' the girls insisted.

'Let us see if your father agrees,' I said, handing him the teacup. 'Look at this. Breathe in its scent. What do you think it is?'

He did as requested. His response to the final question was too coarse to reproduce here, but suffice to say that it was composed of four letters and referred to the natural waste liquid of the body.

'Maria? Susannah?' He sought an explanation.

'Papa, we have done nothing wrong. We went to the kitchen, asked for the tray to be made up, and brought it. That was all we did.'

He turned to me, gruff, not meeting my eye.

'You see. They are not guilty of any wrongdoing.'

I was speechless. I could do no more than look wildly from husband to stepdaughters until my neck began to ache with tension.

It has been useless to mention the subject to David ever since this scene was played out. He insists that somebody below-stairs was playing a prank, and he refuses to take the matter further. The girls, at least, have not been insufferable about it, but have kept away from me. Is this the most I can ask?

It is unfair. Unfair and unjust, and I feel like the enemy in my own home.

What am I to do? What could anybody do?

These unnatural children have had nothing but kindness from me, but I resolve from henceforth to have no more to do with them. I will leave them to their own devices and be a stranger to them until their father deigns to take my part, or they start at their new school in September.

What more can be done?

'Shit,' said Jason, apparently impressed. 'They actually pissed in her teacup? That's hardcore.'

'They do seem awfully disturbed,' said Jenna. 'They need therapy. If only the Victorians believed in it. I feel sorry for them. And her. All of them. Except stupid Harville, of course, turning a blind eye. That won't do anyone any favours.'

'Who do you think kills her then? Surely not the kids. That's crazy.'

Jenna shook her head. 'You're very convinced it's murder. It could be an accident. It might not even be her.'

'So what was the diary doing in the cellar then? She took it down with her. Perhaps she knew they were going to kill her and she left it there as evidence. Come on. What's the next entry?'

May 12th

At last I have won out and persuaded David that the girls must be sent away to school sooner than the autumn.

I made no more mention of the last incident and all was quiet until two days since, when I joined David in the study after supper in order to speak seriously with him.

'My love,' I said, scarcely knowing how to say what was in my thoughts.

'Do you care for brandy?' he asked me, and I rather thought I did. Perhaps it would nerve me.

'There is something I really must tell you,' I continued.

He looked displeased, as if he expected me to launch into a diatribe against the girls again, but I waved my hand to show this was not my intention.

'No, I have nothing to say about the girls, not on this occasion.'

'Then what, my love? Have we received an invitation?'

'No. It is simply that this month, that which I would normally expect to come has not come and . . .'

He looked more impatient still.

'What do you expect to come? A letter? Some form of package?'

I laughed with frustration and relief.

'No, no, I merely mean . . . I think I may be . . . That is I cannot be sure . . . but . . .'

At last his visage showed signs of comprehension.

'Do you mean to tell me that . . .?' He rose from his chair, and I rose to accept his outstretched hands. 'A son?'

'Well . . . a child,' I said, laughing at his excitement.

'Yes, yes, of course. What am I doing? What am I saying? Sit down, you must sit down, in your condition . . .'

'Of course, it is very early yet. Probably too early even to call the doctor.'

'Nonsense, I shall have him called at once.' He rang the bell pull above the mantel and a servant was dispatched to fetch the doctor straight away.

'Oh no,' I protested. 'He must not let us disturb his evening. Another day will do just as well.'

But David would not be dissuaded.

What a happy evening, what kisses and fond words, what talk of names and schools followed.

It was only interrupted by a loud crash from outside the door.

Upon investigation, a bust had fallen from its plinth on to the hall floor. The sound of scurrying footsteps on the stairs could be heard as we picked it up and replaced it.

'Walls have ears,' said David grimly.

'Oh, leave them be,' I said. 'They are to be big sisters. It is exciting news for them as well.'

But the next day, after the doctor had been and gone and declared it too early to say for sure, but possible, if not even probable that I was expecting a baby, a terrible thing happened.

I walked out on to the patio for my customary hour of reading. Before I had gone two steps, a large, heavy item fell and hit me upon the shoulder, later shattering upon the paving stones beside me. It proved to be a large pitcher of the sort used to fill the washbasins in the *bedrooms. It did not quite knock me out, but I fell to my knees, shocked, and there cut my hand on a shard of the pottery.*

'Oh help,' I managed to cry, but nobody came to my relief for some time.

It was Eliza who found me, still on my hands and knees, bleeding on to the patio stones.

'Gracious heavens, ma'am, whatever's happened?'

She tore off a strip of her apron to bind my hand, then helped me to the patio chair.

'Did you drop it?' she asked, indicating the pitcher before going to clear up the worst of the breakage. 'Why would you bring a thing like that out here?'

'No, no,' I said, once my breath had settled. 'It fell. Or was thrown. From an upstairs window.'

I looked up, but whoever may have been there was long gone.

'Thrown? Oh, who would be so wicked?'

She collected each shard in her apron and tied it tight.

'Shall I bring you some water, ma'am? Or should I call the doctor? You look awful pale.'

'Oh, I can't disturb him again for nothing. He is already vexed with me for having him called out before.'

Eliza smiled at me – the first time I think she had ever shown me more than indifference.

'Blow him,' she said. 'If you needs a medic, you needs one.'

'I don't need one. Could you . . . Could you find my husband, please?'

Eliza's smile froze.

'Yes, ma'am. Of course, ma'am.'

After much fussing and fretting, and the establish-
ment that I was really no more than bruised, accounting
for the gash on my hand, David sat grave-faced opposite
me in the drawing room.

'I shall send for the girls,' he said.

'Oh, they will deny it . . .'

'I know.' He sent for them and, when they stood
before him, told them of his intention to send them away
to school.

What alarum, what sobbing and wailing and protes-
tations of innocence followed. But David was resolute.
They even tried to appeal to me, but I could no longer
bear to look upon them. What they had done could have
killed me, or caused the loss of my child. It still might.
What sympathy I had for them is now gone, and can
never return.

'God, this is awful,' muttered Jenna. 'What a household.'

'Harville life,' said Jason. 'Born under bad stars, the lot of them. So I'm guessing the girls are innocent then, if they get sent away. They couldn't have killed her.'

'Maybe in the vacation? Or perhaps they manage to stay at home. Though I do find it hard to believe that two such young girls would . . .'

'What about the jug though? That could've killed her. They were lucky not to be up for murder.'

'It could just as easily have been an accident.'

'Why would they have taken the jug over to the window? Leave it out.'

'No, I suppose it's a bit unlikely. Oh dear. Perhaps a prank that went wrong?'

'Anyway, my money's on his lordship himself. How many more entries are there? Are we getting near the end?'

Jenna looked ahead. There were only two more entries. She swallowed, her eyes flicking away from the looping script as if it might taint her with guilt by association.

'Yes,' she said. 'But there's still no guarantee it'll give us an answer.'

'It might give us another clue.'

'Yes. All right. Let's finish it.'

May 23rd

What an altered atmosphere is in this house! The girls left a week ago, for Miss Marsham's Academy for Young Ladies in Buxton, and there is such peace. I relish the simple pleasures of taking a turn in my garden without having to look over my shoulder or all about me for signs of ambush. No giggling in obscure corners, no fear of assault.

David is at once more affectionate and he speaks incessantly of the baby's arrival and how he shall be welcomed to the world. But his affections are sometimes too much for me, especially in the bedchamber. I do not welcome them there, for I fear damage to my child. He tries to persuade me otherwise but we have kept to our separate bedrooms these past few nights.

Truth to tell, I am so excessively bilious that I can scarcely go two hours together without requiring a basin in which to expel the contents of my stomach. It is extremely difficult to maintain the appearance of elegance and grace in these circumstances, and I know the servants laugh about it behind my back.

Unfortunately, their demeanour is no less surly than it ever was. Once the child is born, I will insist on David speaking to them about it. I feel that, once he has his son, he will deny me nothing.

'Not many clues there,' admitted Jason. 'Unless he kills her for not putting out.'

'At least he isn't a rapist,' noted Jenna. 'Some husbands wouldn't have taken no for an answer.' She shuddered. 'Awful times to be a woman.'

June 10th
    All is over. Everything is done with. My life has changed beyond comprehension and will never be the same again.

'Oho.' Jason sat up. 'Now we're getting to it.'
Jenna's heart raced. She was surprised at how sick to the stomach she felt, and her fingers trembled on the flyleaf of the journal.

'God, I'm not sure I can read this,' she whispered. 'I feel as if I know her now.'

Jason stroked her arm.

'I know what you mean. I'm kind of dreading it myself. But we have to know the worst. Perhaps, when we know it, we can get a decent burial for the poor cow.'

'That's a good point. Right.' She took a long, deep breath and read on.

My existence now will be one of mourning and of evasion. In one stroke, I am reduced once more from lady to nobody. Worse than nobody. A fugitive.

Last night, the evening being excessively hot, I had difficulty in sleeping. I tossed and turned in perspiration-soaked sheets, using a bedpan to relieve my nausea. I think I was a little feverish. I fell into half-sleeps, with broken dreams in which my child was born a monster.

Waking, sobbing, from one such nightmare, I resolved to put off the search for sleep until my mind was clearer. I got out of bed and thought I would go outside and walk in the moonlit garden until my senses were less fogged and my skin cooled.

But as I walked along the corridor past David's room, I heard the sound of voices. His voice, low as it is when he is amorous, and then a woman's, languid in tone.

I could not move, or breathe, or think.

Why was a woman in my husband's bedchamber? Was he ill? Did she attend to him?

I clung to a dozen such tenuous explanations, but in the end I could not deceive myself.

I bent and put my eye to the keyhole.

Little could be seen, but what I could see was damning.

I saw my husband's back and his rear perspective. He was crouching over another body, the legs of which were over his shoulders. He lay on top of her. They were kissing, and as they kissed, he thrust forwards then retreated, over and again.

There was nothing else they could be doing.

I could not see who she was but I was determined to find out.

Shaking and fearful of giving myself away by

uttering a cry or bending over to retch, I hid myself in a curtained alcove and waited.

The heat of the night was now my ally, for it kept me from wanting to move or wrap myself up. I could wait and wait, and while I did, my head cleared, my heart slowed and I was able to consider my position.

I had an unfaithful husband. In that, I was not unusual.

But I had an unfaithful husband who felt able to commit his infidelity in this very house, while I lay in my bed mere yards away.

What wife could bear such humiliation? Not this one.

And yet, what could I do? I could reproach him with it, but his reply would be that I had deprived him of his conjugal rights and thus had no grounds for complaint if he sought relief elsewhere. Many would agree with him and say that the blame lay with me. Perhaps it does.

Nonetheless, adultery is adultery, and a vow is a vow.

I heard their cries, his grunts, her cackling laugh. It pierced me deep, and I wondered if my child felt the pain of it through me, in his innocent sleep.

I stood in my place and held myself still until at last the door handle turned and a woman in a coarse white gown came out. I saw her plait dangle down her back as she turned to kiss my husband a fond goodnight.

Eliza.

I did not come out of my hiding place until the door was shut and my husband out of view. I followed Eliza, softly, barefoot, down the back stairs. I had thought she might go to the attic, but she descended instead to the kitchen and went out into the garden, just as I had intended before coming upon the adulterers.

The thought that she, too, needed to cool down, entered my head, enraging me beyond endurance.

'Eliza.' I spoke from the kitchen doorway, taking a grim pleasure in the little squawk of shock she uttered before turning to face me. 'Does your own bed not suit you tonight?'

A look of blank surprise was superseded by a hateful smirk.

'Why, no, ma'am,' she said in a low voice. 'It's ever such a hot night and a body needs the cool air after all that sweating.'

'You . . .' I could barely speak. 'Hussy,' came eventually on to my tongue.

'Oh, me, is it? Me that's the hussy? When you're the one what came into this house and turned his head away from me.'

'What do you mean?' I came down from the doorstep and let my soles feel the grave cool of the patio flags. It was helpful in its way, giving me a sense of being anchored to the ground. Before, I had had the strangest feeling of weightlessness, as if I might fly up into the sky like a balloon.

'Me and David. We've been lovers a long time. Ever since I first came here as under-housemaid. He was still in mourning then, but I soon soothed him. Years, I've loved him. Years, I've lived in hope, or as much as I dared. I suppose I knew, deep down, that if he married again it wouldn't be me. Some fine lady, some rich

widow. And then . . .' She choked on the words. 'You! A bloody governess. A nobody, no better'n me.'

'You . . . You're jealous?' All sorts of intrusive thoughts crowded into my head, precipitated by the expression of naked hatred on her face.

'I'm wronged,' she said. 'And I'm robbed. Robbed of what's mine by right.'

'You mean Lord Harville? Oh, then the girls . . .?' I said, hideous light dawning.

'Poor mites,' said Eliza with a bitter laugh. 'They ain't done nothing to deserve what they've got in life. Let me show you something.'

'Show me what?'

'Wait.'

She went over to the round iron cover that concealed the entrance to the wine cellar and performed some kind of manoeuvre to open it.

'I'll show you something that'll make you see,' she said.

'What can you show me? I already see,' I said. 'I see that you are the one responsible for all those horrible tricks, and you intend to steal my husband from me once again. But it will not work. I can give him a son, born in wedlock, and that is his heart's desire, far more than to bed some servant girl whenever he wants.'

With a suppressed cry of fury, she rushed at me and knocked me to the ground, where we struggled desperately, hand against hand, with much scratching and biting and pulling of hair. I got free of her and rose again to my feet, but she launched herself once more, and her arms and legs flailed at me with such murderous intent that I feared for my life.

I cannot recall exactly how it came to pass, but somewhere in the milling chaos of fingernails and teeth, I pushed her off me with the last vestiges of my strength.

She went backwards, over the cellar opening and fell headlong into its gaping maw.

For a moment I could do nothing but stand there with my hand over my mouth. She made no sound. I called her name, tentatively. Still, silence.

I went into the kitchen for a lantern and took it with me, down the slippery cold rungs of the ladder. Halfway down, I shone it into the darkness. Eliza lay there, her neck at a sickening angle. I had killed her.

I went down to sit with her. I know not why. I sat with her for an hour, perhaps two, even three, then I realised I had this diary in the pocket of my nightgown and I thought to write it all down and leave this testimony with her.

I leave it now. I place it beside her and I leave this cellar, this house and this town. I will pack a bag and be away from here with the morning mail.

What will become of me, and my child, I cannot say.

I place our destinies in the hands of a merciful God. He will need no diary to understand my motives, for He will see what is in my heart, and so, farewell.

Jenna put the book aside and for a moment neither of them spoke.

'Fucking hell,' said Jason at last, with feeling.

'So the body wasn't hers,' said Jenna. 'God. What a mess.'

'And guess what,' said Jason, sounding so savage that

Jenna turned to him in concern. 'The only one who gets away with it all is Harville.'

'Oh, well, but does he? He loses his wife and the son he longed for. So, not really.'

'You think he wouldn't go out and remarry straight away?'

'How could he? Frances was still alive. He'd need her death certificate before he could do that. Although, maybe a divorce on grounds of desertion? But I'm shaky on divorce law back then. I'm sure it took a very long time.'

Jason shook his head. 'But what the hell happened to her? Them? I mean, if she had the baby. She might have lost it, what with all that fighting and stress.'

Jenna leant her head back against the wall, her brain working furiously.

'I don't know. But I think we need to dig deeper. I can't just let it end like that. I need to know what happened to them all – to Frances and the baby, to Lord Harville, to those poor girls. And Eliza's family! Did they know? Were they told? Everything suggests that it was totally hushed up, since Eliza's body has lain there ever since. The cellar was sealed and it was left that way. Although . . . somebody put all those boxes of papers down there. Harvilles have known, all the way down the years.'

'How the hell are we supposed to find out though? We can't exactly bring any of 'em back to life to ask them.'

'I don't know. Parish records. Births, deaths and marriages. I'm going to look into it, Jay. Just as soon as this exhibition's off my hands.'

'Yeah, I think it's got to be done. I'll help you.'

They clasped hands, each looking for some comfort from the other from the awful story they had just read.

'We'll sort this out,' said Jenna, and they embraced.

Chapter Twelve

Late August had come to Bledburn, and with it the first break in the weeks of summer heat that had tyrannised the town since Jenna's return from London.

On the day of the exhibition, the skies were darker and fat raindrops fell singly or in pairs before changing their minds and withholding the ever-promised cloud-burst. The uncertainty did nothing to help Jenna's mood, already jittery, as she rushed around the house and garden supervising the final touches.

'Jen, chill,' said Kayley, laughing, as she unpacked a box of champagne glasses in the kitchen. 'Leave it to the team. Tabitha's got the paintings covered and I can cope with the other bits and bobs. Take five before your blood pressure goes through the roof.'

'I could do with finding Jason,' she muttered, picking up a handful of invoices and gazing unseeingly at the figures. 'Where's he gone? Doesn't he care that this is his big night?'

'Go and find him. He's probably a bag of nerves too. Honestly, everything's in hand.'

Jenna nodded and put down the papers.

'Thanks, Kayl,' she muttered, wandering out into the back garden.

She hadn't felt comfortable out here since the discovery of the body and, now she knew the story behind it, she felt even less so, imagining Frances's footsteps underneath hers, seeing the spot where Eliza had been toppled into the cellar mouth. But people were busy stringing fairy-lights between the trees and setting out folding tables and chairs. In the past fortnight, she had worked like mad to get the wilderness into a more presentable state. Jason had spent every day stripped to the waist, hacking back bushes with a chainsaw. Not that that had been such a bad sight . . .

Where was he, though?

She wandered vaguely through the old formal garden, rather less formal than it used to be. Potted shrubs and miniature trees had been placed in the flowerbeds, which next year would hopefully have blooms of their own to show.

She reached the tree trunk with the entwined initials and turned back, her skin suddenly cold.

Frances's happiness had been so short-lived.

She looked back at the house, raising her eyes from the hectic business on the patio and lifting them all the way to the roof.

Ah. That could be her answer.

She went back inside and climbed the stairs to the top floor. Nobody was up here – it was out of bounds to exhibition-goers. They had decided to do the attic frescoes as a separate exhibition, once Jason's name was made. She called up to the attic and was rewarded by the sight of Bowyer leaping out of the door.

'Jason? What are you doing?'

'Come up and see.'

She huffed. 'I haven't got time for this. We've only got three hours before the first guests . . .'

'Come up and see,' he repeated.

She did as she was told, grudgingly, and huffed again when she saw the state of Jason, bare-chested in his old trackpants with paint all over him, even in his hair.

Her scolding words died in her throat when she saw what he was doing.

He had a large canvas in front of him, on which was a half-finished picture. Unusually for him, it was a portrait. Of her.

'Is that . . . me?' she asked uncertainly.

So far, it was just an outline, but she knew from the pose he had put her in and the sketch of her hair and face that it couldn't be anyone else.

'I've made a start,' he said sheepishly. 'I mean, there's a long way to go with it. I'm not used to portraits either.'

'I . . . Well, correct me if I'm wrong, but if you're painting me, shouldn't I be posing for you?'

'You'd have to keep still for five minutes,' he said with an uncharacteristically shy little laugh. 'When does that ever happen?'

'I could do it for you,' she said, looking closer. 'Are you going to put clothes on me?'

He reached over to ruffle her hair with a paint-stained finger.

'What do you think?'

'Jason!'

'It's only a sketch. I'm nowhere near ready to paint the real thing yet. I'm kind of hoping you will pose for me when I get that far.'

'If this exhibition does what it's meant to do, you'll be a hot property. And so will any picture you paint of me. Especially if it's nude!'

'Yeah, and? There's a gorgeous painting I saw once in art class at school of a woman lying on her side, showing her arse. Dead sexy, can't remember the title or the artist, though. But, whoever she was, she's living forever. Everybody gets to see what a beautiful woman she was when she was alive, even centuries after she died. I want that for you. Nobody looks at that painting and goes, ew, I can see her bum, how embarrassing. Do they? They look at it and go, wow, what a beautiful thing.'

Jenna nodded. 'The "Rokeby Venus", maybe?' she suggested. 'Velazquez?'

'Whatever. No, the title was stupid. Made us all laugh.'

'Also known as *The Toilet of Venus*?'

He laughed with recognition. 'Yeah, that was it. You can imagine how a bunch of fourteen year olds from the estate reacted to that. We thought it was hilarious. But you get my point, though?'

She smiled and put a hand in his.

'Yeah, I do.'

'Because I've been thinking a lot since we finished reading that diary, about what lives on after death. My work is the kind that lasts. Yours, not so much. I want you to be remembered as more than a footnote on Deano's Wikipedia entry. You deserve it.'

'Thanks for the vote of confidence,' said Jenna with

a brittle laugh, but she knew what he meant, and she appreciated the sentiment. 'You've made me a bit fat,' she objected, peering again at the outline.

'Get lost. There's nothing of you. Besides, what's wrong with a bit of flesh?'

'Sorry,' she sighed. 'You're right. LA turned me into such a body fascist. I hope I'm growing out of that now. You know, I really resented Deano's fling because I thought she was fat. Isn't that pathetic? What kind of skewed thinking is that?'

'Well, Bledburn's knocking all that crap out of your head,' said Jason. 'So it's good for something.'

'Look, we haven't got long before the show,' she said, glancing at her watch. 'Would you do me a massive favour and come and get showered and changed? People are going to start turning up before we know it and I want everything to be perfect when they do.'

'Oh, yes. Time for me to practise all my handshakes and manners and polite conversation,' said Jason, rolling his eyes. 'Don't worry. I'll behave myself at the exhibition. Can't promise anything for afterwards though . . .'

He caught her round the waist and cupped her face in a rough, white-spirit-smelling hand. 'Unlike you,' he whispered. 'You made me a promise for after the exhibition? Remember?'

A guilty little thrill of arousal hit Jenna right in the pit of the stomach.

Oh yes. She remembered.

Forty-five minutes later, she stood in her bathrobe, taking her dress for the night from its hanger and laying it on the bed.

'That's nice,' commented Jason, standing behind her

in his own dressing gown, slicking gel through his wet hair. 'You're wearing that tonight, are you?'

'Yes, I think so.'

Jason rubbed his hands together then put them on her shoulders. He bent to kiss her neck. She nuzzled against his face instinctively, despite her gathering opening-night nerves.

'Bend over,' he growled.

'Jason, we've just got out of the shower . . .'

'Do it.'

Everything in her responded to his take-no-prisoners tone. She bent straightaway, her hands on the mattress either side of the long spangly dress.

Jason reached underneath to loosen her robe, so he could run his hands over her belly and breasts. He lifted it clear of her bottom and spread her cheeks with his thumbs.

'Do you remember what you're getting tonight?' he said, as if this rude exposure hadn't provided the perfect reminder.

The thought made Jenna wet and squirmy between her legs, much as she clenched her muscles.

'Of course,' she whispered.

'Good. Cos I don't want you forgetting. As a little reminder, you're going commando at the exhibition tonight.'

'Jason,' she gasped, looking at the high split in the skirt of her dress, calculating the chances of wardrobe malfunction. They were slim, but all the same . . .

'No arguments,' he said, with a light pat to her bottom. 'You'll do as you're told. I'm your performing monkey downstairs, after all. You made that deal, babe, and when you make a deal with the devil . . . well . . .' He put his fingers between her legs and rubbed her pussy lips.

'You *are* the bloody devil,' she wailed.

'You'd better believe it.' He continued to finger her steadily while she thought long and hard about wearing no knickers at the exhibition, and what would come afterwards. It made her almost delirious with lustful shame. 'I'm having my way with you tonight, Jen. I'm going to get you good and ready for it. I'm going to start by fucking you here and now, because I want you doing all that hostess with the mostest stuff downstairs with a well-fucked pussy. They won't know, but they might guess. And I'll know. And you'll know.'

He was still speaking when Jenna found herself empty of fingers but suddenly full of something else. She moaned with pleasure at the unexpected fullness his penetration provided, pushing herself back on him instinctively.

'I'll think of this every time I look at you,' he said, thrusting into her, forcing her weight forwards on to her braced arms. 'When you catch my eye tonight, babe, you should know that I'm picturing you, bent over and taking it hard. And I'm thinking about how you're going to get more of it tonight, but . . .'

She whimpered as his thumb delved between her bottom cheeks and pushed at her tight pucker.

'There,' he whispered.

She thought about what he said, thought about it feverishly, adding her hot thoughts to her hot body and all it was going through.

She wanted to suck it all into her and keep the whole of it inside, so she could have it again whenever she wanted. She would hold on to the feeling of him slamming into her, the way his thighs smacked into her and his cock ploughed deep, waking up every nerve ending along her passage as it went. His hands on her, exploring her, squeezing and examining and owning every inch of her skin. His low-spoken dirty words. The reality of her submission and her base need of him. The thought of her, without knickers, and everybody whispering behind their hands, *knowing* what had just been done to her – and, worse, knowing what was still to come.

And it was true; there would be talk. Undoubtedly there already was. That Jason was her lover was common knowledge on five continents. They knew where he'd been. They would probably all be picturing it when they shook hands and exchanged pleasantries over champagne.

This thought was the one to send her over the edge, spasming gratefully around Jason's thick, still-thrusting cock.

'That's it, babe,' he said with fierce triumph. 'You need it. You get it. Lots and lots of it . . . Oh . . .'

He was finally lost for words, his voice breaking into sighs and grunts.

She held tight to the knowledge that he was filling her up, draining every scrap of wanton pleasure from it.

'I love you,' he said, language returning to him. 'And I owe you.'

'Not any more, after tonight,' she said. 'And everything I've done for you has been for love. You do know that, don't you?'

Falling into a heap on the bed, Jenna's dress shoved aside, they kissed in a tangle of wet and salty limbs.

'Either that or you've totally lost your marbles,' he said. 'I like to believe the first one.'

'That's the true one,' she said. 'Oh God. The time. Hand me those tissues.'

With half an hour to go before the exhibition opened to the invited guests, Jenna and Jason were disturbed in their conversation with Tabitha by a loud bang on the door.

'Tell them it's too early,' Jenna called to Kayley as she rushed across the hall to answer it. She turned back to Tabitha. 'So you think this room is the more commercially attractive stuff and the other rooms are for specialists?'

'Yes,' Tabitha confirmed. 'Of course, it's all excellent, but we've used this drawing room for the pieces we think will create the biggest waves. I must say, if you don't make a very substantial impact tonight, I'm putting my gallery on the market.'

'The buzz is absolutely out of this world,' agreed Jenna, shutting her eyes for a moment of professional rapture. 'Have you seen all the speculation in the press and online?'

Jason, who had been looking every inch the well-heeled young sophisticate about town, suddenly dropped the mask and assumed a posture of teenage sulkiness.

'Mum,' he moaned as Kayley, apologetic-faced, ushered Linda Watson into the room. 'I said to come later.'

'What, and miss my own boy's big moment? I'm your mother, Jase. It was me what gave birth to you. Do you think you can fob me off?'

'Didn't security stop you?' asked Tabitha, amused.

'They tried,' said Linda grimly, and Jason rolled his eyes.

'Kayley, take Ms Watson into the kitchen and get her a drink,' suggested Jenna, mouthing, 'Water!' once Linda's back was turned.

'If she gets rat-arsed and shows me up . . .' muttered Jason.

'It'll be fine,' Jenna reassured. 'Kayley'll look after her. All you have to think about is accepting the compliments that will be rolling in all evening.'

'Absolutely,' said Tabitha with a nod. 'Now, if you'll excuse me, I just need to call Shona in London, make sure everything's ticking over at the gallery.'

She went to find a quiet room, pulling her phone from her Vuitton handbag.

Jenna, knowing that this would be her last moment alone with Jason before the world whirled in and plucked them out of their private bubble, turned to him and put her palm to his freshly shaved cheek.

'Are you OK?' she asked softly.

He put his own hand on top of hers. Jenna savoured the quiet togetherness, feeling her rapid heartbeat slow as they stood in silence, knowing nothing but each other.

'I'm nervous,' he admitted. 'I'm tempted to just knock back the champagne, but if I did anything to show you up, I'd never forgive myself.'

'This is your night, not mine,' she reminded him. 'But yes. Probably best to go easy on the booze. Just be yourself and they'll love you. Like I do.'

'Hopefully not *exactly* like you do,' he said with an

impish grin, taking her hand from his cheek and holding it against his crisply laundered white shirt. 'I don't think we want an orgy getting into the papers, do we?'

'Good point.' She tiptoed up to kiss his lips. 'Besides, you've got other things to look forward to. You'll want to keep a clear head for them.'

She winked at him and he put a proprietorial and meaningful hand on her bottom, rubbing it through the jewelled sheath dress she wore.

'Oh yes,' he said, his voice so low it seemed to come from his highly polished shoes. 'I won't be forgetting *that*.'

They leant into one another, and Jenna gloried in his sharply dressed freshness. He looked so incredibly glamorous that she wanted the show to be over already, so she could mess up his impeccable suit and perfect hair. The magazines were going to fall all over themselves with love for him, she knew it.

And yet, she was ambivalent about the idea of being a Celebrity Couple. It just didn't seem to suit what they had, and wanted to keep having.

She tossed the thought from her mind. What would be would be. As long as they were together, it would be OK.

Tabitha popped her head around the door.

'So, then, children,' she said brightly. 'Are we ready? Who's going down to the front gate to declare this unveiling of genius well and truly open?'

'Why don't all three of us go out?' said Jenna, smiling. 'Take care not to get trampled in the stampede, though. Have you seen how many people are out there? The police have had to cordon off the street.'

'Well, if their name's not down, they aren't coming in,' said Tabitha firmly. 'It was a very good idea to hire a top security firm for the gate. Right then. Let's do this.'

They took a moment to let the mixture of exhilaration, fear and awe sink in, then walked together towards the front door.

On opening, the expected battery of bright lights hit Jenna full in the face. She put her hand in Jason's and they walked on, heads high, down the steps and along the path.

Behind them, an enormous banner hung from the front wall, obscuring the upper windows, announcing the exhibition.

A few louder voices called Jenna's name over the general roar.

'Look this way, Jenna.'

'Give us a smile.'

'JENNA!'

She ignored them all but stood, smiling graciously, still hand in hand with Jason, while Tabitha gave the order for the gate to be opened.

She stood, with Jason, behind the ribbon that had been strung between the posts, and gave a short prepared statement about how excited she was to be launching this new talent.

As she moved to step aside for the cutting of the ribbon, Jason unexpectedly punched the air and shouted, 'Bledburn forever!', resulting in a whole lot more flashes and clicks.

'Did you have to do that?' Jenna muttered, walking back up the path in front of the first eager ticket holders.

'What? Just felt like I was being cut out of my own moment there,' he said.

'Sorry. But I knew it was me they wanted out there. Next time it'll be you.'

'Absolutely,' agreed Tabitha, hastening up the steps in search of her first glass of champagne.

'I'm going to hide in the kitchen for the first half hour,' said Jenna, 'like we agreed. I'm not having people looking at me instead of your art.' She tiptoed to kiss his cheek. 'Break a leg, darling. And don't forget your manners.'

He winked back. 'I won't pinch any bums except yours, promise.'

Jenna escaped through the solid oak door behind the great staircase. The kitchen was off-limits to guests, but it was hardly a relaxing place to be, buzzing with caterers and waiting staff who swooped around Jenna with silver trays of champagne and canapés.

Kayley stood in the middle of the whirlwind, directing it all.

'Do they need me out there?' she said, spotting Jenna.

'I don't think so. Tabitha will come and find you if they do,' she said, seating herself at one of the bar stools.

Kayley glanced quickly through the open French doors. The patio was accessible to guests through a side door and already a few were coming outside to socialise – clearly here to network rather than discover a brilliant new talent, thought Jenna crossly, following her friend's gaze.

'I'm a little bit worried about *her*,' said Kayley, dropping her voice.

'Who?'

'Jason's mum. She's out there somewhere and I'm pretty sure she took one of the opened champagne bottles with her. By the time I cottoned on, I was too busy trying to organise the waitresses.'

'Oh God,' said Jenna. 'Shall I try and find her?'

'Oh . . . it'll be fine,' said Kayley. 'I expect she'll just fall asleep under a bush or something.'

'Kayley! I don't think Jason wants pics of his mum snoring on the ground all over Instagram tomorrow. I'm going out to look for her.'

Jenna put aside the glass of champagne she'd been handed and headed outside. She was stopped half a dozen times and made a point of stopping and exchanging a few pleasantries with each group. But her eyes roved continually over the wilder parts of the garden, in search of a small bleach-blonde woman in a faded denim jacket, clutching a bottle.

'Jenna Diamond! You dark horse!'

A famous actress who'd made the transition from British stage to Hollywood stood in front of Jenna, arms outstretched.

'Annabel! I didn't know you were in the country, or I'd have invited you. But . . . clearly I *did* invite you . . .'

'I'm Desmond's plus-one. It's a flying visit. You promised you'd keep in touch, and here I am, depending on the red tops for your news. You look wonderful, darling.'

'So do you.' She paused, feeling awkward. Obviously, everyone was dying for the gossip about her and Jason, and the split with Deano and all the drama in between. But she had no intention of discussing any of it with anyone.

'So, how have you been?' Annabel meant business.

'Well, put it this way. Don't ever take a sabbatical. They're bloody exhausting.'

Annabel's laugh tinkled through the damp, thick air. The rain had stopped but there was still a looming purplish sky overhead.

'I suppose you weren't expecting an artistic genius to fall into your lap,' she said, putting a beautifully manicured hand on Jenna's forearm.

'No, well, quite. Sorry, darling, but would you excuse me for just a moment. There's somebody I have to find.'

'Of course. Catch you later. Mwah.'

They air kissed briefly, then Jenna hurried on, past the fairylights and bay trees in pots, towards the recently-cleared ornamental beds.

Just a little further on stood the tree with the initials carved upon it.

Jenna felt herself drawn there, but not because she expected to find Jason's mother underneath it.

She found the bark, with its clumsily scratched legend, and put out a hand to touch it. When had this been done? In those happy days when the engagement was first announced, she recollected. Harville, from evidence of the diary, didn't seem the kind of man to act the lovesick swain. Perhaps it was Frances who suggested it? It must have driven Eliza and the children wild to see it.

The murmur of chat and the clink of glasses seemed distant, although they were no more than a hundred yards away from her. This section of the grounds was out of bounds to guests, more for their convenience than any other reason, for there was nothing of interest in this tangle of old branches and insect-laden weeds.

A crackling close by made her jump. What was it? A

fox, perhaps, or some other wild animal that had made this jungle its home?

She peered uneasily into the dusky thicket but saw nothing.

Anyway, Linda was clearly not here.

Jenna turned to go, but a hand on her shoulder stopped her. Her scream of surprise was silenced by that same hand covering her mouth.

'Hush. It's only me.'

The voice was one she had never expected to hear again.

She made an angry sound against the confining palm and he raised it just a fraction.

'Don't make a fuss,' he said. 'There's really no need.'

'No need?' she hissed, whirling around to face the interloper. 'What the hell are you doing here?'

Lawrence Harville shook his immaculately-groomed head.

'Why wouldn't I come here, Jenna? It's my home.'

'It is *my* house and you are trespassing. I'm going to call the police.'

'No you aren't. They won't be interested.'

'You're on remand for serious drug offences.'

'No I'm not. The CPS dropped the case this morning. Lack of evidence. So you see, Jenna, you don't get everything your own way after all. You and that alley rat you've shacked up with.'

'How did you get in? You don't have an invitation.'

She looked swiftly over to the back of the house, seeing the fairylights twinkling in the distance, watching people look up at the skies as if they expected rain any moment. It did look likely.

'Oh, I grew up here. I know every little crack in the fortifications, believe me. Anyway, no cause for alarm. I only came to give you the news yourself – save you hearing it from a third party. It's only basic courtesy, don't you agree?'

'Well, I've heard it, so now you can get out.' Jenna was working hard to keep her tone hard and her body language uncompromising, but the strain was starting to get to her. Any moment now, a wobble would tell Harville what she didn't want him to know. That she was afraid.

'Oh, I don't plan to hang around,' said Harville. 'I'm not a fan of the arts, really, and I have celebrating to do. Perhaps your little friend Kayley would like to join us?'

'I think not. And you can leave her out of it.'

'Well, you know, if only she'd left *me* out of it, I'd be happy to return the favour. But she didn't, did she? What is it they say? "Loose lips sink ships." A certain ship might not be as watertight as people think.'

'Oh, stop talking rubbish. Is that supposed to be some kind of threat? Just get out.' Jenna was weary now, tired of keeping herself in check.

Lawrence bowed his head, as if in acquiescence, but then he put his hand against the carved initials on the tree.

'I heard you found our Fairy Fay,' he said softly.

Jenna bristled. 'Yes. The skeleton in the cellar. I suppose you didn't know anything about that?'

'I suppose that's none of your business,' he said, with a maddening smile. 'It's a Harville matter.'

'It's a legal matter,' said Jenna, but she felt she was on shaky ground now. She could hardly implicate Lawrence Harville in a century-old crime.

'Don't be silly. Nothing can possibly be proved this far after the event. I'm assuming it's the bones of my ancestor's second wife, the one who committed suicide but has no grave.'

'Don't assume too much,' said Jenna, satisfied by the thought that she knew more about this particular Harville business than Lawrence did. 'You might be shocked when the truth comes out.'

Harville narrowed his eyes.

'What do you mean? Are you saying you have information about the body? Or are you just bluffing? Of course you are. You've made your entire life and career out of making people think you know something, when you're just a talentless chancer. You're a vampire, Jenna. You've elevated yourself on the back of other people's talent. Yet I bet you think you've earned all this, don't you?'

He waved his hand in the direction of the house, the exhibition, the well-heeled guests and beautifully dressed garden.

'You think you deserve all your success and all your money and all your disgusting sordid goings-on with that rat from the estate. Well, let me tell you, you've earned nothing. You're a leech.'

'Get out.' Jenna could no longer keep the tremble from her voice.

'Ordering me out of my own home? My birthright? How *dare* you?'

'I'm calling the police.' She reached in her handbag for her phone.

Harville knocked her arm away and grasped it so tightly that Jenna gasped.

'Oh, don't worry,' he said. 'I'm off. I've done what I wanted to do, and that's deliver my little snippet of news. You won't see me again.' He paused. 'At least, you won't see me *first*.'

He let go of Jenna and began to wade through the waist-high grasses and brambles.

While she stood there, staring after him, rooted to the spot, he turned and spoke casually over his shoulder.

'Oh, and tell darling Jason and dear Kayley that I can't *wait* to catch up with all their news. Won't you?'

She said nothing, just let out an exhalation of horror and watched him forge his way out of her sight.

For a few moments, she was as still as the tree trunk she stood beside.

It was OK, she told herself. He just wanted to make a nuisance of himself. He wouldn't go any further than that. She wouldn't hesitate to call the police and have him dealt with for harassment if he showed his face here again.

She held the cards.

He held none.

It was OK.

She took a breath and began to wend her way back to the patio, clearing now as the first drops of a shower that promised to be heavy began to fall.

She found Kayley, doing her best to clear anything that might not be waterproof from the patio area.

Jenna helped out, scooping up some bowls of olives from the tables and following Kayley back into the kitchen.

'You'll never guess who I just bumped into,' said Jenna as they slid shut the patio doors.

'Did you find Linda? Is she ratted yet?'

'What? Oh. No. I didn't.'

'So?' Kayley turned to look at Jenna. 'Christ, you're white as a sheet. Who was it then? Tell me.'

'Lawrence Harville.'

Kayley gawped then sank on to a chair as if her legs had turned to rubber.

'You're joking, right?'

'Wrong.'

'But . . . isn't he interfering with witnesses, or whatever they call it? Tell the cops.'

'No,' said Jenna flatly. 'Apparently the CPS dropped the case.'

'Oh, you have *got* to be fucking kidding me!'

'I wish I were. Well, he could be lying, of course. I'll check . . .' She looked around distractedly. Waiting staff glided in and out. 'But I just don't have time yet. Tomorrow. I'll look into it tomorrow.'

'But Jen . . . Where is he then? Is he here now?'

She stood up as if she meant to run back out into the garden in pursuit of him.

'No. He's gone. He just came to . . . I don't know. To warn me? To warn us? He mentioned you. And Jason.'

'You think he wants revenge? I bet he's going to try to get back at us. At *me*. I'm the one who grassed him up. Oh *God*.'

She sat back down and buried her face between her knees, rocking to and fro.

'Kayley, calm down.' Jenna reached down to rub her spine and shoulders. 'It's all right. You've got me on your side and he won't dare come against me. Not with my profile. Not with my *lawyers*. Seriously.'

Kayley breathed deeply then sat up, looking seriously into Jenna's eyes.

'I bloody well hope you're right.'

Jenna smiled sympathetically at her assistant. She had been brave to do what she had done, telling the truth about Harville, despite the risk she ran.

When Jenna had first run into Kayley, at the youth club on the estate, she had been a cheery, skinny lass in a hoodie and threadbare trackpants. It was hard to believe this clear-skinned, shiny-haired woman in a figure-hugging purple satin sheath was the same person. While Jenna had been busy turning Jason into something presentable, it seemed Kayley had been doing the same number on herself.

'You're safe if you stick with me,' Jenna reassured. 'And I'm not about to cut you loose. You've done a brilliant job here tonight. I couldn't have done it without you.'

'Yeah, I'm not bad, am I?' said Kayley with a watery smile.

'You're a diamond.' Jenna lowered her voice, conscious of the busy young ears passing to and fro. 'And I know how much it cost you to come back here. It must be a bit . . .'

Kayley nodded, shutting her eyes.

'It did bring back those times, at first,' she admitted. 'I didn't like to go on about it, because I knew how lucky I was, to get this break with you after everything that went on, but . . . well . . .'

Jenna nodded. Over the weeks, Kayley had let slip more and more about the parties she had come to at Harville's invitation. Parties at which, it seemed, anything went. Harville had numerous tapes of Kayley, off her face, taking part in threesomes and moresomes and all sorts, which he had used to blackmail her into concealing the truth about his drug dealing activities. Jason had been the sacrificial lamb. Only at the eleventh hour had Kayley taken courage and acted selflessly and bravely, to remove Jason from the frame and put Lawrence Harville squarely in it.

But, it seemed, her evidence would not now be enough to remove him from circulation, as they had hoped.

'I hope this evening takes away the bad vibes and replaces them with good vibes,' said Jenna. 'Harville Hall is mine now. Its rotten past is over and done with.'

'I know,' said Kayley. 'I'm glad you've changed the kitchen so much. I seemed to spend a lot of time in the kitchen at those parties for some reason.' She shuddered. 'Getting perved on by creeps. Those friends of his. They never told me their real names. I'd know 'em if I saw 'em though. I bet he's staying with them now. I bet they'll give him all the cover he needs. They'll have to. He's got stuff on them.'

'And they on him,' said Jenna. 'That seems to be how his style of friendship works.' She filled her lungs and stood straight. 'But he's got nothing on us, and he knows it. And doesn't he hate it?'

She smiled.

'That's why he came tonight. All he's got left is the power to creep us out. But we aren't going to let him even do that. Right?'

Kayley saluted.

'Right you are, sister,' she said.

The door to the hall opened again as a waiter came

in to deposit a tray of empty glasses. Over the hubbub of general conversation, a more querulous voice could be heard.

'He's my *boy*. Ain't I allowed to drink to him?'

Jenna and Kayley swapped quick looks.

'Linda,' they both said.

'Time for some damage limitation,' added Jenna, as they headed out into the throng.

'Ah, Jenna, at last,' cried Tabitha, who was propping up a very woozy-looking Linda Watson. 'She keeps trying to go over and monopolise Jason, but he's very busy talking to potential customers and all the top critics. I've told her it isn't really the time, but . . .'

'Sorry, I should have been here,' said Jenna. 'Got side-tracked. Linda, please, why don't you come into the kitchen and have something to eat?'

'I wanna see my boy,' she slurred belligerently, trying to extricate herself from Tabitha's clutches by sheer force.

The force succeeded only in propelling her to her knees on the floor.

Several heads turned, faces expressing a mixture of amusement and concern, to watch the performance.

'Linda,' hissed Jenna, determined not to expose Jason to embarrassment on his big night. 'That's enough. Come with me.'

This time, Linda didn't have enough strength left in her to resist Jenna's firm hand on her elbow, and she followed her into the kitchen.

'Do you know what?' said Jenna, once Linda was safely seated and handed a glass of water. 'This is a very big night for Jason and for me. It would be nice if I could go and join in with it. But apparently, the whole thing's going to end without me enjoying a minute of it.'

'S'not my fault.' Linda sloshed the water around in her tumbler, spilling a fair bit on to the hallowed granite flagstones. 'Big night for me too, ain't it? My boy, ain't he?'

'Yes, he's your boy. So act like a responsible parent and lay off the booze, instead of making him a laughing stock. Because that's what you'll do, Linda, if you don't get a grip on yourself. Is that what you want to see in tomorrow's papers? Big headline? Big photograph of you, paralytic drunk with your knickers on show? How do you think Jason would feel about that?'

''M not drunk,' she insisted. 'Bit merry. Thass all.'

'Stop lying to yourself. You're pissed. And you aren't going anywhere near Jason until you're sober.' She passed a plate of smoked salmon mini frittatas over. 'Here, eat a few of these. They might soak a bit of it up.'

'Don't like fish. Where's me champagne? I had a glass of champagne.'

'No more champagne,' said Jenna firmly. 'You're going to have something to eat and then I'm going to take you up the back stairs for a little lie down.'

'Who do you think you are? Treating me like a, like a . . .' She belched. 'Little kid. I'm not a little kid. I'm his mum. Everything he's put me through . . . I deserve to be here . . .'

Jenna sighed. With any luck, Linda's ramblings would soon subside into snores. Until then, she had to be kept out of harm's way.

She belched again.

'Sorry,' she said, briefly putting a hand to her mouth.

'Them bubbles. Not used to it. Champagne lifestyle from now on, though, eh? All them rich bastards out there, lapping our Jase's work up, they are. Easy street for us, eh? Well, not you. You've always had it easy.'

'How about a piece of toast?' suggested Jenna brightly, moving away from Linda before she was tempted to slap her face. She took half a loaf from the breadbin. Jason's loaf, not hers. Jenna tried to avoid carbs.

'I'll have a champagne, thanks,' replied Linda stubbornly. 'I've had it hard, I have.'

'Yes, I know you have,' said Jenna, deadpan. This was Linda's constant refrain. It might be true enough, but it certainly got tedious to hear. 'But, so long as things go well for Jason tonight, the hard times could well be over.'

She popped a slice of bread in the toaster.

'I fucking well hope so,' muttered Linda. 'Horrible, it were. Never two pennies to scrape together. No money, no work, no dignity. Then our Jase. Getting up to all sorts. He was a good boy really, though. It was just a phase. All kids go through phases, don't they?'

'Oh yes. I certainly did. I was awful to my mum as a teenager.' Jenna turned around and smiled, softening towards Linda, imagining how awkward Jason must have been as an adolescent. She probably did have it pretty hard, back then. 'I cringe when I remember some of the things I said to her. I was a right little cow. And she near enough had a heart attack when I went off with Deano.'

'Yeah, I remember that. Mind you, she's done all right out of it now, hasn't she? Sunning herself over there in Spain. So perhaps your phase was all to the good. Jason's did nothing but land him in hot water.'

Jenna leant against the kitchen counter, giving Linda a long and sympathetic look.

'You brought him up all alone,' she said. 'That can't have been easy.'

Linda reached in her handbag and brought out a packet of cigarettes.

'I'm gasping,' she said. 'Mind if we go outside for a bit? It's stopped raining.' She stood up and Jenna followed her to the patio doors. 'Seeing as you've banned me from drinking,' she added, loudly but without too much rancour. She seemed to have accepted the situation.

They stood on the damp patio slabs while Linda lit up. The place was still empty. Jenna couldn't help straining her eyes for signs of a potentially lurking Harville.

'You're all jumpy. What's up?' said Linda.

'Oh, nothing. You do understand my point of view, don't you?' She held Linda's bloodshot eyes with her gaze. 'This is such an important night for Jason. It could make him. But it could also break him. It's enough to make anyone a bit jumpy. Especially somebody that loves him.'

Linda took a long drag on her cigarette.

'Aye,' she said at last. 'You're all right, you. You do love him, I get it. I wondered at first. Thought you must be using him for something. But you're on the level, I reckon.'

'Yes, I am. Thanks for recognising it.'

There was a crackle in a nearby bush. Jenna jumped forward, then saw it was a bird, rising out of the branches.

'What the heck's up?' Linda flicked ash into a pot holding a perfectly spherical bay tree.

'I saw someone earlier,' Jenna confessed, wanting to

get her spooked feelings off her chest. 'Someone I didn't want to see.'

'Why the bloody hell did you invite them then?'

'I didn't. Look, have you finished that cigarette? Because I need to see Jason and Tabitha. Come upstairs for a little rest, won't you?'

'Oh, come on, I'm fine. I'll just stay out here if I'm showing you up.'

'I don't know if you should stay out here on your own . . .'

'Who is this person you've seen? A hitman?' She was joking but her voice was laden with indignation.

'No, of course not. It . . . OK, if I tell you, don't tell Jason. Not tonight. It can wait till tomorrow.'

'Don't tell Jason what?'

He stood behind them at the open patio door, clutching a bottle of champagne, looking bright-eyed and flushed and full of his brilliant self.

'G'is a swig of that, love,' said Linda, snatching the bottle from him and upending it into her mouth.

Jenna rolled her eyes.

'Nothing. How are you doing? I've hardly had a moment to . . .'

Jason put his hands on her shoulders and bent to kiss her neck, then her ear.

'They want me,' he murmured. 'They want me real bad.'

'I knew they would,' she said, pleasure flooding in to replace her nervousness. 'I knew it. Didn't I say so?'

'I've sold a few already,' he said. 'Tabitha reckons it's her most successful opening night in years. But we want you out there. I've come to get you.'

'I'll be out, I promise. I was just going to see if your mum wanted a rest.'

Linda took a break from guzzling champagne to practise her best indignant stare.

'I've told you I'm fine, haven't I?'

'Mum, lay off the booze,' said Jason, wearily authoritative. 'Or I'll kick you out myself.'

'Well, can you hear him?' Linda's indignant stare went into 'ultra' mode. 'His own mother. I'm standing lookout here.'

'Lookout? What d'you mean?'

Jason straightened up and peered into the darkening corners of the garden.

'Nothing,' said Jenna hastily, but Linda wouldn't have this.

'Oh, come on. You said yourself. Someone you didn't want to see. Not invited. There's an intruder on . . .' She belched. 'The premises.'

'What? What's this?'

Jason walked out across the patio, squinting in every direction.

'Come back,' said Jenna. 'It's fine. He's gone.'

'Who's gone?'

Kayley appeared through the side door.

'Ah, there you are, Jen. It's OK. He's gone. I had a word with security and they said they'd seen him get in his car and leave.'

'For fuck's sake,' Jason exploded. '*Who*?'

Kayley blinked. 'Lawrence,' she said. 'Did Jenna not say?'

Jenna put her hands to her face and shook her head.

'Lawrence? You aren't telling me . . .?'

Jason stared wildly at each of the three women.

'Don't look at me,' slurred Linda. 'Nobody told me.'

'He's been *here*? Lawrence Harville? Tonight?'

'But he's gone now,' said Kayley urgently.

'Just as well,' seethed Jason. 'Or I'd have belted the fucker into next week. What was he doing? Jen?'

Jenna shook her head.

'Nothing. Just wanted to tell me the CPS had dropped the case. Can we forget about it now, and concentrate on the exhibition?'

But it didn't seem so, not judging by the ferocious light in Jason's eyes.

'Forget about it? That scrote gets off scot free after all he did and you want me to forget about it? Not fucking likely. I'm going to kill him.'

'Then that'll be the shortest-lived artistic success of all time,' urged Jenna. 'Because you'll be straight back in prison.'

'I don't care. I'd happily swing for him. Where is he? Where's he staying?'

'Jason, stop it,' said Jenna.

'You can't kill him,' added Linda. Three-quarters of the champagne had disappeared inside her by now. She hiccupped, keeping a wavering finger pointed at Jason to make it clear that she had more to say on the matter. 'Cos you can't. Cos it's a crime, that's why.'

'Murder? A crime? Well, how about that? Jen, did he touch you? Did he threaten you?' Jason grabbed hold of Jenna's arms, searching her face for the answers.

'No, s'not what I mean,' insisted Linda loudly. 'Course murder's a crime. But it's worse, ain't it, when you kill, like, there's a special name for it, like, when you . . .'

'What are you on about? Zip it,' said Jason impatiently.

'Like a something-cide,' she continued undaunted.

'Homicide?' suggested Kayley.

'No, it's a different one, and you can't kill Lawrence Harville cos the thing is, that'd be it. The thingy-cide.'

'Shut up, Ma, if you can't talk sense. This is between me and Jen.'

'When you kill your brother,' shouted Linda over the top of him. 'What's it called when you kill your brother?'

There was a moment of silence.

'What do you mean?' said Jason.

'Fratricide,' said Jenna helpfully, though she was sure now that Linda must be raving, out of her mind with champagne.

'I ain't got a brother,' said Jason.

'That's what I'm saying,' said Linda, as if she had been patiently explaining something for a long time. 'You see. You can't kill Lawrence Harville cos it's – what she said – icide.'

'You're not making sense,' said Jason, and Jenna nodded her agreement, though a creeping kind of sick feeling was unfurling in her stomach.

'No? Well, make sense of this. You've got the same dad. You and him. He's no better'n you. Never was.'

'This . . . Come on, Mum. This is bullshit. You've had too much to drink and you're making up stories. Go and have a lie down, yeah?'

'Don't you talk down to me, son!' she shouted, suddenly furious. 'Don't you call me a liar! I've sat on this for near-on thirty years and it's killed me, d'you hear? Killed me, not saying anything. Killed me!'

'Then why didn't you say it?' Jason shouted in return.

'Please, can we keep it down?' begged Jenna, picturing a dozen hidden hands with tape recorders around every corner.

'Because I was scared to,' she said, suddenly breaking down in tears. 'I couldn't tell you. I wanted to. I couldn't do it.'

'This is *bollocks*,' said Jason, rolling his eyes. 'You've told me so many different stories about my dad, I can't believe a word you say any more. First he's this bloke, then he's that bloke, then you don't know, it could be anyone – and now it's Lord fucking Harville? Well, excuse me for not falling for it, but I'm sick of being spun all these lines. Fuck it, I'm going back to find Tabitha. I need some sanity. Jen, come with me. Everyone's asking for you.'

'Oh. I'll be there. Give me a minute. I'll just take your mum up to bed.'

'Let Kayley do it, for God's sake.'

'No, it's OK,' said Jenna. 'I want to. Tell Tabitha I'll be out in a minute.'

Jason stormed off with Kayley at his heels, leaving Jenna with a wailing, champagne-swigging Linda.

'Here.' Jenna handed her a tissue from her handbag. 'You . . . Did you mean that?'

Linda nodded, catching her breath.

'I've never told him. At first, I daren't. I thought I'd lose him. Harville would have him taken off me. That's why I made out like I'd had five different fellas it could have been. When I got pregnant, it put him off the scent. But there weren't no one else. Only George. Harville, that is.'

'How did you . . .? I mean, you can't have moved in the same circles.'

'At the Gala. I were with a group, majorettes. I were only sixteen. You wouldn't know it, to look at me, but I used to turn heads.'

Good God, was Linda really only forty-five? Jenna had to look hard, to see the girl she must have been.

'I mean, I used it,' said Linda. 'Won't claim I were an angel. My looks were all I had in life, so I got the most out of 'em. If I fancied a lad, I had him, and that were that. So George wasn't my first, not at all.'

'Surely he was married?'

'Yeah, with a little lad, three years old. But that wasn't going to stop him taking what he liked the look of. Took me up into the attic, he did, the old servants' quarters. I felt like Lady Muck, even though it was a dirty little secret thing. We met up a few times after that, in the fields, or down by the reservoir. Then I fell pregnant with Jason and I got scared. I told him it were over. He didn't argue with me. A few months later, he sent me a letter, said he'd heard I was pregnant and I'd better not say a word to anyone about us or he'd have the kid taken off me and adopted by a childless couple he knew. I told him the kid probably weren't his, and he seemed happy about that.'

'And you never told Jason?'

'I was going to tell him on his eighteenth birthday. But by then, he was so angry and everyone was so anti-Harville. I thought it'd only make things worse.'

'I see. Yes. Fancy growing up on that estate and then finding out you were related to your worst enemies. Oh, Linda. What a thing to carry around with you all these years.'

Linda staggered gratefully into Jenna's embrace. As she hugged the woman, her mind raced. This was crazy. Jason was a Harville, possibly even conceived here at Harville Hall, in the very attic where she had first found him.

'God knows,' sniffed Linda, 'I don't like the shower of bastards any more than the rest of Bledburn does. But they're his family. What am I going to do?'

'There's nothing you can do,' said Jenna. 'Leave it now. The decisions all lie with Jason. Oh *God*.' The little outburst was brought on by the repeated thought that Lawrence Harville was Jason's half-brother. It was hard to say which of them would be more revolted by the idea.

'Tell you what,' said Linda. 'I could murder a good strong brandy.'

And I could murder you, thought Jenna grimly. *Turning Jason's big night into some kind of alcoholic Jeremy Kyle turn.*

Instead, she escorted the shambolic Linda to the back staircase and helped her up to the only bedroom that was properly habitable at the moment – hers and Jason's.

Leaving her half-conscious on the bed, she went back down the front stairs to do the mingling she had once been looking forward to.

But how difficult it was to be charming and effervescent when her mind swarmed with thoughts of Lawrence Harville's and Jason's parentage. She went to stand by Jason, to join him amidst a crowd of potential investors from eight different countries.

He seemed to have shaken off his mother's words and he laughed and joked with the art dealers as if nothing had been said at all.

As the group broke up so that Jason and Jenna could pose for magazine photographs, she spoke to him, low and without altering her expression.

'Are you OK?'

'Of course. Why wouldn't I be?'

'Your mum . . . what she said . . .'

'Pack of lies. Bound to be.'

He smiled for the camera, remembering everything he had been taught in his modelling session three weeks earlier.

'And if you turn out to be a Harville?' she said, once a variety of poses had been captured for posterity.

'I'm not. It's not happening. Drop it, eh, Jen?'

His tone suggested that to do otherwise would be unwise.

'Get yourself a champagne and let's try to get these freeloaders out of here,' he said through gritted teeth. 'I want you upstairs, as soon as I can. Mum, Lawrence Harville, and everyone else can all bugger off. I need to be alone with you.'

Jenna was taking a flute glass from a tray when the doorbell rang.

'A latecomer?' she said, frowning, as Kayley went to answer it.

There was a mad battery of flashbulbs and a man strode in, followed by a panting and apologetic security guard.

'I know he's not on the list but . . .' the security guard managed to blurt, before the newcomer spoke on his own behalf.

'I didn't think you'd mind,' he said, looking around the room until his eyes alighted on Jenna, at which point he broke into a perfectly dazzling smile. 'After all, I am your husband.'

Jenna sat down on the bottom step of the staircase, overwhelmed.

'Deano,' she said.

'Angel!' he replied, all emotion and enthusiasm. 'I've come home to you.'

Hungry for more?

Read on for an excerpt from Justine Elyot's
historical novel

FALLEN

Available from Black Lace

BLACK
LACE

Chapter One

A small crowd was gathered outside the premises of Thos. Stratton, Antiquarian and Dealer in Rare Books, of Holywell Street, Strand. Largely composed of legal clerks taking their lunch hour, it jostled and catcalled beneath the Elizabethan gables from which one still expected to hear a cry of 'gardy loo' before slops were emptied onto the cobbles.

Some would argue that the shop itself was little better than those aforementioned slops, an abyss of moral putrefaction and decay. Despite the passing of the Obscene Publications Act some ten years previously, many windows still displayed explicit postcards and graphic line drawings. The object of the crowd's interest today was a tintype image of a young woman. She was naked and sprawled in an armchair, luxuriant flesh hand-tinted to look warm and inviting. One of her legs dangled over a chair arm, revealing split pinkened lips beneath a dark bush of hair. Her nipples had been touched up, too – in a figurative sense – improbably roseate against alabaster skin. Most shocking was the positioning of her hands, one of which cupped a breast while the other delved inside that displayed furrow. If she had derived any pleasure from her explorations, it did not show on her face, which was blank and stony. But nobody was looking at her face.

A woman, smartly but not showily dressed all in black, cut a path through the grinning throng. The young men fell back naturally, tipping hats and begging her pardon. A less formidable-looking woman might have found herself joshed or even groped, but nobody would have dreamt of doing any such thing to this lady.

She paused to evaluate what had been creating the sensation and the men around her looked away or to their boots, suddenly sheepish.

'For shame,' she said, then she put her hand to the door of the shop and entered to the dull jink of rusty bells.

A pasty young man whom nobody had cautioned against the excessive use of pomade double-took at the sight of her.

No woman had ever crossed the threshold of the shop before.

Panicking, he came out from the behind the counter.

'I think you may have the wrong address, madam,' he said, placing himself between her and a display of inflammatory postcards from which a portly woman wielding a whip glared out.

'I wish to speak with Mr Stratton.'

'Oh.' The youth found himself at a loss, his eyes darting wildly around the room at all the potentially feminine-sensibility-violating material on display. 'He is out.'

'When do you expect him back? I am able to wait if he will not be too long.'

Two of the clerks entered, throwing the shop boy into worse throes of confusion.

'Oh dear, customers. Perhaps you might wait in the back room? But it is not comfortable and . . . oh, it is not a place for a lady. Pray, put that down, please, gentlemen, it is not for common perusal.'

He spoke the word 'perusal' with absurd emphasis, as if bringing out a rare jewel from the duller stones of his workaday vocabulary.

'What, is it too dirty for the likes of us?' said one, sniggering.

'Please bear in mind that there is a lady present,' begged the shop boy.

The lady in question simply swept onwards into the back room.

Oh, if the clerks could have come in here, then they would see how tame, how positively innocent the self-loving young lady in the window display was.

The woman in black sat by the grimy back window and cast her eye over a box of postcards. Far from averting her gaze, she picked one out and examined it. A woman in a form of leather harness knelt behind another, younger, girl. This one smiled sweetly and broadly towards the camera whilst on her hands and knees. And behind her, the other woman pivoted her hips forward, ready to drive a thick wooden phallus directly into the rounded bottom of her playmate.

The visitor's lips curved upwards.

'Lovely,' she breathed.

The rooms above the shop had been used, over the years, for various purposes. They had been stock cupboards, brothels and family dwellings but never, until that late spring day in 1865, had they been used as a schoolroom.

On that afternoon, however, James Stratton had tidied away all the ink-stained papers from his well-worn desk and replaced them with a slate and chalk and an alphabet primer, with which he was doing his utmost to teach the buxom young woman beside him to read.

'I do know me letters, though, Jem,' she said, declining to place her finger beside his underneath the *A*. 'I can tell that much. It's just putting 'em together I 'as trouble with.'

'So if I wrote a simple three letter word, such as this . . .' He paused to write the word *cat* in as perfect a copperplate hand as the sliding chalk would allow. 'You could tell me what it said?'

She leant closer to him, very close, so that he could smell that cheap musky perfume all the fallen girls wore, mixed in with sweat and last night's gin and last night's men and, way beneath it all, a faint whiff of soap. He knew why she was doing it. She wanted to distract him with her breasts, and very fine breasts they were too, but today he was fixed in his purpose and he intended to achieve it.

'Why, that curly one's a *c*, I think, and the middle is definitely an *a*. Yes, definitely. The one at the end, I don't know, it might be an *f* or a . . . but *caf* don't make sense, so it must be a *t*. *Cat*!' She spoke the word triumphantly, beaming up at him with teeth that were still good, lips that were still soft and plump.

'Very good, Annie. I'll make a scholar of you yet.'

'That you won't. Who wants a whore what's read the classics anyway?'

'You'd be surprised,' he said, his lips twitching into a smile. Annie always had this uniquely cheering effect upon him for some reason, though what kind of a man this made him he didn't dare explore. She'd made her living on her back since she was fifteen and now, at twenty-two, she was quite an old hand at the game, yet somehow she refreshed him.

'Would you think better of me if I could quote yards of Latin while I rode your cock horse?'

'Hush, Annie,' he tutted, regarding his slate with resigned despair. It was clear she was not in the mood for concentration.

'Besides, I've usually got my mouth full when you're around,' she continued cheerfully.

'Now, I won't hear this,' he said sternly, jabbing a finger at the primer. 'Eyes down, Annie, or I shall have to take measures.'

'Ooh, "take measures"? Like in them stories you write? I'd far rather you read me one of those. Go on, Jem. It's too hot for this, and I didn't get much in the way of sleep last night and me head's all stuffed with rags. Tell me one of your stories.'

He ran a hand through luxuriant dark hair, exasperated at how easy it was for her to tempt him off his virtuous path. Truly, the road to hell was paved with good intentions, and he drew ever closer to the fiery void. But she was right. It was too hot and the buzzing of a fly against the grimy window played his nerves like a fiddle.

Besides, he needed a final read through of that latest story before he dispatched it. Annie made a splendid captive audience, always hanging on his every word. Perhaps she could be captive in more than one sense, if he bound her wrists to the bedstead . . . but no. Much as she pestered him for his latest chapters, she had never shown the slightest sign of sharing his darker proclivities. She was a girl of simple tastes, at heart.

'Oh, all right,' he said, closing up the ranks of upper and lower case letters with a thump. 'But tomorrow we must study in earnest, Annie, and I will accept no excuses. Do you mind me?'

'Of course, sir,' she said, the sweet little word of deference stirring him more than he cared to admit.

'Good. Well, then. Go and sit on the bed and I shall bring it to you.'

She scampered up, her gaudy skirts swishing, and climbed up on to the high bed that took up the greater part of the room, plumping up pillows behind her.

James opened a desk drawer and took out a sheaf of papers, all covered in his tightly packed script, tied with a scarlet ribbon.

'Is it the one about the dairymaid who went to the bad?' asked Annie, unlacing her much-patched boots and throwing them off the end of the bed. 'That's my favourite. Poor girl, though.'

'My clients pay a premium for exquisite distress,' said James, taking his place beside her. 'This unfortunate dairymaid has kept me in shirt linen and port wine for upwards of a year now. Speaking of port wine, would you care for a drop?'

'Oh . . . maybe afterwards. Come, I want to know what will happen to her. Had she not just been tied to a fence post and whipped by four swells on a spree in the country?'

'Indeed she had.' James released the papers from their ribbon and held them before his face.

Annie laid her head on his shoulder, settling into his chest with a comfortable sigh. He had to put one arm around her so as to have the freedom of its movement.

He cleared his throat and began to read.

'*A high-set sun illuminated the meadows and hedgerows, its rays roving over the breathing and the inanimate alike. It bathed cow and sheep, parsley and nettle in its golden warmth, but today, could it but know it, there was a fascinating addition to the bucolic serenity—*'

'Never mind that, what about Emma?' said Annie.

'Don't interrupt, or you may find that you share her fate.'

She wriggled delightedly against him and James wondered, not for the first time, why his idle threats excited her so.

'How pitiless that post-noon heat felt to Emma as she tried in vain to extinguish the fire that raged at her rear. Those fellows, all four of whom still stood about her, leering and laughing at her fate, had plied the whip with a most diabolical will and her poor little round bum was all welted and throbbing, as if stung by a swarm of bees.'

'Poor creature,' murmured Annie, but James chose to ignore her this time.

'As if it were not enough that the quartet's insolent eyes roamed at will over her naked body, Emma feared that any moment a cart from one of the neighbouring farms would pass by, its wheels throwing up a cloud of dust, while the men on the box would see her bare, whipped bottom and, should they choose to alter the angle of view, her breasts squashed against the post to boot. Worst of all, the ringleader of that devilish coterie had made her spread her thighs apart, so that he could flick the tip of his whip lazily over the soft flesh located within, thus opening her tender little cunny to the gaze of whomever chose to feast upon the sight. And such a passer-by would see the swollen lips and the fat red bud that nestled inside, all downed with Emma's pale, sparse hairs. They would also see that little portal, once so tightly guarded, now the happy resting place of many an eager cockstand while Emma lay on her back or her belly, welcoming all to her glistening quim.'

'Heavens, Jem, how does it all come to you? It's too rich for me. I never thought my ears was delicate, but you make me blush.'

'Should I stop reading?'

'Oh no, go on, do.'

'*No matter how she strained against her thick rope bonds, she could not alter her shameful position, nor could her hands, tied high above her head, reach down to shield or soothe the agonies of her posterior.*

"*Sirs," she begged, "I have paid the price for my wanton behaviour at the inn last night, and heavy toll you have exacted from my poor sore bottom. Won't you please release me now and I will thank each of you on my knees, with my mouth.*"

"*Why, that's a fine offer, naughty maid," spoke the chief of the swells. "But we have another means of showing your gratitude in mind. For when a man helps a maid understand how she has erred by applying merited chastisement, he has surely earned the right to take such payment from her as he desires.*"'

'What client is this?' asked Annie. 'Who reads this story?'

'I have no idea,' said James truthfully. 'My uncle makes all the arrangements, by correspondence. It could be anybody.'

'You don't know their names?'

'I know nothing about them. I picture a lonely, wealthy old gentleman alone at a bureau, for some reason, but it could be anybody. I write what I myself would care to read and, by some stroke of fortune, it appeals to people I shall never know nor meet.'

'But it ain't made you rich, or you wouldn't be living here.'

'No,' he said, with a tight smile. 'It will never make me rich. But it pays my bills while I am writing my other material.'

'Oh yes. Your novel. You'll remember me when you're as famous as Mr Dickens, won't you?'

'Is that sarcasm I detect?'

'No, indeed! I believe you will be famous one day. But I hope you won't put me in none of your books.'

'I might put you in this one. Then perhaps I will have the means to whip you into silence.'

Her mouth formed an 'O' and she sucked in a breath, her cheeks flaring red.

'Carry on, I'm sure,' she said.

'"*Oh, Sir, I wonder what you can mean,*" *the fearful dairy girl said. For never before had her offer to bathe a manhood in the luxurious warmth of her mouth and tongue been rejected. Many dozens of pricks had she sucked in her dissolute life, and many gallons of their creamy issue had she swallowed, licking her lips with satisfaction of a task well completed.*'

'Stop there.' Annie's voice was a whisper.

'Is it not to your taste?'

'It's dreadful hot in here. Help me loosen these stays.'

'Annie . . .'

James knew what his neighbour was about when she knelt before him, thrusting out that plump white bosom of hers, but he tugged at the thinning lace all the same with a world-weary air.

'I reckon that Emma doesn't have the lips for it,' said Annie, holding James' gaze with bold intent. 'Those black-guards would've been queuing up to get in my mouth. Don't you reckon?'

She puckered her generous lips and James, having pulled the sides of her bodice apart to free some of that tight-bound flesh, patted her cheek.

'Really, Annie, I don't expect payment for teaching you. There is no need.'

'It wouldn't be payment, Jem. It'd be for friendship. For comfort.'

'Comfort,' echoed James, looking down at the delicious slopes of her cleavage.

'You know I've always liked you.'

'And I you, Annie, very much, but don't you tire of it?'

'Tire of . . . well, in the ordinary way. But this ain't the ordinary way, not when it's you and me.'

She dared a little dart up and a peck on the lips.

He grabbed her by the elbow and held her face close to his.

'You're too good to me, Annie,' he said. Their mouths brushed, tasting closeness, a salt-sweet flavour.

'I want to be good to you, lovey,' she whispered. 'I want you.'

Surely, thought James, it would take a man of stone to resist a pretty girl's offer to slide her pink, wet lips down the length of his shaft and suck it to completion. And he was no man of stone.

He made no move to stop her when her fingers began tugging his chemise from his waistband, nor when she unbuttoned his braces.

'That Emma should come to me,' she said under her breath. 'I could show her how to keep her lips always soft with beeswax.'

'Beeswax?' said James, tickling her behind her ear with his forefinger.

Annie had his trousers and undergarments around his knees now.

All he had to do was lie back and . . .

'Feel the softness,' she breathed.

He did. He felt the softness, as she kissed him from tip to root and then with her saucy tongue bathed his heavy sacs.

'Oh, you're too good,' he muttered when the wet ring of her lips sealed itself around his girth.

He shut his eyes, slowly feeding every inch of his erection into her, imagining it as something medicinal that would benefit her health. It was what she needed, a good mouthful, a swallow of cream to keep her warm for the rest of the day.

He opened one eye and watched her head of brassy ringlets bob up and down. The curls were falling loose after the exertions of the night before and needed re-twisting into papers before she put on her working clothes again. James liked the effect, though; the metaphor of it. He was like one of those ringlets, once so coiled and taut, now snaking down into perfect laxity. Where would it end? Where would his life go, now that it was all in a day's work to write obscene literature and get himself sucked off by his best friend, the whore next door?

He put his hands to her head, positioning her so that he could watch her hard at work, see that scandalously painted mouth staining his cock red with whatever bizarre compound of beetroot juice and berry she had put on her lips before coming to his room.

Lord, but she was a good little cocksucker, getting his blood up to just the exquisite degree he liked before he plunged into that final rush. And here was his crisis, high up above him, way down beneath him, meeting in the middle and roaring out of him.

He took a fistful of ringlets and emptied himself into her, feeling his strength drain out of him in short bursts until he was fatally sapped, wasted by pleasure again.

Spent, he watched her take his cock from her mouth and swallow ostentatiously. Then she lay down on her back, stretching like a cat, and looked up at him, licking her lips.

'Yum yum,' she said.

She reached up and grazed his whiskers with her knuckles.

'Was that good?'

He bent to kiss the mouth that tasted of him.

'You know it, minx,' he said.

He felt for the hem of her skirts, all mud-spattered and stained from the street, and began to raise them, knowing in advance that she would not be wearing drawers underneath.

'What you got in mind, my bad boy?' she asked, eyes like mischievous saucers.

'Less of the boy, if you please. I'm five years your senior.'

'Old enough to know better then.'

'Old enough to know.'

He placed his fingers on her exposed thigh. How soft the flesh, giving the illusion of spotlessness, a virginal air that would deceive the worst of roués. He bent his head and kissed the marble-like skin, his lips drifting up and further up.

'Oh, Jem,' she whispered, leaning back, throwing her arms above her head.

Last night's men.

A loud rapping on the door broke and swept away the vague disgust that had made its unwelcome presence felt via his nostrils.

'Christ,' he hissed, kneeling up and shaking his head at a crestfallen Annie. 'Who is there?' he called.

'It's me, James.'

His uncle – his employer, landlord and instigator of his Faustian pact.

'What do you want?'

'I have a visitor for you.'

'Oh?'

James tugged down Annie's skirts and hauled her off the bed, sending her back to the desk with a pat on her rump.

Standing by the door, fastening his clothes back into a state of decency, he said, 'I don't expect anybody.'

'I dare say, but please let us in.'

James opened the door halfway and peered out on to the gloomy landing. He almost didn't see his uncle's companion, so perfectly did her black attire blend with the lightless surroundings.

'A lady,' he said, nonplussed. 'Please come in.'

'I see you already have company,' sniffed his uncle.

'Annie, you may leave now. Put the book away until next time.' He smiled weakly at his guests. 'I am teaching her,' he said.

'No doubt,' said his uncle.

James' eyes fell, rather injudiciously, to his crotch, just at the very moment his uncle's did. The younger man coloured and looked away, watching Annie skip from the room with a wink.

'Does she have much to learn?'

The question, phrased in a low, ironic voice, diverted James' attention immediately to his female guest.

'Please, take a seat,' he invited, pulling the spindle-backed chairs away from the desk and offering them to the woman and his uncle. He sat himself on the edge of his bed, the only other available place.

'Thank you.' She was perfectly economical in her movements, he noticed, as she tucked her black skirts neatly behind her and lowered herself into the chair. Her spine was straight, her shoulders set a little back, her chin raised to display a slender neck.

The face, with its heart shape and quiet grey eyes, possessed an ageless quality – a stillness. James felt he could look into it endlessly and not tire, like looking out to the silver expanse of a calm sea. He supposed himself to be ten years her junior, or more, but she could be anything from twenty-five to forty-five.

'Excuse me,' he said, standing again and holding out his hand. 'I don't believe we have met. James Stratton.'

'Yes,' she said, failing to reciprocate his gesture. 'Your uncle told me your name.'

'And might I ask . . .'

'You might ask, but I'm afraid I cannot tell you my name. If you wish, you may address me as "Madame".'

He looked at his uncle for any clue as to what the purpose of this meeting might be.

'Let me explain,' said Madame. 'Please, sit back down, Mr Stratton.'

He subsided back on to the bed, watching her keenly.

'I am here on behalf of my mistress. She is a wealthy single lady, a client of yours.'

'A client?' For a moment, James could not imagine what she might mean. 'You cannot intend to tell me that . . . a lady . . . commissions my work?'

'I intend to tell you precisely that, Mr Stratton. Furthermore, this lady has formed a desire to make your acquaintance.'

'To make . . . my . . . acquaintance?'

James looked between his uncle and Madame, increasingly bewildered.

'Before I extend any invitation, I must impress upon you the requirement for absolute discretion. Nobody should ever be told of this visit. You must sign a document swearing secrecy. Do you agree to these terms?'

'I, er, well, yes. Yes, I think I do.'

'You must do more than think,' she said severely.

James, by now thoroughly itching with curiosity, simply held out a hand again.

'Give me the document. I will sign it.'

She took from her reticule a small folded paper and gave it over to James, who read it at the desk.

It was clear and simple enough. He, James Stratton, would never speak of what occurred tonight, the 27th inst., to a living soul, the details to include the location of the meeting, the persons met and everything that should transpire.

With a pleasant sense of embarkation on adventure, he signed with a flourish and presented the paper to Madame for her approval.

'Thank you,' she said. 'You will present yourself on the corner of this street and the Strand at eight o'clock this evening, where My Lady's carriage will be waiting to convey you to her place of residence. Do not be late. And dress properly.' She frowned at his shirtsleeves and loosened neckcloth.

'Oh . . . of course,' he said, tightening his collar straight away.

The lady wasted no more time in pleasantry but excused herself, Uncle Thomas Stratton bowing and scraping all the way like a human comic aside.

Also by Justine Elyot:

FALLEN

A lady of pleasure . . .

In the backstreets of London in 1865,
James Stratton makes his living writing saucy
stories for anonymous clients. But then he receives
an enquiry of a far more personal nature.

Lady Augusta Heathcote is blind and has lived a
very sheltered life, overseen by her watchful
companion Mrs Shaw. But Augusta has a yearning
to experience the intimate pleasures of dominance
and submission and she makes James an offer he
finds impossible to refuse . . .

BLACK
LACE

Also by Justine Elyot:

DIAMOND

Her name is Jenna Diamond. She is about to meet her match . . .

Since the painful breakup with her famous musician husband Jenna has returned to England and bought a crumbling old house back in her hometown.

But Jenna discovers a mysterious stranger hiding out at Holderness Hall. Logic suggests she should alert the authorities, but when she looks at her sexy, young house guest Jenna finds it all too easy to let her heart rule her head . . .

Book 1 in the Diamond trilogy, a glamorous erotic romance, from the bestselling author of *On Demand*

BLACK
LACE

Coming soon from Justine Elyot:

DIAMONDS FOREVER

Jenna Diamond and her bad-boy lover Jason
are enjoying an exciting and sensual fling.
But he has skeletons from his past which prove
challenging to overcome.

And when Jenna's rock-star husband returns,
desperate to make amends, she is faced with
a difficult decision: she must choose between her
new life and her old, between her head and
her heart . . .

**The conclusion to the thrillingly erotic
Diamond trilogy, from the author
of *On Demand***

BLACK
LACE